The Heaven Maker
and
other Gruesome Tales

The Heaven Maker
and
other Gruesome Tales

by
Craig Herbertson

Parallel Universe Publications

First published in Great Britain by Parallel Universe Publications

Copyright © Craig Herbertson 2012

Foreword © 2012
Introduction © 2012
Drip © 2011 Originally published in *Big Vault Advent Calendar 2011*
Timeless Love © 2007 Originally published in *Filthy Creations #2*
Synchronicity © 2008 Originally published in *The Third Black Book of Horror*
The Glowing Goblins © 1992 Originally published in *Auguries #16*
New Teacher© 2010 Originally published in *The Seventh Black Book of Horror*
The Janus Door © 2012
The Heaven Maker © 1988 Originally published in *The 29th Pan Book of Horror Stories*
The Waiting Game © 2010 Originally published in *Back from the Dead: The Legacy of the Pan Book of Horror Stories*
The Art of Confiscation ©2012
Farmer Brown © 2012
Not Waving © 2012
Spanish Suite © 2010 Originally published in *The Sixth Black Book of Horror*
The Anninglay Sundial © 2012
Soup © 2009 Originally published in *The Fourth Black Book of Horror*
A Game of Billiards © 2009 Originally published in *Tales from the Smoking Room*
The Navigator © 2011 Originally published in *Big Vault Advent Calendar 2011*
The Tasting © 2012
Steel Works © 2012
Liebniz's Last Puzzle © 2009 Originally published in *The Fifth Black Book of Horror*
Gifts © 2011 Originally published in *Big Vault Advent Calendar 2011*

All rights reserved. No part of this publication may be reproduced, stored in a retrieval system, rebound or transmitted in any form or by any means, electronic, mechanical, photocopying, recording or otherwise, without the prior written permission of the author and publisher. This book is sold subject to the condition that it shall not by way of trade or otherwise be lent, resold, hired out or otherwise circulated without the publisher's prior consent in any form of binding or cover other than that in which it is published.

ISBN: 978-0-9574535-0-0

Parallel Universe Publications, 130 Union Road, Oswaldtwistle, Accrington, Lancashire, BB5 3DR, UK

Contents

Foreword	6
Introduction	7
Timeless Love	10
Synchronicity	11
The Glowing Goblins	24
New Teacher	27
The Janus Door	34
The Heaven Maker	49
The Waiting Game	80
The Art of Confiscation	88
Gertrude	102
Not Waving	108
Spanish Suite	119
The Anninglay Sundial	130
Soup	154
A Game of Billiards	174
The Navigator	180
The Tasting	186
Steel Works	213
Liebniz's Last Puzzle	221
Big Cup, Wee Cup	243
Gifts	247
Afterthoughts	249

Foreword

I've always been a huge fan of Craig Herbertson. It all started at the curious age of five when, apparently (so he tells me) I was ready to slip him thruppence (making us pre-Historic) for a glimpse of him in his vest!

Then through High School we met in the common room, joined the romantic intellectuals to hang about the Lily pond that alas had neither lilies nor water but clung to its poetic name. We talked communism, David Bowie, Lou Reed, Genesis, teachers inspiring and otherwise – and waited for the day we'd make our unique mark on the world; us with our very dark hair, Aquarian free spirit types, leaning into angst, poetry, art, spirituality, music, books, Bowie haircuts – and probably most importantly in a school with over 2000 pupils, nurtured the art of 'being different.'

We succeeded, for better or for worse.

Craig travelled, made music, had kids, wrote – and found his way to Germany. That's where I landed a few years ago, teaching a group of students English poetry. One of the students told me how her partner came from Edinburgh. I nodded and got on with Shelley and Keats. Next day she says he went to Portobello High School – and Duddingston primary, and that he is more or less exactly the same age as me.

So after all these years we met again and immediately could tap into that shared river of Edinburgh, school and a time where it was all beginning. Over kaffee und kuchen we nod, and smile, and understand that the dreams and pie-in-the-sky school hopes, in some way, came true. We both write books. We're both published authors. We both took the path less travelled by – and I'm still a big fan.

Janis Mackay

Introduction

In the early 1970's I first began to pester the late great Van Thal with what I thought were horror stories. The rejection slips were very polite and being very young I wasn't discouraged. Nearly twenty years later, having amassed a collection of rejection slips that would support a new career in papier-mâché sculpting, I decided to quit the short story business. I took up long stories and found the discipline longer, lonelier and drear with unforeseeable endings. I worked in isolation, basically convinced that I was creating a masterpiece. Years later, my novel was miraculously completed and I had almost forgotten why. It was apparent to me, that rather than a masterpiece, I had written a lot of connected words and kissed the best ages of my life goodbye.

It did get me thinking though. I've always liked genre fiction: SF, Fantasy, Horror, Supernatural and Weird. I thought about the stories I like to read and the format in which they come.

With some notable exceptions, SF and fantasy seem to work better as novels or novellas. Horror seems to work better as shorts. Take this example written by my very young nephew,

DRIP by V. Herbertson:

Inspector M. was confused. He was the best detective in London yet he couldn't crack this case.
Drip.
'The tapes have come, Sir!' said M's simple minded assistant Sam.
Drip.
'Put in tape one.'
'Yes, Sir.'
The Tape played. M watched as Inspector L was beheaded.
Drip.
'He was a detective, Sam,' explained Inspector M. 'He had just cracked this very same case'.
Drip.

Tape 2 showed the rising star, Inspector K's head rolling across the floor.

Drip.

'What's that noise' asked M. 'Oh, just the pipes – I'll fix them Sir' answered

Sam.

Drip.

Tape 3 showed Inspector L executed with a huge ornate axe, identical to Sam's beloved family heirloom.

Drip.

Inspector M carefully examined the files and then he noticed that Sam had been their assistant….

DRIP

Inspector M wheeled around in his chair and two things hit him: the realization that it had been simple minded Sam! That, and Sam's axe….

Blood dripped off the axe.

Drip.

At this length it could only be a Horror story. Perhaps that's because in SF and Fantasy the general idea is to get out of the mundane and enter an exciting, desirable world – in both these realms one can be the hero or heroine, all hopes can be fulfilled, all villains vanquished; or if you are of a darker breed, everything can catastrophically collapse around you in a satisfactorily apocalyptic manner. The longer the fantastic world is maintained the better. In contrast, the intention of a Horror story is to crush your desires, vanquish your spirit, make you feel queasy and dislocated, stunned and unhappy; in short, to horrify. Horror is best sustained in quick bursts: it's exciting but also tactile, visceral, disgusting, often amusing, mostly horrible and sometimes nauseating. If it's really good you cringe and shout 'Oh, no!' – As with the terrifying moments in real life, you don't want that feeling to last too long.

So, my Horror novel languishes in a forgotten corner while the short stories - perhaps because they simply are short –get shameless exposure. Some were written long ago and I resisted the temptation to change them. The others? They would never have seen the light of day (or the gibbous moon's reflection on a stagnant haunted mere) if I hadn't encountered the Vault of Evil, the website where all the dastards hang out. I waited half a life-time to see this collection in print and I happily dedicate it to those black-hearted writers, editors, compulsive compilers and enthusiasts from the Vault who inspired my return to Horror writing, and in particular, those who published my work, Charles Black, Demonik, Rog Pile and Johnny Mains.

Yes, it's your fault.

Craig Herbertson, 2012

CRAIG HERBERTSON

TIMELESS LOVE

I'm not afraid, I'm not afraid
I've seen the wondrous cavalcade
The pretty flowers we have laid
To grace our days with light and shade
While others fill the air with death
Rut upon their poisoned breath
Nought and Cross their blackened wreath
We can still be in relief
Silhouettes to sadden grief
With time the pass the parcel thief

I'm not afraid, I'm not afraid
I've been where the darkness bleeds
Where dark farmers rake the seed
So that blackened tractors feed
While others try to cut us down
Grin and bear a cherry frown
They can wear the heavy gown
We will ever be in flight
Spectral suns suffusing light
With time the ill-appointed knight

SYNCHRONICITY

'Synchronicity,'
  'Pardon?'
It amused me to watch Peters, the class intellectual, utilise a word that contained more than two syllables, in the presence of Dermott, the class philistine, whose vocabulary extended as far as immediate needs.

The others hadn't remarked Dermott's baffled exclamation, their faces buried in the menu in urbane contemplation of the starter.

'Synchronicity,' repeated Peters, never one to let go of conversation when it was he who spoke. 'The conjunction of events. Why we are all here at this time and place.'

'Not 'invitation' then,' said Campbell caustically. 'Nothing to do with all being forty-eight years old and this date marking our departure from Bellport High?'

'Not all forty-eight,' said Peters weakly. Despite his intellect, he had never been quicker than Campbell in riposte.

'The ladies, the good wives and our venerable teacher of Mathematics, Mr. Weasel.' Peters indicated the aged figure of Weasel whose much-mimicked hand movements, were illustrating to Mrs. Chalmers, wife of the head boy, how to square a hypotenuse.

'Poor Chalmers,' muttered Mulholland. 'You'd think Weasel would be able to leave the subject behind after twenty-five years of retirement.'

I contemplated Mulholland for a moment. He had been immediately recognisable outside the Dome Restaurant. The ancient steps of the converted bank building had lent his spare figure a certain grandeur. He was clad in tweeds, plus fours, a hunting cap pulled down to shade one side of his face. In short, his anachronistic clothes were a far cry from the scruffy, ripped and smelling garments of his youth. He looked almost elegant between the colonnades of the posh Italian restaurant:

An utter contrast to the gauche, bullied teenager who had cowered through the corridors of Bellport High.

How did I recognise him? The missing eye did the trick; frozen in an eternal wink that lurked beneath the cap with a kind of raw, sexual ugliness. I was surprised he hadn't covered

it with a patch but then his whole demeanour surprised me.

Thirty years had clearly wrought a remarkable change in

Mulholland. Time had dealt less severely with him than the rest of us, I supposed.

He spoke again 'I always understood synchronicity to mean our experience of events that occur in a meaningful manner, but which are causally unrelated. If Campbell wrote a merry little poem and I were to produce the same lyric, at the same time but in a different place, that would be synchronous.'

I looked at Mulholland in some astonishment, recalling a day at school, over thirty years before, where I had found him hiding in a stock cupboard. He had been unable to speak for tears. Thankfully, he appeared now to have grown where others had shrunk. Peters for example, whose hair was thinner, his bulbous head shining luminous between the strands like one of those Scandinavian lamps: his voice still betraying the same irritating tones. A voice that was certainly irritating Dermott who understood very little beyond food and drink.

Nothing much changed there. Not even his trim waistline or penchant for tight pants. Campbell was still cracking jokes, mostly with Dermott's attractive wife. Nothing whatsoever changed there on the surface. But looking down the line of all the old school leavers was like attending a Warhol exhibition of 'Dorian Grays'. Aristotle would have had a field day demonstrating how depravity and apathy had left their marks.

I supposed I looked as decrepit as the rest. Perhaps I held a unique position. I seemed to be the only one who would have to select between the rent money and this ridiculously priced Italian meal. I became even more conscious of the ragged edges of my cuffs and collar.

At least I hadn't married. Half the company seemed to be saddled with dull wives all of whom were contemplating Ravioli with academia barilla pecorino gran cru as a main meal. Must be herd instinct, I reflected, wincing at their varied incompetence in pronunciation. I glanced at the incomprehensible menu, written only in Italian. As with the tables, everything sparse as though simplicity and elegance were a fair substitute for sumptuous excess. For this price, naked, dancing ladies wouldn't be unfair.

I could avoid a starter but then I had no doubt that, if I did, we would end up mucking in. Dermott would steer us in that direction if he had a starter and several beers. If he had no starter and went light on the alcohol, he'd somehow engineer that we pay separately. That was always his skill at school: the art of justifying everything he did.

Compromise. What was the cheapest? Prawn cocktail? Do they still do that? What's it called in Italian? I glanced up.

Hopefully, someone across the other side would give some kind of culinary clues. Chalmers was talking a little too loudly in Italian just to show he could do it. Good old headboy.

Campbell had left off his wife and was eyeing the table to the left, which seemed to have commandeered most of the remaining single women. You could see in his eye that he was reflecting on past triumphs. Slim pickings there my boy: mostly divorced with three kids or exceptionally obvious reasons for still being single.

Mr. Weasel tried to catch my eye across the two empty chairs. I managed to feign interest in the menu. It's amazing how heinous crimes seem to fade into playful mischievousness after the passage of years. That tottering old bastard, who looked like someone's favourite grandfather, had whupped us liberally with the tawse. Sore hands for months afterwards.

And his habit of strolling the corridors swishing dawdling arses with his hickory cane. It must have been illegal even then, but he got away with it. Interesting that he wasn't keen to sit with the ladies. I established to myself that I hated him as much now as I did then. There was only one person from Bellport High who I could possibly hate more than Weasel but fortunately, he hadn't turned up.

I couldn't imagine school reunions held much appeal for

Gray. Gray was an orphan. He'd arrived from somewhere else having been expelled for something awful. Bellport High seemed to be the natural dumping ground for maniacs.

I once speculated that Gray had killed his parents or they had run away from home. I kept that speculation to myself then, as you didn't want to draw unwelcome attention from Gray. He wasn't a big lad or particularly strong but one glance at his eyes was enough to shake you. He was utterly immoral; unpredictable, quick, inhuman; worse still, a creative sadist with an inventive collection of tortures that would have shamed De Sade. Eighteen years old… it seemed incredible looking around the faces around the table… these empty chairs would probably have been filled if Gray hadn't shortened the life span of half the school.

'Anyone know what happened to Gray?' The words had spilled unwilling from my mouth.

'Ask him,' said Campbell with a smile. I sensed a shadow, an aura, something behind me, and looked up.

Have you ever experienced it? You stick your head down a rabbit hole and something with eyes springs out; you turn around while walking, and when you look back, your face hits a lamppost. Or maybe one of those tricks at school where they stick a worm in your hand. It was partly the unexpected, the shock of seeing his face above me as I had seen it so many times before: Peters' claptrap about synchronicity. But then it was also the fact that the face had changed so much in thirty years.

Gray wasn't leering down with anticipation. His face was still darkly handsome but it was careworn, chiselled with lines that lent his fine cheekbones a sort of tired elegance.

Remarkably, the eyes had changed: Where hate and glee had

battled for supremacy there was only a kind of haunted stillness. 'Sorry I'm late,' he said. He removed his expensive

German greatcoat and his dark eyes swept the table with a view to sitting.

I confess I laughed. It was shock, relief, absurdity. Gray and 'sorry'. Like Hitler saying, 'I didn't mean to upset people'. I managed to kind of smother it into a welcome and indicated the empty chairs opposite.

Gray's entrance silenced us. Chalmers, the one boy who had tried to stand up to him at school, and that, only because his position demanded it, gave a kind of frozen nod to the empty chair at his side. The wives were giving him the once over as they would any handsome stranger. Peters, Campbell and Dermott had all been drawn into his perverse circle in varying degrees of complicity. Still they said nothing. Only Dermott, incapable of guilt, gave a slight nod. Mulholland, whose lost eye was a victim of one of Gray's sportive exploits, pursed his lips and looked back at the menu.

It was Weasel, a teacher after all, and a sadist to boot, who broke the silence. 'Gunney? Geld? I'm terribly sorry but…'

'Gray, it's quite understandable. I wasn't in your class, sir…'

'Gray,' said Weasel half to himself, liking the 'sir'. Gray had always avoided being beaten at school so Weasel was unlikely to remember him. I had a gut feeling that Weasel's nights were spent in sweaty dreams consumed by the pain-filled features of young boys. Now two of the school's old monsters shared a table with us like camp commandants partying with their prisoners.

Time heals, they say. So, we were all going to be civilised under the rococo lights, with the piped Domingo, over some fancy meal whose name I would never master. After some

Friuli wine, we would doubtless recount the old horrors with a laugh and a smile. I looked at Mulholland's disfigured face and wondered how he felt behind that impassive mask.

Probably like me, faintly sick.

'Mind if we order, Gray?' said Chalmers. He was trying to establish himself. Strange after all these years the same old predatory instincts surfaced. Gray's simple acquiescence drew an undisguised relaxation from Chalmers.

I thought back to their numerous confrontations. That time in Physics when Gray had electrified some water and was forcing that poor sap… what was his name… Angel, that was it, Angel. He was forcing Angel's hand into the water. Angel was screaming piteously as he always did. Chalmers came through and ordered him to stop. Then Gray with his glee-filled eyes said 'Stop what? This?' Without hesitation, he had placed his own hand in the electrified water and simply held it there. Chalmers, not for the first or last time, looked like a sanctimonious fool. Then the bucket of water over the door; only Gray had not used water but a single glass of beer, which left Chalmers, its unhappy victim, with some ridiculous explanations to do later.

But these were innocuous bagatelles. How many times had I walked into the form room to see Mulholland upside down in a wastepaper basket while the others looked and laughed and hit? Or that skinny fellow, Angel, undoubtedly the school wimp, pants at ankles, tied to a post in the playground.

Once he had tattooed Angel's back and stomach with a Biro: 'front' and 'back' only in Gray's peculiar world of humour the words were in the wrong position. That poor kid… man now… must still bear the scars.

'And what do you do nowadays, Gray?' Weasel was still placing Gray. The name must surely have filtered through the staffroom at some point. You couldn't hold the entire student body in thrall without a flame from the inferno disturbing the pipe smoke.

'Offshore Banking,' said Gray. 'I think I'll miss the starter and try this ravioli with the ladies. I believe it's especially good here.' He had caught their choice in their muted table talk and seemed to relax a little. He looked composed, sat in his expensive French shirt, sporting gold cufflinks and a conservative tie. Still, there was just a faint echo of the driven boy emerging with his laconic voice. And the voice, the taunting, teasing voice of the torturer as he forced poor Angel to eat a spit-covered sweet, Mulholland to drink the lav water, me to whistle while he pinched my nipple. Better not dwell on the voice, I reflected. Might as well try to enjoy this Italian extravaganza before facing the financial music next month.

'What's your line, Chalmers?'

Chalmers hesitated a fraction, 'Insurance,' he said quietly.

'Oh, now I recall. I met… oh, I forget… but he said our head boy was a clerk with…' Gray drummed his fingers on the table.

Did I see a familiar light in his eyes? It was the way he had voiced 'clerk', just a bare hint of contempt. Not enough to be rude, not enough for anyone inattentive to really hear; only that apparently haphazard conjunction of the words 'boy' and 'clerk' to make Chalmers uneasy. Now, observing Chalmers, I could see that he had saved for this meal whereas Gray looked every inch the man who could buy and sell the restaurant.

Dermott piped up. In anyone else, it would have been an attempt to steer the conversation to safer waters. Dermott simply wanted to know.

'What's this synchronicity you're blabbing about, Peters?'

'Well, I was just going to point out… what a perfect example. We're all wondering what happened to Gray? And there he stands, just at that moment. It's a Jungian concept, the conjunction of events all melding together in one instant.'

Dermott's face took on the solid mask of indifference; immediately dismissing 'synchronicity' as something that could be neither bought nor sold.

Mulholland quietly interjected. 'I think I just mentioned that it refers to our experience of events that occur in a meaningful manner, but which have no causal relation. An historical example is that Lincoln dreamed of his assassination just before he actually was…'

Peters was off expounding his genius to the table behind.

Mulholland raised his eyebrows in a dismissive gesture.

'I'm somewhat famished,' croaked Weasel, for once gauging the mood. Campbell and the other men sought the attention of a waiter. I didn't bother. I had tried on numerous unsuccessful occasions to effect that trick. Gray's hands were up in an instant. His compelling personality drew a waiter as easily as an angler plays a caught salmon.

The waiter came up. 'We're all, I believe ready to order,' said Gray competently. 'Ladies?' There was brief flurry.

'Starters: Bruschetta for me, a prawn cocktail, two Carpaccio, one Prosciutto Bruschetta Fegatini, that's that toast with chicken liver… let me see.' He continued the order with the assurance of a seasoned epicure. The waiter was having difficulty keeping up as he pushed on to the main menu:

Ravioli for the girls and the rest; Mulholland, the veal. Me? I settled, optimistically, for poor man's spaghetti bolognaise.

Gray was quietly ordering the most expensive champagne in the house when there was a sudden gasp from Chalmers.

'Angel,' he said.

The waiter stiffened. It was only then that we all looked up.

Waiters are just waiters aren't they? Even on a busy night, their job is to blend into the background. Like dodgems, they weave around you. On a successful night, you would hardly remember they were there, never mind a face. But Chalmers had remembered. All of thirty years and here was Angel, beggar at the feast, and our head boy had recognised him.

I vividly recall Mulholland's expression in that moment.

Angel had saved Mulholland from being the most contemptible boy in the school. Both had been the victims of endless torture, the human canvas for Gray's Machiavellian art. Mulholland's eyes reflected what we all thought. Here was Angel, at the age of forty-eight, a menial waiter, still offering his humble services to his old classmates. Physical torture was passé. Now he would spend the evening serving our expensive culinary wants like some despised Southern Slave. I speculated what we should tip him.

Gray was the first to react. 'Sit down, Angel, won't you.'

Angel shook his head quickly. 'Can't, working'.

That was the problem with Angel. I was just thankful that I had been a decent enough bloke at school. I don't think there was anyone throughout the filled tables of the restaurant who hadn't participated in, or at least gained vicarious pleasure from, Angel's career of humiliation. Mulholland, dressed behind his lordly façade, perhaps understood better than most that Angel's deferential obsequiousness had brought the pain to his own door. Weakness is like a magnet. It attracts bullies and Angel had been unfortunate in encountering the worst of them all.

'Drink?' said Campbell.

'Synchronicity,' this before Angel had a chance to refuse. Peters, a man with a chasm where others had social sense, betrayed his delight. 'Angel here, serving the very boy who…'

What he would have carried on to say is anyone's guess.

Chalmers managed to ejaculate something about stopping for a drink after and Angel began to take the order. His hands shook. His distress was utterly painful. He made several mistakes. You could tell that seasoned epicures like Gray and Campbell would have made mince of him in other circumstances. By about the fourth effort Angel had somehow interpreted our needs and was slinking off to the kitchen. We all seemed to be getting our starters and the spaghetti, veal, ravioli and, most importantly, Champagne was hopefully en route. I needed a drink to numb the pain.

'Not a very happy boy,' said Weasel absentmindedly. I restrained the impulse to mention that his state of mind might have been improved with even a little help from those responsible for his protection. What was the point? All water under the bridge. Then Mulholland said. 'Not a very happy school.'

I suppose you don't say this kind of thing at a school reunion. Jolly, cheery remarks like 'I remember when you had hair' or 'putting on a bit around the middle' filled the bill.

Mulholland had broken a rule beyond old school rules but, as I said earlier, he seemed to have grown with the passing years and looked well able to forge a new set.

'How do you mean?' said Weasel.

'The petty torture, the beatings, the sadistic boys and masters.'

Jesus! Mulholland wasn't beating about the bush. I got that sudden vertigo, almost like the precipitation of an LSD rush, where the whole evening seemed about to be swept away like a conjurer doing the plates and tablecloth trick.

'Come,' said Weasel, next to Gray the last person to have the right to comment. 'The old school was a super environment for young minds.'

As if to illustrate the point Angel returned. He spilled part of my prawn cocktail on my sleeve, dropped Gray's Bruschetta and failed to open the champagne. Everybody tried to minimise his misadventures and Gray finally took the bottle and opened it with a flourish. Perhaps it was Gray's nature.

Perhaps he was simply born to torture others even had he wished otherwise. Angel stood for a moment. There was a terrible silence.

I tried. 'Angel, is there a cigarette machine here?' I didn't smoke. I was just putting enough words together to make any conceivable sentence.

'No,' said Angel. He hovered.

'My Bruschetta?' said Gray. I felt then that I had hit the nail on the head. Gray and Angel were like some ill-fated duo. An eternity could come and go and Angel would still be the mouse to his cat. Angel stood, lost for a second. I felt he might be confused about his role: old school wimp or incompetent waiter. Finally, he left for the kitchen to an immediate lightening of the atmosphere.

Mulholland, however, had had no interest in a lightened atmosphere. 'There's an example of our beneficent school system,' he said, toying with his crab.

'Well,' said Dermott getting down to brass tacks, 'you don't seem to have done so badly out of it. Nor the rest of us for that matter.' He indicated the crowd of us, slouched in the comfy chairs, picking at our hors d'oeuvre and sipping champagne.

'Despite rather than because of Bellport High,' said Mulholland.

'Oh come, come,' said Weasel.

'A place of petty torture and sadistic bullying. You were there, Mr. Weasel when I lost my eye. Do you recall the incident?'

Angel had returned with a second bottle of champagne. He hovered on the edge of the crowd, seemingly indecisive as to whether he should attempt to open the bottle or surrender to Gray's surer hand.

'Yes, vaguely.' It was the wrong thing to say but of course, Mulholland had broken every code in the book.

'You'll remember though, Gray?' The table went silent.

Gray eased back in the chair a little. He eyed Mulholland with something like respect. 'It was the last day at school. We dangled you from the sixth floor stairwell. Campbell, Dermott and I. You were upside down screaming, a stupid schoolboy prank, which I intensely regret now. There was some confusion afterwards. In the struggle, you might have hit your head on the banister or something of the sort. Poked out your eye. Very regrettable.'

'Yes, I recall very well now,' said Weasel. I was on corridor duty and was on hand to give you first aid. Regrettable accident, horseplay and the like and very fortunate I was immediately on hand. Such, sadly, is life…'

'Regrettable, yes, unfortunate, yes,' said Mulholland. 'Not so regrettable that Gray didn't manage to make it to the dining room for lunch, neatly covering his tracks. And unfortunate that you were never able to establish who was to blame. Nice to find out after all these years.'

'Yes,' said Weasel, not listening, 'a regrettable and unfortunate incident. But time heals all. Now we can sit together like old chums and laugh about it all.'

Angel had contrived to remove the starters. He had given up with the champagne and the bottle lay conveniently within Gray's reach. He took it deliberately. An uncomfortable silence followed the popped cork. Angel laid out the main courses and stood just behind me facing Gray with Weasel on his right. The dishes looked surprisingly good, although bigger portions would have suited me and as always with sod's law, the others' ravioli looked a lot better than my miserable portion of spaghetti.

Gray began to pour the wine. I gripped Angel's arm and whispered. 'Have a drink with us.' He kind of hovered but didn't pick up a glass. I'd done my best.

Nobody seemed inclined to start. Then Peters guffawed.

'Why, synchronicity! All this ravioli. Precisely the meal we had for lunch on our last day.'

'How jolly,' said Mulholland with heavy irony. 'That fine example of conjunctive events has fairly cheered my soul.'

'I have a better.' said Angel suddenly.

We paused, forks raised. Even the tables beyond us hushed.

'I was on the corridor at the time Mulholland was injured,' said Angel quietly. 'Mr. Weasel lashed at me with his cane. He missed. At the same instant you were being lowered down the stairwell by your legs. Gray and his crew had done that to me so many times it was almost fun to watch it happen to someone else. Except that when Mr. Weasel struck out with his hickory cane he caught your eye.'

Mulholland quailed for a moment. Pursed his lips and determinedly, poured himself a large glass.

The silence deepened into something dreadful.

'I saw Gray run.' Angel continued with enthusiasm. 'He was obviously after an alibi.' He looked at me with a beaming smile. 'He elbowed you out of your seat at the dining table.'

Angel looked at the air above his old classmates, following an imagined parabola. He said: 'I watched that eye hurtle through the air like a comet, out of the corridor, through the open door of the dining room and splash! Straight into a plate of ravioli. Your ravioli, Gray.'

Angel smiled, realising perhaps, that the unusual circumstances had encouraged him to overstep the boundary between customer and waiter.

In the ensuing silence, he coughed and said politely. 'Enjoy your meal.'

Mulholland gave me a queer look and we both picked up our forks. 'That,' he said, piercing a glistering sliver of veal, 'is what I would call synchronicity.'

THE GLOWING GOBLINS

As a child Colin had been most unpopular….especially with his parents. They took a grim pleasure in locking him in the cupboard below the stairs for most of the night and, when occasion demanded, some of the day. The occasion was usually 'the wetting of the bed', but it could often be something else – 'the not washing behind the ears,' 'the crying in the kitchen', 'the telling lies', 'the telling the truth'; sometimes they would lock him in the cupboard for 'the nothing at all'.

At first he would scream. Then cry, then sob. And then the silence would denote one of two things. Either he was asleep or he was too frightened to do anything but sit still and listen.

Although there was nothing in the cupboard it was Colin's belief, inspired by his parents that if he made any noise, horrible little goblins with no eyes and gaping toothless mouths would come to torment him. In the early years this is exactly what would happen. At first the Goblins would sit silently on the extremities of the vast cupboard and then they would creep towards him on their hands, knees or backs. As the nights went by and Colin invariably erred, the goblins would crawl closer, their wide toothless mouths opening and shutting like fish out of water, while Colin moaned in terror.

Outside cupboard-world, life rolled miserably on. Winter nights were dim-lit bridge games. Colin's father was always a starched white shirt, black suit and patent leather shoes. Colin's mother was always ill. She lurched from room to room like a slowly sinking ship, cleaning and dusting the cheap old furniture, watched forlornly by Colin and the peeling flower wallpaper.

She died one afternoon.

Dry eyed, father summoned doctor, obtained death certificate, phoned undertaker, phoned friends and cancelled bridge games indefinitely. After the unaccustomed break in routine, he put Colin in the cupboard for 'the nothing at all' occasion and sat in the kitchen drinking whisky from a clay mug.

It was also a break in the routine for Colin. Instead of merely darkness and goblins in the cupboard he was amazed and terrified to see his mother had joined him. She lay screaming on the floor in the centre of the cupboard. Well, her mouth opened and shut and her face contorted with fear although no sound emerged.

For about an hour Colin sat cowering in a corner and then it eventually came to him that there was nothing to be frightened of; the goblins no longer crawled towards him; they sat alongside him, their mouths opening and shutting, but their obscenely witless faces pointed towards mother.

After another hour he discovered that he was exuding a faintly luminous light. It was then that he began to open and shut his own mouth.

Outside cupboard-world, life was slowly changing. Father spent much of his time sitting in the kitchen with his whisky... now drinking straight from the bottle. A pile of unwashed dishes towered above him and scrawny grey mice scampered unnoticed at his feet. He tried unsuccessfully to teach Colin how to play bridge and even less successfully to talk to the boy. In frustration he would lock him in the cupboard for days and nights on end. Colin was unperturbed and even a little annoyed when his father at infrequent intervals broke the door open to push in a dirty bowl of cold stale porridge. At breakfast time, if Colin had been dragged form the dark sanctuary of the cupboard, his father would stare at him over the bleak table.

Colin would stare back, unspeaking, unmoved.

Each morning, Colin observed his father's deterioration. Soon he would fail to rise from his unmade bed. Then one day, after a long silence, he would be taken a way by grown ups, taken away and put in a hole in the ground.

And that night when relatives had put Colin safely in bed

and were humming and hawing and sharing out the cheap furniture, he would sneak downstairs and quietly and carefully open the cupboard door,

And there on the threshold between light and dark, he would pause, for a breathtaking moment when the silence carried the ghost-echo of two horrified whispers.

'Colin?'

NEW TEACHER

In Room Three the screams had reached a scale suggestive of the last knock in a pig's abattoir. Perhaps the only comparable level of human suffering might be the fall of Jerusalem. In either case the penultimate moments of the music lesson were blithely ignored by Peters the mathematics' teacher and his younger companion, Mr. Clark of history, as they strolled past the door and onwards down the sloping corridors of Bellport High School

As they passed the firmly closed door an exceptionally bestial shout pierced the air. Peters, an experienced sadist and virtuoso of the tawse, merely paused momentarily in his stride as Mr. Clark, known for his moderate views, glanced upwards with a single raised eyebrow. Neither said a thing until they reached the smoker's staff room. It was at that moment, with an appreciable distance from the screaming and a decent interval for the mind to settle, that Mr. Clark ventured a remark.

'The new teacher?'

'Music,' said Peters with a hollow smile.

'Having a bit of a rough time?'

'I'm afraid it's been three days of gymnastic, vocal and pugilistic exercise for the boys… at Mr. Nugent's expense.'

Peters searched for his pipe. 'They've just transferred him to Room Three, next to the smokers' staff room, so that any passing masters can pop their heads around the door if the situation appears to be plummeting beyond control.'

Clark found his lighter buried in his trousers. Another distant whoop of exhilaration thrilled the air. There was a sound much like a violin exploding into fragments. 'Must pop in to see if he needs assistance,' said Clark lighting a Capstan.

'Yes, someone will need to give him a hint or two…in a bit. After you?'

It was difficult to make out any inhabitants of the smokers staff room. In actuality, there was no non-smokers staff room but a series of minor skirmishes over the two designated rooms between Miss Hawthorn, the head of religious instruction (a grim and unremitting harridan) and her picked battalion from the German language department had seen off a more inventive, but less cohesive defence by mathematics, French and art. Now an uneasy stand-off existed. On the rare occasions where necessity demanded Miss Hawthorn's presence on the ground floor, she was treated to a sporadic but dense attack of foul pipe smoke, cigarette fumes and general fug by whichever of the weaker party was *in situ* – regardless of whether they desired to smoke or not. The upper storey staff room was defended by bunches of insipid flowers, a set of graphic cancer posters, a battery of perfume sprays and a range of hidden ambushes beyond even the colourful imagination of the smokers. Each side had adopted a siege mentality and at present all bets were off as to the victor.

Through the smoke, a huddle of teachers could be seen hunched over a variety of drinks that ranged from black tea through to instant coffee, to pale beverages recognizable only by a heady smell of cheap spirit. Peters and Clark, moving, like experienced skirmishers in trench warfare, manoeuvred through the battered chairs and tables to the more comfortable set of dilapidated couches.

'What's that infernal racket?' Simmons, head of art and the after-school film club, had just woken from a nightmare.

'The new music teacher,' said Clark. He pushed aside a pile of ragged exam papers and a collection of filthy mugs and placed his feet precariously in the gap. 'What's the film tomorrow?'

'*Deep Throat*,' said Simmons absently. He pulled a flask from his overcoat. 'What a bloody noise!'

'What's the new man's name?' said Mr. Ball unexpectedly.

'Why on earth do you want to know?' replied Peters. 'He won't be around long enough to need a name.'

'You never know,' said Ball: He ran the weekly sweepstake

on the football results. 'A new face could well want to invest a couple of quid in the tote.'

An almost imperceptible movement of cheek and lip indicated a wave of enthusiastic interest rippling across a series of drawn visages.

'His name's Nugent,' said Clark. 'I just remembered that I helped interview him in the summer break. He expressed a profound interest in church liturgy, the early history of bird watching and something about choirs. I don't recall that he demonstrated a predilection for sport…'

The enthusiastic interest collapsed like a deflating balloon.

'Did our revered Head participate in that interview or was it McVicars, our less esteemed but more intimidating deputy?'

'It was the Head,' said Clark.

'That explains the appointment,' said Ball languidly. 'The Head's recruited a batch this term that would make Mormons look like veterans of the hellfire club.'

'What's the bloody time?' Simmons had dropped off again and only awakened when an object had struck the wall behind him with some force.

'It's only second period,' said Clark. 'Shouldn't you be teaching?'

'It's on the eighth floor,' said Simmons with a trace of pique. ''I think the lift might be broken.'

The others lapsed into silence. Peters took a morning paper from his bag, placed his worn tawse on the table, and began to flick through the horses with a professional eye.

Mr. Clark scowled at his coffee. His initial enthusiasm for the teaching profession had waned to the point of extinction. Looking back, he thought the enthusiasm might have last about a week. Now, two years down the road, Bellport High had utterly done for him. Slouching back in the seat he could see the horrific façade of the main school building reflected in the windows of the Assembly room. The towering blocks rose like a concrete insult to good taste. The flickering shadows of pupils and teachers trapped in the straitjacket of education, flitted across countless windows like demonic shadow plays; boxed theatre sets that included thousands of pupils and hundreds of teachers locked in an unrelenting battle for survival and dominance.

Thank God for free periods and thank God that that mercenary bastard, Ball. He had organized a racing excursion to Musselburgh the following morning. Perhaps if he put his entire salary on a lucky horse he could jack the whole thing in. If he lost he could borrow a few quid and bury himself in beer.

Ball's friend from Manchester, an untidy man of no apparent fixed address or job, had come up to watch Musselburgh races. He stared at the tawse with a perplexed look. 'What the bloody hell is that?' he said.

Peter's glanced up from his paper and took the long belt in his hand and gave it a thump on the desk. Cups rattled. 'It's a tawse, my good man.'

'A belt, used for corporal punishment. A bit different from the cane in England,' said Clark. 'I don't approve of their use,'

'You *hit* them with that?'

'As often as possible,' said Peters. 'They stand up so...' he demonstrated with more pleasure than decency allowed. 'They hold their hands up before you so, palms doubled over and then you whack them as hard as you're able.'

'And that stops the little bastards misbehaving?' said the Mancunian.

'Sometimes,' said Peters regaining his seat. 'But in any case its one of the few pleasures I maintain at Bellport.'

Clark shook his head slowly and mournfully. The sound of a trumpet ripped into the air. It was quickly stifled, fading with the slow fall of a dying elephant.

'Do you remember your probationary year as a teacher, Peters?' said Ball unexpectedly. A few faces turned the colour of semolina. Peters said tersely 'Vividly. Twenty years ago it must have been. It was awful. New teacher-'

'No, no; the actual year. I need it for that horse who won the National the year you started. I'm completely stuck with this one....'

Clark stared into space. 'It was only two years ago for me,' he said in a whisper, 'but I still remember it as a living hell.'

'You get less for common assault,' agreed Simmons putting a newspaper on his face.

The door opened. All hands who were not asleep reached reflexively for tobacco. It was only Miss Caruthers of geography. She lit a cigarillo with a shaking hand. 'What's that bloody noise?' she said coughing irritably.

'New Teacher,' came a limp chorus.

'Nugent! Jesus wept; they haven't given him that Year 1 class have they – with Dermot, Campbell and Spawn of Satan.' Miss Caruthers moved nervously towards the window. She paused for a minute to stare across the wasteland of the playground.

'Gray's class,' said Clark, 'No I think Gray's off for hitting the janitor with a bucket. In any case, even the Head couldn't be...what's the big word for stupidly overconfident?'

There was a thoughtful but barren silence. From Room Three a rising murmur of insanity began to infiltrate the ether.

Peters grimaced as he tried to relight his pipe. For a second he looked vaguely dreamy. 'I think he's got that class with young Farantino and thon sweet little cherub with the scar on his cheek.'

'You did that didn't you?' said Ball a little unkindly. The newspaper had just revealed several call-offs in a team he had been relying on heavily for the weekend.

'Absolutely not,' replied Peters. 'I only damaged his wrist. A mere flesh wound.' He fingered the tawse, which he kept tucked under his jacket above the shoulder. 'I think it's his class. Let me see; period three yesterday I saw them drag all the chairs into the corridor.'

'What were you doing near the music rooms?'

'I had to slip out for a bit.'

'I saw him on Monday in the afternoon being trailed by a couple of lads who had attached a donkey's tail to his jacket,' said Miss Caruthers absently.

'That *was* Dermot,' said Clark. 'But he should have been in my class.'

'It *is* Farantino's class. That smug little bastard,' said Simmons. He had woken up again. 'They have music in the morning then after break…is it break time?' He held his forehead histrionically, '…they come to me then, the little bastards. At least they'll have worn themselves out on this new fellow'

'Break in ten minutes,' said Clark dismally. 'Just a warning in case anyone has corridor duty.'

Ball laughed. 'A warning?'

'In the sense of warning that you *should* be on the corridors. I'm free next period,' he said smugly.

'Rule one in teaching,' said Simmons taking a long dram.' Never be seen on the corridor or indeed any public place when there may be pupils in the vicinity.'

'Don't suppose the new fellow, Nugent – what a stupid name - has discovered that particular gem of truth in the manual,' said Peters.

'Well look at this,' said Miss Caruthers gleefully. 'It's old Hawthorn heading across the playground looking like someone's offered to test her virginity.'

'Christ,' said Ball. 'Don't do that. What a mental picture to take into the break. It's worse than that bloody racket.'

'Get your baccy out folks.'

Those teachers who had not lit up began to prepare a hasty assault on the atmosphere. A few moments later Miss Hawthorn broached the doorway. She stood for a second, visibly intimidated by the curls of grim smoke that swept across the staff room like a spewing belt of satanic mills, then with a shrug like a lioness, she stepped one pace forward staring myopically into the room while holding the door open as wide as was possible. 'What on earth is that awful noise,' she said in her brittle voice.'

'Noise,' said Peters. 'Do you hear something Clark? You have the younger ears. A noise of some description.'

Clark's face took on a stoic calm. He glanced down at his newspaper.

'There is an awful noise coming from Room Three,' said Miss Hawthorne with a look of baffled incomprehension.

'I think I hear something,' said Ball calculating the odds on a rather complex treble.

'Yes,' said Simmons in a theatrical voice. 'I rather think it might be coming from that new fellow's class – Nugget, Ungent?'

'It is unlikely to be Mr. Nugent's class,' said Miss Hawthorne in a strident voice, 'because the Head has advised me to inform you that Mr. Clark will have to cover for our colleague as he has phoned in sick this morning.'

'Then who on earth is in his classroom?' said Peters. 'I heard an adult's voice a moment ago. There, didn't you hear it?'

A gruff voice seemed to be grunting and bellowing at a volume loud enough to penetrate the smoke stained division between Room Three and the staff room. Something shattered against the wall and there was a strange silence filled only by a low and disturbing chuckle.

Suddenly, Clark, who had only been idly skimming the newspaper while he thought of a way of weaselling out of lesson cover, went quite white. He dropped his newspaper. It fell open at a stark photo of a lunatic escapee and a rather lurid headline which warned against approaching him under any circumstances.

Even as the staff raised their eyes towards the open staff room door a thin trickle of dark blood was visible, snaking its way down the sloping corridor like the first grim intimation of a rupture in a dam.

It came from the general direction of Room Three.

THE JANUS DOOR

As I walked up to the third floor of our new flat I could still hear Jan screaming at me from the foot of the stairs. The whine in her voice seemed to be garrotting the sentries in my brain who defended that private dreamworld known only to despondent husbands. For the tenth time in the day I prayed for a means to escape, for a door out of this sordid existence. Instead, I was faced with the door to our new home.

It was an ordinary door, but to me doors are never really ordinary. They are entrances to places, and you never know what is going to happen when you walk through one: New door - new life. Hopefully, a better life; me and Jan, happy, like we were before I missed my promotion chance and was left stranded with another thirty clerks in the 'steady worker but lacks talent' class.

I put the key in the lock and turned it. The tumblers were noiseless, as though the lock had been recently oiled. I placed my hand on the old fashioned door knob, and as I did I felt a tingling sensation as though a ghost girl had licked my spine. The sensation melted. Taking a deep breath, I pushed open the door.

Surprisingly, it creaked as it swung on its hinges: a wailing, tearing sound: the sound you might expect in an old mansion, not a new flat in a suburban area.

I made a mental note to oil the hinges, and then walked in to survey the flat. Thankfully, inside I could no longer hear Jan. She must have turned her attention to the removal men who had broken one of her pots on the stair landing, an event she apparently expected me to anticipate and prevent.

A cough behind me made me jump. For a second I thought Jan had found a new means of locomotion which dispensed with the need for stairs, but it was only a man standing hesitant in the doorway. He was big, thick set with grey-white hair. In his hand he carried an oil can.

'Hello,' he said. 'Richard. New neighbour?'

I didn't answer, sarcastic retorts sizzling in my head.

'Heard the door,' he continued unabashed. 'Thought this might be just the ticket.' Without asking he began oiling the hinges in a methodical manner. 'Like to be neighbourly,' he said smiling.

I didn't return the smile. I hate practical people, perhaps because I can't saw straight, and my thumb seems to swell up even before I pick up a hammer and nails. I particularly disliked the pushy practical type.

'Lovely door this,' he said. 'Original pine. Unusual for these types of flats. See it's never been painted...'

I left him and padded down the hall. My footprints made eerie ghost steps in the dust creating a chill mood which was reinforced by the scene in a dining room as bereft of presence as the cabins of the Mary Celeste. I drew open a curtain sending dancing moths out into the steaming sunlight. The light almost made the room appear like a still life.

The big man had followed me in uninvited. He wiped some dust from the table top on to his hand. 'Need a bit of cleaning this; professional would charge the earth. I might be able to give you a bit of hand. How come the estate agents didn't...'

'...I bought the place quick at a rock bottom price; I work for a firm.' The big man looked as though the office jargon would leapfrog his head. 'I did a deal and got it cheap. Part of the deal was I do my own clean up.'

He still looked lost, defeated by his own narrow sense of doing things. I asked a question.

'Did you know much about the previous occupant?'

He smiled, now on familiar ground. 'I knew him well. We were very friendly. In fact, I keep expecting him to walk through that door.' His bright little eyes directed me to the open door.

'It's hardly likely,' I said. 'The man's dead ...or so they told me at the office.'

He gave me a look.
Just then Jan walked in and started shouting.

All morning I had been working on the flat, cleaning and dusting and polishing while Jan towered over me like some sort of demented southern overseer. In the afternoon she left to go to the shops, dumping me with instructions to clean up the spare room. It was the worst of several bad tasks - the room was full of what looked like radio equipment in various stages of decomposition - but I still felt that pall of relief at her departure. Now I could be on my own; my own man, taking my time, pottering around.

I put the kettle on and dropped a cup. It smashed on the floor, and I grinned as I scooped up the bits. I dropped the pieces in the swing-bin, wishing I could do the same thing with our marriage.

I paused for a second, thinking about the good times. How attractive Jan had appeared when I first met her. The times we did it in the car when her folks were home. How she always smelled sweet. Then the transformation as things got out of hand at the office. From an angel to a monster in three easy stages.

It started with the first argument. How I looked sloppy, needed a shave. Then I seemed to wear out suits more than the normal guys. I - how did she put it? - inhabited clothes. That's no way to get on, looking like a tramp. She built me a cage, a cage of words locking me in. Rules and orders. How to do this. What not to do. When to say this. And, from a happy go lucky guy I became one of the trapped.

When I thought back to the pre-Jan days they seemed full of light and glory. I kicked the bin. Thinking makes you bitter.

The spare room was a jumbled mess. But there was something satisfying about being in it. I spent a few moments sitting at a desk heaped with wires and transistors considering what had inspired my sense of ease: The door was closed; it was a quiet room, one window, a small desk lamp creating a halo of light around the penumbra of which the giant speakers and mixing desks loomed like a metal jungle. I picked up a sheet of wiring instructions and felt the years slipping away from my shoulders. That was the centre of the satisfaction. It was a man's room; a totally masculine domain. The sort of room where favourite uncles built model railways; great landscapes of papier-mâché mountains and moss hedgerows with tiny tracks leading into tunnels and disappearing who knows where. The room was for adults who never grew up.

I decided then it was my room. Jan or no Jan, I was going to make it my own.

Jan invited the pushy neighbour in. The two of them sat at the table laughing about my lack of practical skills; typical neighbourly talk. 'He can't hammer a nail.' Laughter. 'I remember once he wired the electric plug on the kettle the opposite way round'. The big man made little grunting noises and kept offering practical help. All the while he kept nodding across at me like an inane puppet. I smiled - resisting the temptation to make funny faces or smash a vase - and made a pot of tea. The subject got around to the spare room. I heard Richard butting in with suggestions about shelving and the right way to hang a tapestry on the wall.

'The spare room is mine.' I said. 'I'm going to clear it out and use it as an ...office.'

'Office,' laughed Jan. 'You've got an office at work.'

'I need to work at home. There is a big project on...' the idea was building in my head, '...it's a real chance. The boss has given me a special dispensation. He told me specially, took me aside. I'll not get another chance.'

There was a pause. Jan looked impressed. She always looked impressed when the prospect of money hovered in the air.

'Well...'

'I could help you set out some real bureaus.' said Richard.' There's a space...'

'That's kind of you. But I'll have no time to set up anything. I've got to get down to it now.'

I saw Richard to the door. The creaking wail was still pronounced as the door swung on its hinges. 'Oil didn't do much good,' I said smiling.

'Can't understand it,' he replied. 'I'll have another look tomorrow.'

'Please do.' I shut the door. The hollow echo of its wail resounded faintly in the hall.

That night I felt Jan's fingers running across my body. We made love for the first time in weeks. After, she asked me about the work. I kept things vague and looked tight lipped and forceful; the sort of ambitious dick Jan wanted to share her life with. She seemed happier.

I got up to go to the bathroom. Pacing down the hall I caught a faint whisper coming from the spare room like a hustle of dust. I opened the door and walked in. Around me the speakers and amplifiers towered like castle battlements. Paper fluttered across the desks like ghosts. I breathed in the still air, heard what seemed like an answering breath. Then I saw the red light of the main amplifier. I walked across the floor sending up clouds of dust and echoes. Somehow, although I didn't remember doing it, I'd left the amplifier on. There must have been a hidden microphone somewhere, catching my movements and pushing them back through the speakers. I switched it off.

I began to spend time in the spare room. The only window was shielded by blinds. The struts of these blinds were entangled, and it was clearly impossible to open the window without removing the blind. The entangled struts cast a web of shadows across the room, and the shadows made the air seem full of movement. It was as though something was moving in the corner of your vision. You turned to see it, and it was gone, only to be replaced by another stirring just out of reach.

Apart from the speakers and the amplifiers, there was a range of unusual electrical equipment that banked the walls. The effect reminded me of a museum of ancient radiograms, all shapes and sizes. From some of the 'radiograms' ticker tapes hung giving the faint impression that a party had finished fifty years before, and no one had cleaned up. The words 'finished' seemed to reverberate in my ears as though the speakers had been momentarily activated, and I had spoken the word aloud. My eyes were drawn by some instinct to the open door. For a second, no, less than a second, a ghostly figure like a hologram seemed suspended between the door jambs. The figure disappeared, but for the first time I sensed that I had company. Someone else, probably the previous occupant, had left his more-than-physical traces in the immediate environment. Suddenly, I felt a warmth as though a friend had caressed my head, and my eyes were drawn inexorably to an old desk beneath the window. The desk was engulfed in papers which waved softly as I walked towards them.

I sat down in the swivel chair. The chair swung noiselessly beneath my weight. I examined the array of papers in silence, contemplating where to begin.

Then like the voice of a hated relative squeaking from under a coffin lid, Jan's screech disturbed the peace.

Richard and Jan were sitting in the lounge discussing wallpaper. 'Richard's just offered to wallpaper the bedroom, but I've told him we can't possibly accept. Can we?'

'Of course we can't,' I said, 'But…'

'It's no trouble to me…' said Richard.

'Well…' said Jan indicating me 'He's so useless. Perhaps you could give him a hand.'

When I got back to the spare room the presence had gone.

At the office the boss called me in to his room. 'This is crap,' he said holding out my portfolio. 'Do it again. Do it right or you'll be looking elsewhere. I'm carrying no one here. Young men are breathing down your shoulder. Young men who cost less and give more. Think about it.'

I couldn't think about it. Instead I clocked out and paid a call to the library and then registrar house. I searched out through archives.

A door is a moveable frame used to open and close a space. It is also an opening through which people leave or enter a building. The latter definition appealed to me. My fascination with doors extended to unreal doors - gates. I'd read my Science Fiction. I knew that at least in imagination, it was possible to find a door which opened on another world. There are times in your life when such a door appeals strongly. When I was little I often wanted to escape into a secret garden. When I was an adolescent I needed that door and it wasn't there. Now, with my work and my marriage crumbling I was looking again.

Only this time I felt there was a chance I wouldn't be disappointed.

I unearthed some illustrations. Ghiberti's East Doors in the Florentine Baptisery. In 14th century Tuscany, Ghiberti created doors so beautiful that people called them the gates of paradise. I felt that I could touch the paper and my hand would disappear through the gateways and touch heaven. But these illustrations were too small for a whole body to get through; to touch heaven wasn't enough.

I researched the history of the block of flats. It had been made earlier than I suspected - 1968. The architect was a woman called Hossana. It was unusual in those days for a woman to have achieved such prominence, but then it appeared she was an unusual woman. Her plans had been grandiose. They included a series of stepped fountains in the central quadrangle but, like most architects, she had been thwarted by the investors. Unlike most architects she had committed suicide when the plans had been amended during construction. She had thrown herself from a third storey window. The room wasn't mentioned but I could guess where it was located. Her reasons for suicide were not entirely clear. She had been young, successful; there were no personal problems. The only clue was her apparent obsession with mythic archetypes. Her original designs were lodged at a small, private office on the other side of town.

I called Jan and told her I would be working late and took a bus to the small office. There, after a few flattering lies about writing an article, an old secretary let me examine the papers. I pored through documented accounts of the suicide, old newspaper editions, financial transactions and finally the original drafts of the flats.

When the old girl came through with a cup of tea, apparently pleased to have someone to talk to after her initial suspicion, I had just finished reading. I sipped her metallic tea as she engaged me in conversation. It was dark evening when I took the last bus back to the flat. From the records and the conversation I'd found what I wanted to know.

Hossana had thrown herself from the window of my spare room. The impetus for her suicide had been the final refusal of the investors to allow a mythic theme of gateways to be embellished above each doorway. Hossana had even offered to fund the work herself. The investors had taken the view that the strange gargoyles and mythological creatures perching above the door lintel in each flat would undoubtedly offend and even scare some potential occupants.

The old secretary had met Hossana and spoken with her. The young architect had been beautiful, dark eyed, half Italian. A moody person to work for, given to depressions and melancholy, but with an insatiable energy and will. It was apparent that the small office had become a kind of shrine to Hossana.

I was inclined to believe that the spare room in my flat might have taken on a similar function.

The flat was in darkness when I returned. My instincts told me that Jan was not there, but they also told me that someone else was. I didn't know where Jan had gone, unless she had phoned the office, discovered my deceit and ran back to mother. I knew where the other presence was. When I walked down the hall the door of the spare room swung open with an almost human wail. I hesitated for a second on the threshold. I whispered 'Hossana' and from the vast speakers like a hushed wave the word echoed back to me.

Then I walked into the room.

The face of the full moon glared like a prisoner through the horizontal struts of the blinds. Its light was echoed by those of the amplifiers; green, white and red lights like cats' eyes amazed and staring. The banks of speakers seemed like immense stone gods frozen in impassive postures. Each breath I took was shussshed back at me through the speakers like a giant mother comforting a child. I knew that she was there.

A zephyr drifting through the window, which I had not opened, caught the ticker tape and sent it moving. The papers on the desk waved softly and then in ones and twos began to float to the floor. I had the sense that something incredible and beyond imagination was about to happen. Suddenly, brutally, a harsh light flashed through the room from the hall, I heard a loud cackle and turned fully expecting to see the door way to some kind of heaven.

Instead I saw Jan laughing. 'Whatever are you doing in the dark?' Richard the neighbour, peered over her shoulder like an ogre.

'I came in to switch things off.' I said quickly. Jan gave me a curious look.

The amplifier lights had faded, the speakers were silent. 'I don't know how you can work in this mess,' she said.

Richard nodded gravely as though he could actually see the envisaged bureaus in their appropriate space.

'I've no time to clean up. I have the space at the desk. This job gives me no time.'

'Well, I hope we see some profit from it,' said Jan. 'All the evenings you've been out.'

In the morning I phoned work, and cancelled all appointments. Jan had shopping to do, and I spent the hours at the desk beneath the window sorting papers. Most were circuit diagrams or complex mathematical equations on superstring theory which were beyond me. There were several files and binders containing abstracts for personal computer programmes, and some notes in languages which I recognised as French, Italian, Dutch and Arabic. Most of the texts were out of my grasp; of them all I followed the French reasonably well; mostly it spoke of metaphysical philosophy, some rather abstruse, but there were many references to doors: The Hagia Sophia Cathedral in Constantinople, the introduction of Bronze doors in Northern Europe. The use of doors to spell out a narrative, usually mystical or religious.

The construction of doors seemed to be the main subject of the Dutch texts. I caught references to casing, vertical beams, rails, but most of the terms were too technical.

The Arabic again was mainly philosophical. I understood very little of this, but there were diagrams and mathematical principles which had a vague familiarity. The graphic material would sometimes seem accessible; it combined ancient cryptic pictures and cabala with strikingly modern symbolism.

Although it was impossible to determine in such a short review of the materials, it seemed that the previous occupant was researching a description of the universe using superstring theory and mysticism that reduced grand unification theory to five dimensions; a startling if implausible conclusion.

After a few hours I was exhausted with the strain of examining the transcriptions. I felt unable to eat. Instead I wandered down to the inner quadrangle to see if I could see the window of the flat from the ground. This I found impossible. The quadrangle was overgrown, the fountains dried out. Although the step formation had been retained in principle, the materials were cheap and shoddy. It was clear that it would have been impossible to make the fountains workable and I wondered how Hossana had persuaded the investors to go as far as they had.

I stood on the central fountain, trying to see the window, but the view was obscured by both the narrow perspective and ivy.

On a whim I wandered up the opposite stairwell and found myself on the parallel floor to my own flat. For some architectural reason which I am utterly unable to explain it was impossible to see my flat window from this side. Yet it should have been possible. I tried straining my head around the open stair window to no effect. I could only see the windows of my neighbour.

Beneath me about a metre downwards there was a space on the lintel; a space of about twenty centimetres wide. Beneath that there was a drop of around thirty-five metres to the stone pavings of the quadrangle. I felt an impulse which I could not reject. Grasping the casing of the window I pulled myself out and onto the lintel. I perched on this tiny platform and, facing the wall, began to edge around the quadrangle. For some five metres I travelled in this manner until I came to a drainpipe. Clutching the pipe I turned.

Whether it was the height, my empty belly or something beyond explanation I don't know, but when I turned I felt nausea grip me by the shoulders, the world seem to reel and yaw. I knew I was gripping the pipe with all my strength but it seemed as though I was barely touching it. The ground beneath me swelled upwards as though a great force was pushing through the quadrangle, and the sky seemed suddenly crushed downwards in response. Staring across the open space was an immense, inhuman effort but I did it.

I saw the flats as though through a hall of mirrors, distorted and unreal. It seemed the opposing windows were literally staring at me. The whole edifice took on an unreal quality as though it were at once ancient and futuristic.

Before I passed out, or maybe as I began to fall, I am sure I saw through the ragged struts of my window a vision of blinding light from the doorway beyond.

What I'm less sure about is the figures: Strange, ethereal silhouettes like crucified saints crowding the door frame; tormented angels grasping outwards, begging me to enter.

It was a vision of angels that woke me. The angels became a female doctor and nurse bending over my hospital bed. 'You're lucky to be alive,' said the doctor. 'Badly bruised, a minor fracture of the tibia. A somewhat miraculous escape.'

Apparently, I'd been out for two days. Because of the concussion they kept me in observation for another three. Jan dutifully visited, keeping her eyes fixed on me as though I was a reptile set to strike. I chose not to explain my fall, so Jan explained it for me. 'You should have watched out. You know these stairwells are slippy. You're clumsy and stupid.' This in the face of the impossibility of falling out of the window by chance.

My boss was less sympathetic. When I returned to the flat on the floor in the hall was a letter from the office. I got to it before Jan. 'What does it say?' she said.

'It's from the office. The boss has given me time off to recover and to finish the project.' I neglected to mention the time off was on a permanent, unpaid basis.

Richard popped in with some boring books on making ships out of matchsticks. He felt this might help me through my convalescence While Jan was making coffee in the kitchen I steered the conversation around to the previous occupant of my flat.

'He was a quiet fellow,' said Richard. 'Rather morose. He rarely left the flat. He was always working on some outlandish theory about the flats.'

'What theory was that?'

'He was obsessed with the architecture,' said Richard flatly.

'How did he die?'

Richard gave me that keen look. 'Oh, he didn't die.' Jan walked in with the coffee. 'He's a missing person.' Richard grinned.

That night, while Jan slept, I pored through the binders and files on the desk. I knew the answer lay somewhere amongst these papers. The man had walked into another world. Not dead, not missing but escaped - free. Somewhere there was an avenue to this freedom. If one man could do it, another could follow.

The search proved fruitless. The room seemed empty, the presence gone.

In the morning I purchased dictionaries, and for a further two days I remained in the spare room working feverishly, only exiting to eat. At first Jan was pleased. She and Richard would exchange glances when I emerged. I took these glances to be ones of sympathy for the dedicated worker. I later found this to be a mistake.

The unpaid bills began to drop through the door. I manage to stop the first of them but it was a futile task.

I felt that I was on the verge of cracking the ciphers and codes of the documents. A coherent picture was emerging, a startling picture of alternate reality based on complex applied mathematics and a mysticism inspired by the architectural features of the flats. It was like being trapped in a maze. Our own four dimensions were inadequate to hold the physical presence of a man with the appropriate map. I was constructing my own symbolic referents, mapping this maze, when I heard the door open. I turned hoping, and half expecting, to see a blinding light. Jan stood in the doorway, blocking the entrance.

'What is this?' She held out an envelope.

We shouted, argued. I remember her beating me with her open palms. I covered my head unable to defend myself. Then I struck her. From somewhere, Richard intervened. Gripping me by the arms as Jan struck me repeatedly. They left me on the floor, my blood darkening the carpet. I lay for some time, half conscious, breathing in gasps. Then, in the darkness, I heard a hollow click, the room seemed at once to expand and contract in time with my lungs. One by one the amplifier lights blinked on. I felt I could hear the paper breathing, the very words chanting from the pages.

By some trick of acoustics I could hear distant voices, whispering. At first I thought the voices were emanating from the doorway, but then I heard my name, laughter. It was Jan and Richard.

They were discussing my death.

My mind was drawn back to several telling incidents in the past few months. Times I'd come back early and Richard had been hanging around, little asides between the two of them.

And Jan sorting out the details of our life assurance forms. They were going to kill me.

I tried to get up. Couldn't. Richard was talking about disposing of the body. It was my body he was talking about. I pushed myself on to my hands, felt wracking pain surge through me. Their voices were silent. I heard footsteps, the sound of movement beyond the spare room. The speakers around me began to hum into life. The sounds of my own breathing began to mask all other sounds; a great rolling ocean composed of sighs. Painfully, I rose from my hands, tottered, lurched towards the door of the spare room, trying desperately to remember the knowledge I had assimilated, knowing that only through full understanding could I hope to escape.

Slowly, like the pages of an awesome book the door began to open. Light surged from the exposed space, unearthly light. My hands outstretched, were lost in the radiance as though a whiteout had blanketed my vision. The door was flung wide I fell the last few steps, smiling as I crashed through the gateway of paradise.

I had a sense of being nothing. Then I saw in two directions at once: Outwards to the hall and inwards to the spare room. Jan and Richard walked through me into the room. Richard said simply 'He's gone. We pushed him to the conceptual breakthrough.' He laughed, and Jan threw her arms around him.

I tried to move. Something was wrong.

'They can't escape,' said Richard staring at the door. 'Almost like gold fish, except that the fish can move in the bowl. They can't move - ever. They can hear, they can smell, they can see.'

He grinned, and slowly began to close the door. 'But they can't escape.'

I knew then, too late, why some doors wail with such terror when opened.

The people inside are screaming to get out.

THE HEAVEN MAKER

The Accident

The night of the terrible accident was one of heat and sweat. The sultry air was summer's assault on Morden's overtaxed lungs and the faint rap of his heart had a muffled quality as though an old clock had been wrapped in a heavy blanket and packaged in his chest. As he struggled through the hospital doorway he dropped his cane and had to be assisted by a young nurse.

'I was asked to come,' he said. 'I have to authorise a caesarean section on the body of my daughter. I believe that although she is dead, it might be possible to save the child.'

A young doctor with a calm demeanour and a gentle face ushered him into a small ante room. The doctor took a seat alongside the Senior Surgeon on duty who let a sepia file slip from the grasp of his large hands and filled three glasses with water from a crystal decanter. He pushed one towards Morden.

'I'm very sorry to have dragged you out of your bed at this late hour, especially in view of the tragic events of tonight and your obvious ill health. As you know we were unable to save the lives of your daughter or her husband. We have kept Mrs. Ward on a life support system but she is quite dead. Her brain is not providing any impulse. We are keeping her heart and lungs working so her vital organs will supply her unborn child with sustenance. In this manner, although there can be no guarantees, we have a possibility of preserving the life of the unborn child.'

He took a small sip of water. 'I'll be direct with you Mr. Morden. We cannot make any promises. A caesarean birth might be performed in three weeks giving us a very premature baby and an outside chance of a surviving child. On the other hand we might simply be raising you hopes in vain. I need to know your decision now as the equipment we use can be made available to other patients. These are hard times Mr. Morden. I'm afraid I must press you.'

Morden cleared his throat before answering. His voice was a faint whisper barely heard above the hum of the air conditioning. 'May I see my daughter?'

'Of course, Mr. Morden.' The older surgeon paused as the doctor whispered in his ear. He frowned and looked directly in to Morden's eyes. 'It seems we must anticipate an inquiry because of the circumstances of the accident Mr. Morden. In view of this it would be of great benefit to the hospital if we could impose on you to identify the body of your daughter's husband.'

Morden nodded.

'In that case we'll have his body transferred to ward 7 so that we don't have to shuttle you from here to the morgue. Dr Baptiste here will escort

Dr Baptiste supported Morden as they walked through the long corridors. It seemed to the older man that they moved in a surreal motion separate from the speeding world around them. Apparently a kind of blindness had afflicted the rest of humanity. The nurses and patients hurried by the two unheeding though Morden thought his anguish must burn like a beacon for all to see.

Coarse laughter resonated in the corridor. Morden started involuntarily. Ward 7. He found himself gazing into a wide chamber. Beds, emptied and covered in white sheets stood on either side like the slabs of a mausoleum. At the far end three porters stood idle, hands in pockets. One was talking loudly and gesticulating with a free hand. In front of him two trolleys broke the symmetrical line of the beds. On each trolley the shape of a body could be seen. Around the nearer trolley stood an artificial respirator and a number of machines.

The porters became aware of Morden and Dr Baptiste and as the two advanced their voices dropped and faded. The young doctor gestured at the porters and they backed away from the bodies glancing at Morden with curiosity. The doctor pulled back the sheeting from the first body.

A maze of wiring extended from beneath her and several drips were inserted in her nose and mouth. Her face however, was uninjured and to Morden it seemed that she might simply open her eyes and speak to him. She had always been a beautiful girl and here, now, Morden saw the years of her youth and childhood stretching backwards like a series of fleeting images.

He bent to touch her and the images weakened and were gone. 'She...,' he said incoherently.

'I'm afraid she's quite dead Mr. Morden. It's an artificial life we have given her, for the sake of the unborn child.'

Morden shook his head. 'Cover her again if you please,' he said, struggling to gather himself. 'Make every effort to save the child. I'm sure she would have wanted that for John.' He looked at the next trolley.

'There's just the final identification Mr. Morden, and then we'll get you home.'

As he walked round the dead girl with downcast eyes Morden heard one of the porters gasp. From beneath the white sheeting of the second trolley a pale arm had fallen twitching. A gout of blood appeared on the region near the head. With a terrible fascination Morden watched as the corpse rose upwards and the sheet slipped from its shoulders. The dead eyes opened with a convulsive snap and stared into his own. The jaws gaped wide spewing dark blood and the mouth began to scream and scream and scream.

'John Ward, My son-in-law,' said Morden as he passed out.

Howard

It was late afternoon. Morden was sitting in his chair staring out of the window at the leaden sky. He heard the gate shutting in the garden and looked down to observe a spare figure clad in a tweed suit walking up the pathway towards the house. With a sigh he arranged the tartan blanket around his legs. He heard the door open and his housekeeper's tremulous voice rising in surprise. There was a brief interchange. In its aftermath came the tread of footsteps making there way upstairs. The door was pushed open and the man hesitated at the doorway.

'Come in Howard,' said Morden. 'I expected you but not this soon.'

Howard entered and slumped into the chair opposing Morden. After a space he said 'I've already been to the hospital. John's still in a coma. They wouldn't let me see him.' His watery eyes searched for those of Morden but the old man turned his head and stared again at the grey skies. Howard lowered his head again. 'You must be devastated.'

'Somewhat,' said Morden.

'John was dead for over three hours you know. It seems incredible. I would have thought his brain would have been damaged yet the doctors say he was lucid for a few brief seconds.... of course, you were there.' Howard stammered.

'Yes, I was there Howard.'

'I would have been there only-.'

'Only you were drunk.'

'I-.'

'You're always drunk Howard. Don't bore me by attempting to deny it. My son. A useless, futile drunk.'

Howard started out of his chair but thought better of it. 'Would it have made any difference if it had been me driving the car?'

'Perhaps you might have gone instead of Cathy. God forgive me for saying it but I wish you had. I wish you were in the ground now and she was sitting here instead of lying wired to those damned machines.'

'God I could use a drink now,' said Howard.

'You'll have your drink Howard after you have told how she ... how Cathy died.

Outside the clouds had gathered, lined with streaks of crimson. As Howard talked Morden watched the sun sink like a suppurating wound into the swollen belly of the sky.

Howard began in a hesitant, throaty voice but as he was caught in the narrative he began to illustrate the words with tiny nervous gestures.

'We were all supposed to be going to the theatre. Cathy, John and myself. I couldn't make it in the end. I got held up, met some friends in the Bridgewater and well... missed the train.' Howard looked down at his grey shoes. 'Yes, I was drunk. Perhaps if I hadn't been stewing in a gutter, perhaps if I'd been sober I would have caught the train. But I was drunk and missed it and so John waited with Cathy and because he waited he was late and it was dark and he must have driven fast on the wet roads.' He licked his lips, fumbled for cigarettes. Finding none he continued.

'They hit a rough patch on the cobbles in Palace Lane and John lost control of the car. Straight through the chains at that weak point by the bridge. Witnesses say the car hung for a second suspended and then lurched over into the water like a rat. God the water must have been cold. Cold and dark. The windscreen smashed, caught by one of the chain links and that cold water rushed in throwing them back in their seats. John's immense physique stuck fast, trapped by the steering wheel and held in by his seat belt but Cathy was seen reeling over into the rear.

'The car sunk rapidly. John must have struggled like a maniac to free himself, fighting against that rush of water. They say that every window except the back was smashed to pieces and one of the doors was broken off its hinges. Anyway, that wasn't the worst of it. They were down in those waters for nearly ten minutes. There was a pocket of air trapped in the rear.

'I can imagine John keeping half calm even then. His bloody army training and his composure. Well, he did it. He kept her head up, waited till the car was full of water. He could have got out himself but you know what he thought of Cathy; he kept her head up until the air was near gone and then struck out through the door he had kicked away. But he must have been disorientated. The car was upside down when they hauled it out this afternoon. I've no doubt in that first few vital seconds he tried to go the wrong way. Perhaps he was caught in the tangled rubbish on the silt bed. In any event, when he reached the surface he was nigh unconscious.

'God, let me have a drink father.' Howard paused to plead with Morden but the old man was adamant. He took a small key from his pocket and placed it on the glass table before him. It was the key to the drinks cabinet and Howard knew it. He stared at the small key for some time before continuing.

'When he reached the surface he must have been totally confused. An old couple who'd seen everything started shouting to him. He struck out for their voices, still holding Cathy. I've no idea where he got his strength from but he managed to reach the other side. He reached the side and when he got there his hands scrabbled on the slimy bank of the canal trying to pull himself up. The old couple looked on helpless. If he'd gone the other way he would have been safe but he followed their voices and found four feet of bank between him and the tow path.

'They watched him sink back into the water and they watched as Cathy slipped out of his grasp and down into the black.

'They picked him up a hundred yards down from the Bridgewater lock gates. John was dead when they found him but Cathy died in the ambulance on the way to the Hospital.' Howard, unable to hold himself back bent over and picked up the small key. He looked at Morden but the old man made no sign. He took they key over to the cabinet behind him, found a bottle of whisky and filled a large glass, drank it and then filled it again.

'You know the rest father. They've got Cathy on that machine waiting to pluck the child out in some ghastly fashion while John lies comatose in the next ward waiting for his rebirth.'

Howard took another mouthful of whiskey and topped the glass up. 'He should be dead by all rights. He should be dead as a doornail. I mean he was dead wasn't he; for three hours he was cold. His brain must be destroyed. It can't survive can it? I mean mine's done in enough with this bloody stuff.' He tipped up the glass for emphasis. 'What's it like if you're out cold like that for ...'

'Shut up Howard.' Morden looked at the young man with distaste. 'I have often considered the sins I must have committed to be cursed with a son like you. I won't put up with your drunken gibberish in my house. Take the bottle if you like. But take it out of my house and out of my sight.'

Howard's perception seemed inflamed rather than subdued by the drink. He gripped the neck of the bottle and stared into the eyes of his father. 'You saw him didn't you? He sat up in front of you and looked you in the face. What did you see?'

'Get out Howard. Get out and stay out.'

'I'll go father,' He picked up the bottle,' I'll take this and I'll see you in hospital. We can visit out deranged hero together.'

Morden said nothing as the young man left. The sun sunk had without trace behind the backdrop of clouds. He stared out at the darkness.

'He wasn't mad,' he said to himself. 'It was something close to madness I saw in his eyes.'

For a long while he sat in the still room waiting and watching as the lights gradually winked out in the surrounding streets.

The Vigil

Despite his parting remarks Howard did not appear at the hospital.

For a month Morden kept a solitary vigil by John's bed. On a few occasions he had found himself outside ward 7 where Cathy's body lay in its artificial limbo between life and death: He had been unable to enter the ward alone. It was enough to gaze for a few seconds through the tinted windows. He would see the inert body with its trailing wires and sentinel machines crouching by the bed, and, then he would return, drained and depressed, to sit in John's chill room with nothing but the constant pip of the oscilloscope to break the silence.

The nurses would come at intervals to bring tea or perform routine tasks around John's body. Morden would watch three of them struggling with the young man's ponderous frame. Even relaxed it seemed vital and formidable. They spilled him over on to his side and he would face Morden, eyes closed like a marble statue. Sometimes Morden would sense a well of power emanating from behind the shell of the eyelids as though a giant lay recumbent, his spirit locked by a spell but still living and breathing in the dungeon of his body. At other times there would be an absence of power as though the energy which clung to life was fighting an unseen battle in some hidden recess, as though the power was soaking away into a spirit world out of reach.

The nights were worst. The long, silent nights. John's body was veiled by a thin transparent gauze. The gauze and the trailing wires of drips and monitors seemed like a tangled web in which had fallen an ancient crusader draped in stone. The small private room had the feel of a tomb, an unearthly disturbing peace.

Often he thought of the terrible accident, his own labouring breath reminding him of those minutes John and Cathy had endured trapped in a pocket of air beneath the waters of the dark canal.

In those evening vigils Morden would sweat in the clammy antiseptic room, the borderlands of his mind dwelling on the events of the past month; the terrible accident, the morgue with its conflicting smells, the sultry nights, the draped beds and endless corridors. All seemed confused in his mind.

But one memory came stark to him in the quiet times: the face of John contorted in agony and terror as though a blindfold had been ripped from his eyes and he had seen something that no man should see.

This face haunted Morden's evenings and screamed in his nightmares. It was then that he would hear Howard's voice whispering down the avenues of his mind and a vivid picture of the waters of the dark canal would at first appear then grow monstrously until it enveloped him in a satanical oblivion.

As the days slipped by Morden found it difficult to keep a grip of reality. He seemed to be balanced between two impossibles - his daughter sleeping in a death it was impossible to disturb yet her body still functioning, her heart beating, her lungs heaving in and out, even her womb filled with a growing fruit ready to be plucked;, She was the past kept precariously in the present. And then there was John, sunk in his own unquiet slumber, breathing, alive yet unaware. He might never waken, might never live. Lost in the present he was the uncertain future.

Morden found that he too was retreating into a private world. A world where his emotions and senses could no longer be assaulted by the horrors of the present, where the evenings bore no fresh nightmares to taunt him and the mornings no omens of disaster and personal tragedy.

The visits had become a series of endless repetitions of the same scenario. The afternoons and mornings he found he could cope with. Often in these visiting hours he found himself speculating on the past, no longer involved with John, who would always present the same blank visage to the world. Morden sat beside him and stare at the walls, forming happy pictures from the indentations and marks on the smooth surface. Then his eyes travelled to the sleeping giant on the bed and he found himself surprised to see a man lying there. At these times he would have difficulty recognising John, as though the young man's features were being slowly washed away like a crumbling cliff face against the onslaught of the sea.

Despite the protests of the doctors Morden started the

evening vigil at the regular hour of seven thirty. Then he sat through until around one o'clock before returning to his own home. Often, in the earlier part of this visit he fell asleep, nodding off for ten or twenty minutes before jerking upwards, startled to find his surroundings unchanged. He had taken to bringing a bible with him and he read its passages in his lucid moments trying to find some comfort from the words. Comfort he found there and also, an aura of protection seemed to emanate from the book as though the pages themselves had been invested with sacred property.

Dr Baptiste seemed to have taken a personal interest in Morden and would sometimes drop in to the room to see him. On one such occasion he remarked on the appearance of the bible.

'It's strange how suffering always brings with it an amplification of religious beliefs.'

'This isn't an amplification of religious beliefs I'm afraid,' replied Morden tapping the bible with his finger. If anything I'm a humanist with a little private corner reserved for mysticism. This is my concession to the wisdom of the ages not an immersion in religious propaganda.'

The doctor seemed disappointed but he smiled. 'I have found a great deal of strength in Christianity. In a job like mine it's good to have something to depend on.'

'Well, the bible, like all works of its stature, gives one the comfort of the reactions of others to tragedy. Its very presence, even for an old unbeliever like me, seems to cast an aura of warmth in this chill room.'

The doctor shivered. 'This is a cold room. It's as though there is a draught creeping in from somewhere.' He shrugged. 'Well, the bible to me is the word of God.'

'Perhaps,' said Morden:' or perhaps the words of several inspired men.'

The doctor gave a low laugh. 'Well, I can see we are at odds here Mr. Morden. We can't agree on the true value of the bible on the philosophical plane but perhaps we can put its words to a more practical use.' His calm face took on an expression of pity mingled with determination. He indicated John who lay face upwards on the bed. 'Mr. Ward is in a deep coma. He may emerge from that coma tomorrow, ten years from now or, god forbid, never. Medical science can do very little for him. However, we have had results in the past out with science. The sound of a familiar voice, the playing of a favourite song, anything indeed that he might recognise, that might give him the strength to come back'

He looked down at the resting man. 'He could be anywhere Morden. In a dark sleep. Perhaps he is looking for a beacon in that darkness. Your words might be all he needs. Read him the bible. It could be the sound of your voice or perhaps another greater voice which draws him out of the dark sleep. Try it Mr. Morden. Read him the bible. You might hear something yourself.'

Dr Baptiste left. The room seemed dimmer and Morden huddled into himself. His eyes caught the gold leaf on the binding of the bible. On a whim he flipped over the pages. They fell open by chance on Zechariah.

> 'And the angel that talked with me came again, and
> waked me, as a man that is wakened out of his sleep,'

For the next week all evening Morden read aloud from the bible. On the seventh day, just before twelve he finished the last chapter of revelations. He shut the book. The young doctor standing in the doorway asked him if he had observed any change in the patient.

'None,' replied Morden' except perhaps he has sunk further into his own head.'

'And yourself?' said the doctor.

'If anything my humanism has been transformed into a bleak cynicism.' said Morden. He rose to his feet. 'I think I'll make my way home doctor. I've had enough for tonight. Oh' you could do me a favour.' He indicated a portable tape recorder and some tapes. 'I brought these intending to play them after I had finished reading. These are some tapes made by my daughter Cathy. They're dissertation notes on witchcraft. Some work she was doing at university. A bit morbid I fear under the circumstances but they're the only tapes I have of her voice. Could you organise them for tomorrow. I shan't be coming in. Frankly, I'm worn out.

Dr Baptiste smiled. 'I'll cancel your appointment with the surgeon then.'

'Damn, I forgot. He isn't there now is he?'

The old surgeon was seated at his desk in the anteroom. A pyramid of files rose above his head displacing the decanter of water which lay on the floor beside him.

'You've had a diabolical time of it these last two weeks" he said. 'I'm afraid I'm not in a position to relieve the gloom. However, due to some difficulties which I needn't go in to we've rescheduled the birth of your grandchild. We'll operate in three days time, with your permission of course.' The surgeon steepled his large hands. 'I'm afraid we can't make any guarantees about the survival of the child. Scans have shown ...well, at the very least it will resolve matters as far as your daughter is concerned. She can be laid to rest with dignity.'

In the reception area Morden felt a sense of relief pervade him. He felt light headed, almost feverish. Baptiste helped him to the doors. Outside he could see the rain lashing down, obscuring the taxi lights in a dancing curtain of orange beads.

'You don't look well Morden.' said Baptiste. 'Couple of days rest will do you good. 'He opened the doors and Morden brushed aside his offers of assistance. The old man walked out alone into the torrent but as he reached the last step he turned and shouted. 'Don't forget the tapes. Her voice might make all the difference. Don't forget the tapes.'

The Fever

The long vigil had exhausted Morden. His heart stuttered along like a vintage car and a fever, echoing the heat of summer, embraced him in clammy arms. Confined to bed his housekeeper ensured he had no visitors.

She was unable to prevent Howard from entering. He came at night breaking in through one of the lower windows. Morden first became aware of him when he heard the drinks cabinet rattling in the next room. Morden's fever had lent him a kind of heightened sensory awareness. He was not surprised when he heard a second pane of glass shatter. When Howard staggered into the bedroom carrying a bottle of whiskey, Morden had propped himself up on the bed and was facing his son with a look of disdain. He said nothing when the young man slumped down at the foot of the bed.

Howard opened the bottle with difficulty, looked for a glass and finding none took a swig from the neck.

'She's dead.' he said finally. His voice was hoarse from hours of drinking.

Morden knew without further words that the machine had been switched off. They had both known that Cathy would never come back to life but the machine had sustained kind of myth that she was not dead.

Morden felt as if a weight had been lifted from his mind.

'The child?' he said.

'That bastard killed it.' Howard took another swig. 'John, he killed it.'

'John is wakened?' said Morden trying to unravel the meaning behind Howard's drunken rambling.

'Well, he didn't kill it. He said he didn't want it born. They tried to stop him. They tried to reason with him. Wanted him to sign papers and give authority. Then they said he was mad when he wouldn't sign the stupid papers; they left him to cool down. He walked out the ward and turned the bloody machine off himself.' Howard started to laugh; a high broken sound like some sort of small animal.

Morden felt unmoved by what he had heard. It was if he was no longer personally involved. 'John turned the machine off and killed his own child?'

'It was funny.' said Howard. 'I've never seen anything so funny.' He tried to muffle the laughter. 'They called him a miracle. They all stood round, the doctors, the nurses and that old surgeon. He sat up and looked at them. He looked fine, as if he'd been asleep for a while. And that pompous old surgeon said that he'd been dead for over three hours and that there should be irreparable brain damage and here he was as right as rain and a walking bloody miracle, nothing wrong with him at all.

'Two hours later he gets up out of his bed and switches off the machine that's keeping his kid alive. And then...' Howard gagged on a throat choked with laughter, '...and then he tells them he's just been to Hell.'

Morden gave Howard a keen glance but the drunk was immersed in his appropriated whiskey.

'Did he say why he switched off the machine?'

For a time Howard did not reply. When he spoke his voice had recovered some of its composure. 'He said, ' What has not lived cannot die. What cannot die can have no soul. What had no soul cannot suffer.' Howard chanted the words like a rehearsed litany. It was apparent he had repeated them a number of times. Morden glanced at Howard. His son seemed to have sunk into some sort of reverie. In the dim light he might have been a large rag doll with no motivating force, no intelligence to animate him. Morden had often thought of his son as an empty shell and here, in the half-light, the impression was more pronounced. He found himself comparing Howard to John.

John had always been a man of striking abilities, a handsome athlete gifted with a keen intelligence. Morden tried to equate his memories of John with the picture that Howard presented him. The only conclusion seemed to be that John had temporarily lost his mind. He had always been the most rational of men and above all things he had loved Cathy. That he would kill the product of their love was unthinkable; he was a scientific man who believed in the advance of medicine. He would find nothing unnatural in the manner in which his child had been preserved.

Morden could only conjecture that John had been swept away by madness grief. Again he recalled the look of horror he had seen in the young man's eyes when he had risen from the trolley to confront the world once more.

What had he seen in that dark sleep?

Morden roused himself from his own, almost clinical examination of this latest tragedy. Howard was muttering to himself in a low sing-song voice.

'He said he'd been through Hell?' said Morden trying to raise some intelligence from Howard.

'No. No, you old fool. He'd been to Hell. He'd been to Hell and back.' Howard took another swig from the bottle. 'He'd gone there, didn't like it much and thought he'd better let the rest of us know so we can cross it off our visiting list.' Howard tried to get to his feet, swayed uncertainly then fell back on the bed laughing. 'Oh God that was a morbid trick you played on him father. I couldn't have thought out anything quite so morbid myself. These bloody tapes. Oh God, that was so evil.'

'What do you mean Howard? Tell me man?'

'He must have thought she was alive you fool. That's what sent him over the edge. When he heard Cathy's voice he must have thought she was alive.'

Morden felt a rush of blood to his head as though the fever, which had been diminishing was making one final furious assault on his body.

'I have to see him.' he whispered 'I must visit him and explain?' Morden's hands clenched and unclenched in sudden anxiety. Howard looked up with his dulled eyes and a leer of exultation spread over his pasty face.

'You want to see him father? You want to explain?'

Morden's hands ceased their futile motion. Howard took a last swig from the bottle and threw it on the floor. He stood to his feet engorged and triumphant.

'He's gone father. He disappeared without trace.'

The Dead

The cemetery had been built in the early 1800's when the city's churches had been swollen to capacity with the bodies of the dead. Bought by a large private firm its emphasis was on space. The churchyards of the inner city were congested with bodies. Coffins lay atop each other, their contents often exposed to the eye. Drunken mutes and sextons made their profit from the deceased where they could, removing bones and rotten carcasses to make room for those newly dead. They sold coffin handles and even nails while body snatchers had an easy time of it rejoicing in the shallowness of the graves and the accessibility of their natural resources. Outbreaks of the plague finally forced the authorities to rise above religious prejudice and consider an alternative to churchyard burial.

Outside the city wall the new community of dead took seed. They spread until tombstones and cenotaphs swept up to the new boundaries and more space had to be found. The owners instructed their sextons to find it at the extremities of the cemetery and then to find sites in those places which had been overlooked by earlier generations.

It was thus that Catherine was buried in a forgotten corner, near the centre of the cemetery, among the old and mouldering graves of Edwardian merchants. Beneath the shade of an ancient oak her small grave stood, dwarfed by the black slabs of the surrounding stones.

Morden was glad that she had been buried in this secluded

backwater. It was a place of solitude. A place where he could weep undisturbed. The solemn stones seemed more comforting in their numbers and silence than the many relatives who had attended the funeral and he felt at ease here among the dead. They made no demands on him, nor had they the potential to cause him unexpected suffering. Their lives had passed, the river had moved on leaving them behind like the stilled waters of deep pools. Like memories, the stones would never twist and change but would only erode.

He felt at peace here. Perhaps because he knew that his days were numbered, that his interests were bound up in death. He would soon join the congregation of dead and leave the living to their trials. It was not an unwelcome thought. He cast his mind back over the events of the past week. That awful night when Howard had broken into his home with the news of John's disappearance.

Howard, despite his earlier flippancy, had been badly scared by John. Perhaps he had seen something of that look which Morden had witnessed in ward 7. A look not of madness but bordering it. A look of terrible knowledge, a burden too great to be carried by one man.

He had become hysterical; shouting that he wanted to hide from John. Morden let him sleep at the bottom of the bed and resolved to visit the hospital the following morning.

Dr Baptiste had lost some of his tranquillity when Morden met him at the reception. The old surgeon was unavailable from some unspecified reason and the two men occupied his room. Files lay scattered on the floor in disarray and Morden noticed the decanter and several glasses heaped in the small green pail by the desk. Some small shards of glass were embedded in the carpet.

Baptiste stroked his beard in a distracted manner and seemed unwilling to begin the conversation.

'What happened?' said Morden.

Baptiste walked to the window. 'It's difficult to know where to begin. Events seem to have taken on a life of their own since last we met.' He turned from the window and faced Morden. 'I can tell you frankly that we have had many cases where people have died and been brought back to life but none as inexplicable as the case of your son-in-law.'

Baptiste picked up a file from the desk and threw it open. 'Here, in these scattered files, you'll find over thirty cases from this hospital alone. They're all remarkably consistent in their reports of after death memories. All experienced a review of their past lives encapsulated in a single moment of time. All talk of a silver cord or web which emerges from the head or feet and acts as a kind of chain between the physical body and the soul. All talk of a sensation of duality. Many have been able to report words said by those close to the death bed at a time when it is indubitable that they were not conscious, that they could not have heard the words spoken.'

'And you believe these reports?' said Morden incredulous.

'I had given them no thought... until now.' He closed the file and sat in the surgeon's chair. 'As you know John Ward was dead for two to three hours. We long suspected that he was simply in a catatonic state. That is, he had slipped into a coma and gave the appearance of being dead.'

'You must know if a man is dead or alive,' expostulated Morden.

'Death is difficult to define. Classically death occurs when the heartbeat stops and breathing ceases. This was the case with John. However, when a body has been immersed in very cold water it is possible that it may become hypothermic to a degree that pulse and breathing are undetectable even by trained observers.' 'But surely you have men trained to recognise these difficulties. They would suspect something of the sort and take measures to resuscitate the victim?'

'I assure you Mr. Morden that every effort was made to resuscitate John and your daughter. Both of them were wrapped in blankets, their bodies warmed until their temperatures reached normal levels and then-.'

'I thought immediate artificial respiration-'

'That is a layman's misconception, Mr. Morden. In cases of hypothermia the heart is often still pulsing feebly and any prolonged cardiac compression could only damage chances of survival. I assure you that every attempt was made to save them and that when they arrived in the hospital both were dead. In your daughter's case we were able to sustain her heart beat and lungs by artificial respirator because of the child.' Here the doctor looked away from Morden. 'In John's case by all the evidence at our disposal it should have been futile...'

'He was dead you say and yet now you suspect he was in some sort of coma?'

'The other doctors, my seniors, think he was in a coma. I... I am not sure.'

'What are you saying?'

Baptiste stood to his feet. 'I'm saying that I saw his body minutes before you arrived in the hospital. His facial muscles had sagged. His skin was white; when I pressed it no colour suffused the point of pressure. The skin of his finger webs had lost its pink transparency. Everything pointed to his being dead. Furthermore, when I entered ward 7 for the second time that night I noticed that the blood had settled in his trunk and back. When he rose up before us I clearly saw it. He was galvanised by something *unhuman*. His body seemed to be jerked into life by some impossible force. I have never seen anything like it. The man was dead'

'My superiors disagree,' He continued,' despite the evidence. They think I'm mistaken.'

'Perhaps you are,' ventured Morden.

'You were with him while he lay comatose. Did you notice anything about him then?'

'Only that at times he appeared to be full of some vital force. As though part of him was awake. At other times he appeared drained and defenceless, near death.'

'His musculature remained healthy and undamaged despite a three week period of inactivity. The muscles did not atrophy. No-one has been able to account for this.'

Baptiste had lost himself in an inner debate. It was as though he was trying to convince himself of his own veracity.

Morden drew him back to his own personal concerns. 'Were you present when John emerged from the coma?' Baptiste nodded. 'Please explain as clearly as you can his first reactions. I have to know because I may have made a terrible error.' Morden had steeled himself for this moment.

'The first thing he said was 'don't cremate Cathy'. He looked drained, like a man who has been through much and intends some drastic action.'

'How did he know that Cathy had died, I thought the tapes...'

Baptiste shrugged in defeat. 'The tapes of her voice had been playing for a few seconds. I had just put them on myself. It is another mystery. Without doubt he knew for certain that she was dead.'

Relief suffused Morden but in that instant it gave way to consternation. 'How could he have known she was dead?'

For a moment Baptiste paused. Morden had never seen a man with so much indecision on his face. It seemed he had been wrestling with the argument even as he spoke to Morden. A look of resolve swept over his young face.

'He knew she was dead because he was with her in Hell.'

Hell, thought Morden. He stared down at the wreath of immortelle held in his thin, worn hands. It will last forever like these flowers. Baptiste had believed it. In that final moment he had not been explaining events to Morden. He had been arguing with himself. Putting forward the important points in his head, weighing up the evidence he had been given. It was all improbable as his colleagues had doubtless informed him, but in the end he had believed John. He had believed that a man had gone to Hell.

Morden tried to reason with him. He pointed out the probability that John had received Morden's voice while in a coma. That he had heard the bible read from Genesis to Revelations. That perhaps the final chapters had embedded themselves on his unconscious. The apocalypse had been engendered in his dormant psyche. But Baptiste was no longer listening. His faith in a benign Christianity had been supplanted by a morbid spiritualism.

He kept insisting to Morden that one need only see John himself and hear his words to know that he was telling the truth.

Morden could empathise with this in a way. He had seen John's eyes staring into his own. There was something unnerving about it. Perhaps John had seen some sort of truth but Morden knew that this truth must be something in the nature of a vivid nightmare, perhaps from the Hades world of the collective unconscious. In all probability he had seen something hideous but Morden had no doubt that whatever it was, however awful, it could only be the product of his own disturbed mind.

He threw the wreath on to the small mound. It landed lightly by the foot of the gravestone. Morden's eyes took in the epitaph above the tiny flowers.

Rest in Peace

He looked at the slabs of black stone. In their formal postures they surrounded Cathy's grave like gaunt strangers. He almost sensed them waiting for him to go. Waiting for him to leave Cathy to some furtive horror. He looked beyond the first row of graves to the next and then his eyes lifted beyond those to the next again. As far as his vision reached he could see gravestones circling in crooked files, stretching out in their thousands until they disappeared beyond the brow of the hill.

Morden's mood changed. He no longer felt comforted by the presence of the dead. Instead he felt threatened. His heartbeat murmured in his ears as if taunting him with its hesitancy,

What if John was right? What if Hell did exist? How many citizens of its realms had this cemetery provided? Morden felt something snap in his head. A wave of vertigo took him and for a few seconds the stones seemed to be wheeling round like a grotesque merry-go-round. He sank to his knees, almost as though he were being pulled down by a relentless hand. A great pain was swelling out of his chest. It had no more room to expand and he struck the ground. Even as he lost consciousness his mind rallied to the bitter humour of the moment.

If they had only dug a spare grave he could have saved a lot of bother.

Recovery

When Morden came to he found himself by some macabre coincidence lying in ward 7 of St Mary. Half of the beds in the ward were taken up by patients who, like himself, were victims of heart attacks. The other half were empty. A nurse told him there had been an over-spill from the cardiac ward and that he and a few other cases had been given temporary accommodation in the main building.

Morden felt claustrophobic as he stared round at the other inmates; all looked terribly old. Some sat up in their beds, eager to give an impression of health. For the most part pretensions had been thrown aside and the old men lay prone, staring absently at the ceiling, or lying with their eyes unfocussed as though miserable ghosts drained them of enthusiasm through the repetition of invisible antics.

The inevitability of his failing health was a weight on Morden. In the past few weeks his life had seemed outwith his control. It was as though he was constantly being manipulated by others. Like a shoddy puppet he had danced to the tedious melodies until the strings had broken. As he looked round the ward he saw fatalism in the eyes of others as they prepared for their own demise.

He wondered if any looked at him with the same apprehension.

When Baptiste visited him after a month of recuperation Morden felt prepared for anything. The doctor was clothed in a sober suit. When Morden remarked on the absence of his uniform Baptiste smiled and replied in gentle tones.

'I had to give up practice.'

'Surely they didn't strike you off because of one incident.'

'It wasn't forced on me by external powers. I had changed inside.'

He had become some sort of fanatic.

His eyes shone with an inner light and his voice brimmed over with religious exultation. It became apparent that he wanted Morden to be his first convert.

'You saw his eyes. You recognised the agony of a man who has been to Hell.'

Morden, comfortable in the cynicism of recent extraordinary experiences toyed with him.

'I saw something there, yes.'

'If he saw Hell then there must be a God to create it and therefore there must be a heaven.

'A heaven which I assume you will ascend to at the end of this earthly trial?'

'Not just me Mr. Morden but all those who follow Christ our Lord.' His hand was reaching into his pocket for a bible, a gesture reminiscent of a gangster reaching for a gun.

'Heaven,' said Morden staying the young man's hand, 'is an exclusive club to which I have no wish to append my name. I suggest you try to persuade some of the others. It appears I'm temporarily reprieved.' Morden tapped his chest above his damaged but functioning heart.

'But don't you see,' Baptiste continued. 'John died. He was not dead for minutes, but hours. He actually went to Hell and came back. He is a messenger from God himself.'

Morden laughed 'What a marvellous concept young man - the new messiah comes from Hell instead of Heaven.'

Baptiste pressed his argument unheeding.' He died and came back. He saw-.'

'You forget,' said Morden suddenly wearied 'I also died and I came back.'

'What did you see?'

Morden felt that, in this condition, Baptiste was prey to any charlatan with stories from beyond the veil. It was as though he had been robbed of his powers of reason. Morden paused, then spoke with weight. 'I saw my life pass before my eyes, as though I was suspended outwith time. But after that ...nothing ...oblivion.'

Baptise left without a convert. But he seemed undismayed. He had given up a promising career on the strength of a single incident. Like Peter the fisherman or perhaps a naive convert to a dubious creed his whole past had been transformed by what he considered divine engineering, a miracle. He was now an unshakable optimist.

Morden had not been honest with him. He had not fallen into oblivious sleep after seeing his life pass before his eyes. His experience had been similar to those described by Baptiste in the hospital files.

He had left his physical body. He became aware of a grey mist, a fog through which shone muted lights. He saw the subdued outlines of what he had known to be other presences. Then he had felt himself rushed back into his body. After that oblivion claimed him.

It was a calming experience. A profound sense of well being infected him at the time. Although there had also been an undercurrent of something else; another feeling - a feeling that he was being duped.

Winter set in as Morden entered his third month of recuperation. He was in the therapy room when he received visitor who introduced himself as one of the ambulance men who had rushed him to St Mary's after his heart attack. Morden began to thank him for saving his life when the man stopped him.

'That's why I'm here really. The doctors wouldn't let me speak to you until you were well enough. I didn't save your life. At least I wasn't first on the scene. Another gentleman, tall chap with very black hair in his early thirties I'd say. He happened on you. He must have known the drill; got your heart going then sent for us. You'd have never lived if it wasn't for him.' The man shrugged his shoulders in a questioning gesture. 'He wouldn't leave his name, but the strange thing is he seemed to know yours. He gave us a message. Shouted it while we were pulling away. He said ' Tell Morden I'm going back to the Icy land. Tell him August the first I'll meet him.' I don't know what it's all about. Perhaps it means something to you.'

'John,' said Morden quietly. 'It was John my son-in-law. The Icy land is Tibet where he studied for many years. August the first is the anniversary of my daughter's death.'

Howard had been conspicuous by his absence during Morden's incarceration. Morden had assumed that he had succumbed to one of his drunken binges.

The binges had begun in Howard's teens and had continued at irregular but gradually extending intervals throughout his life. The family had disowned him after several relapses in which Howard disappeared for months on end, appearing at the conclusion of each relapse only to borrow money to finance another.

Morden was not unduly surprised when a letter from the Moroccan authorities arrived advising him that Howard had been arrested on charges of Drug abuse and trafficking. It was the same suicidal tendency clothed in a more debilitating vice. He had been given a life sentence but an appeal had been registered.

It seemed that Howard had been indulging in opium for a number of years unbeknown to Morden. According to the lawyer he was addicted and would likely die. He had enclosed a long letter from Howard which, uncharacteristically, did not ask for money.

Howard claimed to have set out after John. He was burning with curiosity after the older man disappeared. Howard had friends in low places and he made use of them to find out where John had gone. It seemed that something in John exercised a powerful attraction on Howard. A force which, although it terrified Howard, compelled him to seek him out.

John had purchased a flight to Hong Kong. Howard raised the money from various sources and followed him. He lost him there and succumbed to the lure of opium. Weeks of drugged confinement damaged his health and made him unaware of anything but the desire to extend his opiated dreams.

Still, tales of filtered down to him from unsavoury sources; tales of a man of frightening abilities, a master of the killing arts, who had burst on the underworld like a nemesis, slaughtering his opponents without mercy or cause. He was a tall man with black hair and piercing grey eyes. The eyes, said the natives, of a madman.

'Somehow I knew it was John,' Howard wrote in erratic script,' and later in one of the poorer brothels I was proven correct.'

Howard was delivering a consignment of opium to the owner. Inside he discovered a Tia master was on the premises choosing some girls for his patron. The man was renowned for his abilities and acknowledged no peers. A white man appeared at the door. He made some esoteric signal and the master turned adopting a fighting stance. It was over in seconds, the master lay with his neck broken, his body snapped over the piano. Howard barely followed the sequence of events but he had no difficulty in recognising John. The brothel emptied at the conclusion of the conflict. John walked up to Howard and beckoned him to follow. The two wandered the back streets, Howard guided by the immense figure of his brother-in-law who paced ahead like a hunting beast.

Lost in a maze of twisting alleys Howard found himself finally under the eaves of a pier by the waterfront.

At first John said nothing. He stared at Howard, the moon glinting in the wells of his eyes. Howard almost panicked. In the silence John looked like some terrible statue and Howard thought he might be insane.

When he finished speaking Howard was certain that he was.

'It seemed he would never stop. I couldn't take it all in at once and even now it confuses me. I'll never forget how he appeared to me under that dripping pier head with the hanging weeds behind him and the rotten smell of dead fish. He was mad too but at the time in that nightmare place I would have believed anything

'He claims that when he died he went to Hell. A real Bosch Hell it was too. Your physical body emerges into this other dimension resurrected in the same form as when you die. An old diseased man goes to Hell old and diseased; a baby goes as a baby and so on. I was fascinated. He actually believed it. He went into incredible detail, bits I forget... there was something about cremation dispersing the body...

'John said he'd being trying to find Cathy in this netherworld but he wasn't powerful enough to do it. I tried to reason with him. I explained about you reading the bible and told him it was simply his unconscious mind absorbing all that nonsense; that he'd conjured up this night mare either as he died or as he was resurrected. But he would have none of it. When I insisted, he went mad. He grew angry with me and began shouting. God, he is so powerful now. He never was a weakling, always a fit man, but now he's like a bloody colossus, and I'd just seen him snap a

Tia master in half. I admit I was terrified of him. He saw me cringing away in fear and something in him snapped. His huge shoulders slumped and he leaned against the pillar.

'He said he had to be a killer; he had to be the greatest killer in the history of mankind. He went silent for a time then. I think there were tears in his eyes but I couldn't bear to look him full in the eyes. There is something in them now, something inhuman. Whatever it is it scares me senseless.'

Howard had written no more. The last words had been disjointed; as though the hand which wrote them had weakened and could write no longer.

The Old Manse

Morden stood breathless at the portals of the old manse adjoining cemetery hill. The sun had just set and the long shadows of the graves were melting into the grey twilight behind him. That morning, eight months since his last cryptic message, John had left a short note on Morden's doorstep. The note said that John had been to Tibet, that he had returned and wanted Morden to come to the Manse to 'finalise matters'. He signed the note in his curt script but added in haste that Morden must steel himself. Inside the note he enclosed a large key.

Morden drew the key from his pocket and inserted into the great wooden door. The door croaked inwards on rusty hinges and Morden faced a long narrow hallway with an uncarpeted floor of old oak planking. There was a musty smell of dead leaves impregnating the air.

At the end of the hallway he could see the outline of a large doorway. Inside the doorway the interior of a room could be discerned by the light from a small oil lamp. As he walked into the hallway the sound of his footsteps seemed loud as though their echoes were disturbing a long kept peace, but he knew by the footprints in the dust before him that another had walked this path in recent times

As he drew near to the room the lamp picked out the figure of a man facing him seated behind a large deal table

From twenty feet away Morden knew it to be John. He sat unmoving, staring ahead, his face shadowed by the low placed lamp. As Morden entered the doorway John's eyes stared back. It was only when he stood in the confines of the tiny room that Morden realised that the eyes were those of a dead man. Their lustre was gone but somehow they retained an aura of horror, as though in the lasts seconds of life the dying man had realized some awful truth and the impression of its impact had seared itself on the shield of his eyes, in the mask of his face.

Morden's nostrils picked out another scent impinging the air and rising above the smell of neglect. He saw that John was not alone. In the shadows beneath the desk where it had fallen from the dying man's arms the frail corpse of Cathy lay exposed. The flesh clung to the face, drawing back form the mouth and the empty sockets of the eyes so that she seemed to be taunting him with a conspiratorial grin. Her hair, always long, had grown longer and the tresses swept over the flaccid shroud and nestled in the hollows where the flesh had sunk from the bones.

Even as he watched a fat pink worm stabbed out from between her half open mouth and then retracted like a tiny pink tongue.

Morden sat down on the nearest chair and vomited between his legs. His heartbeat was rapid and he felt waves of nausea sweeping over him. Every time he tried to raise his head he smelt the creeping odour of dead flesh and again he would retch. Finally he found the strength to look the dead man in the eye.

'How could you do this John?' he whispered.

As if in reply Morden was drawn to John's right hand which was placed palm down on the deal table. Beneath the dirt stained and bloodied fingers lay a manila envelope.

Without taking his eyes from John Morden stretched out his hand and pulled the envelope from beneath the fingers. With the stench of decay in his nostrils and John's unwavering gaze boring in to him Morden took the manuscript from the envelope and began to read.

The clock was striking twelve when he let the manuscript slip to the floor. He had known something of what to expect but not all.

John had claimed that he had died and gone to Hell. Through a superhuman effort he had contrived of his own accord to return.

He was resurrected in the same physical shape that he relinquished on earth; it was thus with all humanity. The agonies of Hell were incomprehensible, beyond the imaginings of the living and Cathy was not resting in peace but burning in agony.

'The real irony is this Morden. There is no God. He has departed and will not return. Once there was a heaven but it has been subdued by the darker forces of Hell. Heaven's machinery is broken and there is no-one left to effect a repair.

'Deprived of the sight of God the angels of death are tormented beyond understanding. So they repay the souls of the damned in kind. They torment us because, lessened though they are they are greater than humanity. So, Hell is all we have; all of us for all time, the evil, the good, the young, the old. Understand me Morden. There is no God and there is no Heaven.

'I came back to this world for one reason, hopeless though it may be. I came back to learn everything it is possible for a human to learn; all knowledge, all skill, East and West, North and South. Futile though it may be it is all I can think to do.

'I am going back to find the women I love. And to do that I have to conquer Hell, to make it into Heaven.

'I will be the maker of a second Heaven. I will be the Heaven maker.'

Morden stared into John's tortured eyes.

Was that look burning in the dead eyes one of naked

revelation, a truth for all mankind? Or was it the look of a lunatic, a man who had succumbed to the horrors of his own subconscious?

Morden felt his weakened heart stutter in his breast. He was about to find out.

THE WAITING GAME

Eduardo tried to move his head. Slowly, ever so slowly; any more to the left and the chain would tear the nasal septum. The agony - it was incredible. No point, for the moment, in making things worse.

Before his face, the tiny iron chain – more of a bracelet – stretched outwards until it disappeared through the hole in the gossamer veil. In the dim lights the veil obscured Maria's face – he assumed it was Maria; she hadn't spoken. He guessed that the chain crossed the gap between their noses like a miniature rope bridge. Eduardo hoped that she was mercifully unconscious. *But why didn't she move?*

It was the kind of thing that would make people laugh at a children's party game. Two people attached together, unable to escape. But of course, in a children's game the chain wasn't penetrating your septum, and you weren't terrified that there was worse to come.

'Maria?' You had to be careful, even when you spoke, or the chain tugged the inners of your nasal passage sending a stab of agony through the forehead. 'Maria?' He could see the vague outline of her head, ghost-like behind the gossamer veil. She was slumped over. *God, was she dead? Had Catherine killed her?* It was too much to bear. She couldn't have…but then the old bitch had been more than angry.

Carefully, Eduardo let his gaze travel upward: Far above, he could vaguely discern a tiny skylight window that let in a pale light. Beneath the dark eaves of the rafters, this hollow light revealed a single, unlit candle in some kind of rusted flambeau holder on the left wall. The right wall was invisible, melting into shadow: In front, only the slumped figure of Maria behind the gauze curtain. Beyond her, a door and what might be a walkway across the chasm below.

Eduardo had heard the door open from that direction - He was relying mostly on sound - His other senses virtually useless:

The taste of blood on his lip where Catherine had slapped him; the immanent odour of damp and decay, the chill of venting winds and draughts; all that remained to the epicure.

Taste and smell had always been so important. Now they were utterly subordinate to sound. Audition had told him that he was propped in some kind of high chair and that the wind blew through hidden recesses below. From this single lonely sense, his fevered mind constructed a vast sprawl of underground chambers leading into hopeless oblivion.

It had taken him about an hour to mentally construct the immediate scene: A large cell. Eduardo and Maria propped up on two facing chairs. The chairs raised on platforms above a pit. A walkway to allow access. Some of this was assumption but the iron chain piercing his septum was an unavoidable reality.

Like Catherine's jealousy.

Eduardo could see her now; her raddled face ugly with anger as she had shouted and struck at the slumped figure of Maria. When he lurched forward, she laughed as a burst of pure white agony fragmented across his face. That had been his first intimation of the horror. The unspeakable realisation that she had pierced and chained his nose and he was fixed like a trapped pig. Then she had left him in the dim lit chamber, effectively alone. And waiting.

Ironically, Eduardo had always played a waiting game. (Once he had liked that English play on words). He worked a restaurant in Montmartre. Head waiter. Good looking, suave and, like most waiters, owning an instinct that sifted the aristocrat from new money, the beggar from the thief and, of course, the stinking rich from the stinking poor.

Eduardo had waited on the rich in more senses than one. He had waited for someone in particular: A rich woman – one old and rich, very rich. Finally, he found her: Catherine Dupont: intelligent, sophisticated – a high-class family with a Florentine bloodline reaching back to castles and kings. She owned a manse in Cheshire, a villa in Marbella and a small Chateau in

Auxerre. Marry these possessions to the private Yacht and the dinky little sports car with the open top, and a whole arena of pleasure opened up for a lucky man. Eduardo wasted no time, and like a sharp, began stacking his cards.

In her day, Catherine had been more than beautiful. Lonely and old now, she still retained the vestiges of that great beauty, like a ruined palace or a wounded swan. Not beautiful like his Maria of course. Maria had youth, vivacity, the shy, natural beauty of the young. *God, why didn't she sit up?* Eduardo shifted a little. The tiny moment sent a new tendril of pain across his forehead. But he could imagine Maria's face now, dimly hinted at, behind the gossamer veil. Her dark eyes, sweet lips, a mouth made for love.

Maria came from the same back streets as Eduardo and in the shrouds of poverty, they had fallen in love. *Why had he been so ambitious?* Maria had hopes but she would never have agreed to his crazy scheme without pressure. Finally though, she *had* agreed; they both came from the gutter and, at root, they shared the pragmatism and practically of the poor. It would hurt Maria that he slept with the old lady but as Eduardo said – they would never truly be man and wife. It was a matter of convenience. In a few months the beast-like coupling would stop. The old dear would only need companionship. At every opportunity, they could meet. Catherine was naive and forgetful. It would be easy.

Eduardo' belly churned with hunger, scratching at his reveries. He saw Catherine's face again, dangling the key, spitting at him as she laughed. She had said something about food. Perhaps it was a lie. *Maria! Why didn't she wake?*

Eduardo had lied, of course, another of his now redundant, skills. He had used every tool in his workbox of deceit to engineer a whirlwind romance, a swift marriage. Catherine was old; her heart was weak. She would succumb to her weakness. Eduardo would wait a decent interval and then marry the love of his life, Maria.

But he had not bargained for Catherine's jealousy or her

sudden revival. She had practised as a doctor in her youth and still had connections with the leading surgeons in Switzerland. Eduardo could still feel the ice of his smile as she announced her intention to try the progressive treatment of her old alumni. It had seemed a God-given piece of fortune. Catherine's condition was hopeless and some *avant garde* operation would doubtless speed her to the grave.

Damn that surgeon and his unholy skill.

The endless days waiting by the bed as she recovered form the operation. All the time thinking of Maria and how she was pining for him. The tedious convalescence where he did more waiting than the busiest day at the restaurant. The plaintive requests. The difficulty in maintaining his optimistic smile. Eduardo was almost relieved when Catherine was able to walk but the relief turned to horror when it became apparent that the operation was a resounding success, that Catherine was renewed and revitalised.

She was a woman in love. She needed him at all times. It was difficult to get outdoors unaccompanied. She was more demanding than he could have imagined.

A thousand schemes had run through his mind as they travelled back on the cruise ship. Catherine insatiable, the strain of hiding his disgust. And then the return to the old French Chateau with its creeping corridors, hidden rooms and ancient ghosts.

There he endured the long evenings, hardly tempered by the expensive wine, the caviar and tapas as he reclined on the renaissance sofa with Catherine, avoiding the gaze of the glowering ancestral portraits. Moment by moment, Catherine became more objectionable, clinging, whining as she demanded little favours and treats. All the while Eduardo had chaffed at delays. One picture in his mind: The beautiful Maria in his arms. He thought of murder, poison, a broken tread on the stairway but he didn't have the guts for it.

Instead, he conceived a plan that seemed an ingenious

compromise.

Catherine always complained about the live-in cleaner. How difficult it was to get anyone good. On the morning when the slovenly girl ruined the Florentine dresser by a misapplication of solvent, Eduardo was suddenly inspired. He had tried to make his voice casual :

'There was a girl at the restaurant in Montmartre, very efficient, reliable. I could give her a call.'

'Is she pretty?' The remark was equally casual; Catherine's smile a mask.

'Pretty?' Eduardo forced a laugh. 'Plain girl, thin, childlike…I don't think *anyone* would consider her pretty…you know how these young things annoy me but good at her job and experienced. Knows her place'

Incredibly, it had worked. Maria was interviewed. Eduardo stayed away, feigning utter indifference. He had to bite his tongue when Catherine announced Maria's appointment.

'Well, just keep her away from me,' he had said. 'I'm not having her underfoot.

The first days were torture. Eduardo stayed completely out of sight: Deliberately avoiding Maria. In the end, it was Catherine who championed her. She became insistent that Eduardo should at least formally introduce himself.

Even now, through the pain, he could see Maria's trembling face, smell the sweat on his body as he prayed Maria would play her part. Catherine hovering, apparently indifferent; her weak eyes hunted any betrayal of interest on his part. Eduardo had played his master card, hardly aware of his own histrionic ability.

'I will make this quite clear once and once only. You are here to serve the mistress of the house. I have no interest in your work as long as it is done well. You are to stay out of my study at all times. That is my preserve and I am capable of cleaning it myself. Now run along.'

Maria had cried; the tears genuine.

Catherine and he almost argued over his curtness. She was insistent he tried to be at least civil. He offered to try. It became an almost enjoyable game to throw out the odd brusque remark when he crossed paths with Maria; to make a big show of the slightest appearance of shoddy work. 'This is simply not clean,' he would insist picking on a random piece of cutlery.

It reached a point where Catherine begged him to temper his attitude. She loved Maria. She could find no fault. Such good company while Eduardo worked so hard on his diaries.

This last was another masterstroke. Eduardo had managed to convince Catherine that he was working on a diary. The preparation for a new romance. In fact, he spent ten minutes scribbling some crap down about how much he loved Catherine - this because he knew she would read it - and the remaining hours loafing around.

Methodically he was creating in Catherine's mind, his need for solitude.

Eduardo began to work odd hours. Occasionally, he would *have* to write it down'; Leap from the bed and rush downstairs. Sometimes, he would come back and wake the old bag. Tell her of his struggles with words and ideas. He pushed it to the point where he knew she was growing tired of the game. The after a long period in which he attempted to gently wake her he found that she would not respond. He had finally worn her down.

Eduardo almost screamed his pleasure. Hands trembling, he sneaked down the long, long stairs. The light rap of his knuckles on the door. Maria's startled face. His hands caressing, voice whispering as he carried her to the bed.

Moments of bliss.

But only moments.

Eduardo had made a terrible miscalculation – he had thought Catherine naïve. The first he had known of this miscalculation was the look in Maria's eyes: The look of utter terror.

Maria Why didn't she wake up? Maria?

A blow to the back of his head he assumed. There had been the acrid smell of chloroform. A scream of rage from Catherine. Then darkness. Later, the awakening. The terrible pain, the horror of seeing the slumped figure before him with all its poignant familiarity.

The hours dragged. The tiny skylight dulled, the vast chamber becoming an impenetrable darkness. Then, far away: footsteps. The glimmer of a candle. The door swung slowly open.

Catherine stood in a white night gown. She held two unlit candles in her left hand and a large tin in her right.

'Comfortable my sweet?' She smiled sourly. 'Lost your tongue. Not yet…' she laughed and approached gingerly on the walkway.

God to be able to move just a little, to send her spinning into the darkness.

'Now, Eduardo. I come from a distinguished family. Lots of skeletons in our cupboards and room for another few.' She placed the candles on Maria's chair and held up her right hand.'

'Please Catherine…'

'I'll make this short like our romance. In my hand a tin. In the tin, maggots. I'm going to place the maggots here. She parted the veils lightly. Eduardo had one sickening vision of Maria's beautiful face, the chain piercing her septum. 'Yes, here on this tiny box just above the chain. Now, you were always clever, Eduardo. Perhaps you can see how this works. The maggots, enterprising creatures, will climb from the tin seeking food. Then emerge into this closed box from which they will drop down the tiny chute onto the chain. Then they are faced with a choice of *aperitif*. The beautiful Maria or the charming Eduardo.'

'God no, Catherine…'

'You can try to stop them of course. You can move your head and shake the chain. You will find that I have implanted the length of it under your cheeks. At some point, perhaps in the general frenzy, you may well rip off your face or that of Maria. Shame, she is beautiful…but even then with you faces hanging like Halloween masks, you will not be able to detach parts of the chain from your skull or prevent the maggots from finally earning their….'

'Catherine!!!'

'Well, a lady must get her rest. Don't wait up late Eduardo. 'Catherine smiled broadly as she took the second candle and began to walk back long the walkway to the open door. 'I expect you'll want to sleep.' She said from the door. 'I wouldn't advise it though, unless Maria is awake.'

The white figure retreated into the darkness ignoring every scream torn from his lungs.

Slowly, Maria's hidden figure raised its head. Through the shifting cloud-grey fabric he sensed her stupefied awakening.

'Maria,' don't move!'

From beneath the veil a long sob, metamorphosed to a high pitched screaming.

At that point, perhaps impelled by the new vibration, the first maggot dropped from the tin. For a second it lay stunned on the surface of a chain link and then, with almost malignant purpose, the blind head began questing for direction.

Eduardo' mind burgeoned with increasingly desperate possibilities of action before accepting that there was little he could do but wait.

THE ART OF CONFISCATION

Sadism was a peculiar form of Art at Bellport High. Some adroit pupils considered the edifice of the school itself to be a visible expression of the sadistic mind. The vast concrete structure rising eight stories into the terrified skies was a modern tower of Babel, its occupants the very embodiment of the vanity ascribed to lost and misguided souls. Within that malignant building, young lives were brutalized and destroyed, innocent minds succumbed to iniquity while guilty minds overwhelmed the innocent with a lavish range of torture and rapine purely for the gratification of illicit pleasure. The deep recesses of the anonymous building were pitted with cells and dungeons termed as classrooms only by the naive. The sprawling corridors led to inferior chambers of evil such as Dentistry (painful extraction), Swimming Baths (drowning), Dining Room (starvation) and The Library (premature burial). Well-trodden paths variegated the building with a gamut of arteries that led to lesser alcoves, arcadia and hallways utilised for spontaneous murder and beating.

The smaller boys whispered that ghosts had been frightened from dark cupboards, vampires had sought mirrors for escape and even spiders had deserted the sinking chambers in favour of safer haven. Each classroom, ruled by a mighty tyrant or mismanaged by a usurped tyro was a black empire of despair; each corridor an arterial gauntlet with no apparent egress; each battered door held secrets that would shame a paedophile and some doors led simply nowhere. But all the snake-sheathed corridors, their shifting maze beset with snares, their damp floors streaked in mucous, their scuffed and windowless walls emblazoned with the graffiti of the institutionally damned, led to a single smoke-stained mahogany door where beat the dark and poisonous heart of Bellport High - the Staffroom.

Inside this squat smoke-choked organ, the beleaguered staff -

dismal creatures of the school - made plans, dreamed dreams and cheapened nightmare as they constructed the means to evade humiliation and the intricacies of its deliverance.

Peters of mathematics, a spindly old master and expert of the leather belt, was at the very moment instructing Mr. Ball in its most efficient use. The grubby coffee table, swathed in lash marks resounded once more to the beat of the tawse.

'So, if he stands with only one hand held so,' said Peters with histrionic emphasis, 'the weight of the tawse will allow the hand to slip downwards, lessening the effective blow but almost certainly giving one an apparently accidental strike to the exposed leg.'

'But,' said Simmons, Head of art, from behind his newspaper, 'the wiser pupils know that they must place one hand beneath the other – a school rule and long established custom.'

'Yes,' said Peters tapping the belt with a gnarled finger. 'My predecessor, dear old Weasel, said the trick is to slightly deepen the angle of the tawse so that the thin edge strikes upwards so.' Another crash sent coffee cups tumbling to the stained carpet. 'Certainly the palm will bruise and one has the added potential of a swollen wrist.'

Clark of history, still fresh to the job, shook his head in despair. 'But belting kids. It's simply sadism, an anachronistic throwback to the dark ages.'

Peters paused in mid-demonstration with a stunned look. 'Simply sadism?' He gave a mournful shake of his silvered head. 'If you want to last the course here young Clark, you'll have to adopt some better defences than humour. Look at Nugent over there.'

Through the fug of tobacco fumes a huddled figure could be seen abjectly clutching his knees as he tipped his body back and forward like a seesaw. The bodily motion of Nugent, the probationary music teacher, was a grim reflection of his teetering mind.

'I'd give him till Friday,' said Simmons idly. He placed the newspaper over his weary head.

Ball who had slouched into apathy suddenly brightened up. 'I'll offer two to one Friday, five to one Monday morning…'

The jaded teachers, provoked into a semblance of life, picked up red pens from the surfaces of homework papers and made some quick calculations. Crumpled bank notes began to exchange hands. Clark gave a dismal shrug and stood to his feet. 'Jesus,' he said to an indifferent audience. 'Give the guy a break.'

'Break,' laughed Simmons from underneath the newspaper. 'How appropriate.'

At the door of the staffroom Miss Caruthers of Geography was stubbing out a cigarillo. She eyed Clark as he made for the corridor. Unmarried and febrile with stress, she recognized in young Clark a kindred spirit of sorts and also the faint prospect of a future bolster against her rising tide of depression.

'The bell's about to go?' she said.

'Yes, best get to classes before the human soup coagulates.' Clark was not indifferent to feminine charms.

'I've got to decide what to do with this pornographic magazine.' Caruthers held up an imported catalogue that depicted a variety of sexual acts in full colour. Clark remarked in the single brief glance afforded, that he recognized at least three of the acts and two of the species.

'Confiscated?' he said.

'Yes my staffroom cupboard has a whole stack of this stuff now. Plus two switchblades, a torch, a whoopee cushion and half the contents of a confectionary shop.'

'You could always sell it to Peters.'

'No one young enough between these pages to tempt that old bastard,' said Caruthers dryly. 'I might have to tell the Head about the porn though. I think Gray, that seventh spawn of Satan, is running a syndicate. He's definitely the source of the new horror craze.'

'Yes, I've found a few of those disgusting anthologies on him last week. You'd think his life was horrible enough.'

A loud whack on the table advertised another demonstration of leather chastisement

'Peters!' Caruthers shouted across the staffroom. 'Does your wife practice on you?'

Peters feigned deafness.

Clark smiled. 'The staffroom's full of De Sade's assistants. Peters and his damned belt. I wonder how many lives he's ruined.'

Miss Caruthers gave a rueful grimace. 'Not as many as MacVicars.'

Clark dropped the smile.

MacVicars, deputy head and acting head of English, was a man who scared adults. Young Clark, in fact was more scared of him than of his students, which was an unusual circumstance at Bellport High.

There was a kind of lunacy to MacVicars that defied description. Where Peters used physical cruelty and violence to establish dominance and to enjoy the humiliation and degradation of young minds, his simplistic efforts were dwarfed by MacVicars' capacity for mental torture. This torture, visible by its effects on the pupils and enhanced by long repute, was all the worse for being concealed behind MacVicars' classroom door so that even the dubious benefit that schoolboy myth and exaggeration lent to hidden practice left unhealthy scope for imagination. The mere sight of MacVicars on the corridor sent staff to scuttle for escape. The tremors and ticks of terror on the faces of small boys and teenagers were a stark and concrete reminder of the efficacy of his methods.

Something went on behind the doors of MacVicars' English classroom and that something was very unpleasant. It was something that infected Clark's fertile imagination and made him shudder as he broached the corridor, and it was the thing that froze him in his tracks as he saw MacVicars himself striding like a black crow towards the staffroom. MacVicars, tall brittle and draconian, seemed to glide down the corridor like a spectre seeking prey.

There was an instant where Clark's mind raced with conflicting emotions – mostly fear and desperation – then with an abject sigh of relief he saw MacVicars take the stairwell. Clark stared for a few moments pale faced. He listened as the stairs rang to the brisk athletic steps like a skeleton playing some crazed xylophone and even his fossilized teacher's heart felt a pang of remorse for the poor boys who would shortly be instructed in some bizarre and awful rite.

'That'll be Farantino's class,' he said to himself. 'Poor little bastards.'

The poor little bastards like schoolboys eternal were blissfully unaware of the tramp of doom. They were engaged in an attempt to glue Angel's bottom to his chair.

MacVicars' classroom like any Roman arena had witnessed pitiable scenes of torment. Doubtless the corrupt citizenry of ancient Rome had acquired a sophisticated taste for gladiatorial torture but amongst themselves the schoolboys of Bellport High made do with simple bullying. MacVicars' polished classroom windows exposed the confines of his prison with a ruthless light as Angel, the school wimp, provided his daily fodder for young minds. It seemed at times that the poor boy's only purpose was to excite sadistic impulse. At that moment Gray, the school bully, was shouting instructions while his cronies sat on Angel's knees and stifled his cries with a snot rag. The peripheral members of the class and those wise enough to think further than immediate entertainment were sat at their desks in regimented apathy. That is, all except Farantino a medium-sized boy with an intelligent but unassuming face. Farantino had just arrived and was standing behind the closed classroom door where he looked on the events and indulged in a momentary reflection about human nature and its foibles.

How strange the turn of events. If Farantino had only advanced a step a whole chain of circumstances would not have linked; lives would have proceeded in an entirely different fashion and some would not have been prematurely ended. As it was, Farantino had time to establish that there was nothing much before him that was out of the ordinary. The classroom was dank and unwelcoming, the pupils were abject and disconsolate and Angel was suffering the accustomed torment. Farantino made a step forward and at that same moment MacVicars thrust the door open as a prelude to dramatic entrance. The drama became an unintended farce as MacVicars wrist battered off the door handle and young Farantino fell to the floor in a sprawling heap. As he fell he dropped his bag and sent its contents spilling to the classroom floor.

Schoolboys at Bellport High were, through necessity, masters of invention. The huddle around Angel seized the momentary confusion and dispersed with all the speed of Brownian motion. In a matter of seconds the desks of the classroom were peopled by an attentive audience – one of whom still struggled to pull his trousers up – as the dreaded space between school desks and the blackboard became the arena for a riveting drama.

The boys were present at an epochal moment and they knew it, for here before them was not only MacVicars but an annoyed, wounded and angry MacVicars and beneath his feet was Farantino, the school genius.

It is an interesting circumstance of school that no matter how sadistic the bent of a master, he can recognize in an instant the mind and character of every boy and their propensity and capacity for meaningless persecution. MacVicars had mostly avoided antagonizing Gray the school bully; Angel the wimp had been a regular but insignificant doormat; Peters Minor, son of the Mathematics teacher, had been disregarded with contempt. All of the boys from the great to the small had at one time or another been psychologically trampled upon by MacVicars' mercurial intellect; all that is with the exception of Farantino.

Farantino, as everyone now knows, was a child prodigy; a

boy of baffling genius. The oldest son of the local vicar and an Italian parishioner - reputedly of the ancient Lombard lineage - Farantino was a boy who would one day be wealthier than many small countries, whose inventions, skills, idiosyncrasies and talent would be the subject of articles, speculations and general envy throughout the world. He had already betrayed his genius in many forms. He had already amassed a small fortune, he had already acquired a team of legitimate and illegitimate employees working at legitimate and illegitimate business and he had never once so much as spoken to a teacher unless he had himself been addressed. He maintained an aristocratic silence in the presence of adults and expressed himself only through his schoolwork, which from domestic science to mathematics was a trail-blazing exemplar of consummate brilliance, incredible invention and creative fireworks.

MacVicars knew all this. Over the years he had read Farantino's essays, composition and interpretation with the growing comprehension that, unbelievable as it seemed, he faced a boy who was an undoubted cognoscente of words; a boy who had read and understood reams of classic literature where others his age read comics, whose vocabulary was as extensive as the limits of the public library and who could interpret and identify any amount or kind of poetry or abstruse philosophy with the ease that another boy spat. He was a boy so clever that English was a mere subset of an astonishing set of academic and practical virtues. He was a boy in short who was far more adroit with the English language than even MacVicars, who himself held two first class honours degrees from Edinburgh University, attic boxes full of merits, ribbons and accolades and several literary prizes reserved for the academic elite.

It was for these reasons that MacVicars had never dared challenge Farantino with his cutting ripostes and displays of cruel brilliance. He knew somewhere deep in his poisoned heart, with the instinct of the born despot, that young Farantino would be more than equal to any challenge and could probably wound him where it hurt most – his vanity. But it was for this reason also that MacVicars, with the hopeless need of the opium addict, was unable to avoid the unexpected opportunity before him.

Perhaps if his wrist had not been bruised, perhaps if he had not been in a hurry and probably if the books had not spilled from Farantino's bag, MacVicars would have let it pass. But to his astonishment and injury his gimlet eyes picked out the paperback book that had fallen from Farantino's bag.

From his lofty position he scanned the exposed title with astonishment and dismay. His mouth, accustomed instinctively to lecture opened before his brain stopped it.

'What is that *thing* on my floor?'

A schoolboy could have made any number of caustic retorts – Polish, spit, chewing-gum, Farantino, Farantino's bag or Farantino's book - but Farantino was far wiser than a schoolboy ought to be and wanted only to get back to his desk with the minimum fuss.

'That sir,' he said in a mild voice, 'is my copy of the *Third Pan Book of Horror Stories* edited by Herbert Van Thal. I purchased it this morning and by accident the book has fallen from my bag.'

'Book?'

'Paperback book, sir. An anthology.'

'Let me see this *book.*'

Farantino raised himself from the floor and carefully picked up the paperback. He handed it to MacVicars.

MacVicars held the book up to the class. 'So, Farantino, perhaps you'd like to describe this lurid cover to your classmates.' As Farantino was related to his 'classmates' as the captain of a battleship is related to a boy who has rented a model boat in that they might conceivably be near the same stretch of water, the remark was implicitly an insult.

Farantino said quietly. 'It's a rather poor portrayal of a monster emerging from a stone coffin sir.'

'Would it give us an idea of the contents?'

'It might point in that direction, sir. It is a horror anthology.'

'Let me see. 'Dennett, *Unburied Bane*', 'Jepson and Gawsworth', *'The Shifting Growth.'* These are tales that one might find in a penny dreadful?'

'Perhaps, sir.'

'And you hope to edify your mind with this rubbish?'

'Amuse myself sir and, if I might be bold, Dunsany, Faulkner and Wells –'

'Dunsany, Faulkner and Wells.' MacVicars voice had begun to rise. '*Amuse* yourself with Dunsany, Faulkner, and Wells!'

'Poe, sir, considered by some -.'

'Considered by some! Considered by which revered body of literary critics? I find this quite unbelievable. Quite, quite beyond belief, that a boy of your talent, a small but growing talent -' (Here Farantino winced) '- should read this bilge, never mind purchase it.'

MacVicars had begun to rifle through the pages. 'From end to end, utter balderdash and here I find to my utter astonishment that you seem to claim some literary merit lurks beneath these objectionable covers.'

'Dunsany -.'

'Do not give me Dunsany, young Farantino.' MacVicars face, normally the colour of bone, had reddened to a florid mask. 'A playboy amateur whose fantasies mock real literature. Wells, a cheap turn-trick for the masses. Of all these *authors*…' His face was rapidly scanning the contents with a show of disbelief, '…perhaps that vulgar eccentric, Mr. Poe, could string a sentence or two together in his dreadful American tongue - a pure debasement of decent language of course - but to impute to this rag-tag collection of tripe some literary merit? Words fail me.'

With a flourish MacVicars sent the *Third Pan Book of Horror Stories* flying through the air. It landed on the edge of the wastepaper basket and, like a ghoul slinking back to its borrowed grave, slowly slipped from view.

There was a long silence. Laughter, not wise or often heard in MacVicars class, remained buried in thirty small breasts.

'You will write me a comparative essay, Farantino. Three thousands words on the merits of James Joyce's 'The Dead'. Your comparison will be any of these, these so called authors whose works you seem to enjoy with such fervour that you must bring them to *my* English class.' MacVicars paused and in a typical moment of irrelevant authority vented at Farantino in pompous tones. 'Longum iter est per praecepta, breve et efficax per exempla.'[1]

Farantino stared back and with quite deliberate emphasis replied 'Damnant quod non intellegunt.'[2]

MacVicars, who had never been challenged by anyone, man or boy, since his third year at university drew back his hand and fetched Farantino a hard slap on the face. Farantino flinched. 'Perhaps you will *comprehend* that. Go to your desk. Bring the completed work on Friday and as your Latin is in such fine form I expect your essay in that dead tongue.'

MacVicars returned to his desk. He lit his pipe with the special lighter that he had received from his cherished Literature group aware that the display of crude violence had somehow diminished him more than the boy. He took advantage of his bad humour to castigate and bully Gray, to humiliate and persecute the hapless Angel. To studiously ignore Peters Minor and to work his sardonic humour on the rest of the class in degrees of brilliance that varied in style but rarely dropped in quality.

Farantino he avoided. The boy's right cheek was swollen and he sat apparently humbled and got on with his work. As always though, the exterior visage of Farantino hid a seething cauldron of plans and schemes. Anyone foolish enough to enter the house

---

[1] The journey is long through advice, efficient through example

[2] They pass judgment on what they do not comprehend.

of his mind would have found not a series of small neural chambers but a virtual palace of grand electric rooms in which the young genius constructed marvels of invention. They would have been surprised during the lesson to find that none of the rooms contained any reference to the *Third Pan Book of Horror Stories* or MacVicars' cruel treatment. Farantino had far larger ambitions that stretched well beyond MacVicars' classroom, the classrooms of other teachers, the whole crumbling edifice of Bellport High and indeed anything about the school that he had long since outgrown. Truth be told, in one of his mental chambers he was already sowing the seeds of his own personal empire – an empire that had the fair face of a thousand legitimate businesses and enterprises, and a hundred shady and horrific cellars. He had simply catalogued the lost book in a small mental cupboard as his property, which would be duly returned. One of the stories had engendered an idea. The theme of Horror held a fascination. He had dismissed MacVicars as the tail of a horse dismisses an irritating fly.

MacVicars, like the fly, proceeded with his life regardless.

At the end of the lesson the boys were allowed to go and with the exception of Angel, who had a whole day of persecution before him, vacated the classroom with profound relief.

MacVicars was surprised and secretly pleased to see that Farantino had come to his desk. He waited an appreciable time before he raised his head from his work.

'Well?'

'Sir, may I have my book back?'

There was an appreciable pause. 'You may retrieve it from the waste paper basket.'

'Thank you sir,' said Farantino. He bent down, found the book amidst the debris and carefully smoothing its cover, made for the door.

MacVicars held out his hand. Farantino paused with a look of uncertainty then reluctantly passed over the book.

MacVicars had long known that the art of confiscation rests

in increasing the victim's immediate desire for an object over its intrinsic value. The victim must feel its injustice and must come to think of the confiscated object as the most important thing he possesses. Most of the skill, as all comedians know, rests in timing. Farantino had fallen for the simple trap with delightful ease.

'I am surprised that you have the temerity Farantino,' he said with heavy delivery. 'You will thank me for saving your mind from such trash. The *book* is confiscated'.

MacVicars was smugly satisfied to observe a brief look of what he interpreted as implacable hatred shift across Farantino's normally placid face. If he had known exactly what was in the boy's mind he would have been deeply offended.

Farantino produced the essay on Friday morning. It required a Latin dictionary, an intense conversation at the Post Graduate Latin club and two weeks of MacVicars' time to establish that it was almost word perfect. The knowledge embittered the master and the seven pedantic mistakes were underlined with red pen and no indication of the correct grammatical construction. It took a further three efforts before Farantino was told the work was 'acceptable'. After the third effort Farantino again had the insolence to ask for the book. Again he was denied. MacVicars, in point of fact, had buried the book somewhere in his cupboard – a vast cornucopia of stolen trophies - and had no idea of and no interest in its specific whereabouts.

MacVicars, having broken the boundary, spent the end of that term and a great deal of the next in an unrelenting attack on Farantino. The attack was subtle, guided by a fine and twisted mind. It took many shapes and forms most of which bypassed the rest of the class but between a master, who prepared each lesson on the premise that he would outwit a pupil, and a boy whose natural intelligence and erudition parried every blow, the duel was as clear as the polished surface of MacVicars' classroom windows.

In fact, MacVicars daily routine was shaped by the contest;

the contest in which he had every advantage, theoretical and practical. He had time to prepare, he had experience he had scholarship, he had a burning intelligence and he was driven. MacVicars knew that his own mind bordered on genius but as the days went by the realisation dawned on him that Farantino's mind did not simply border genius but surpassed it in every sense of the word, to the extent that the young boy was almost supernaturally gifted.

MacVicars took to long walks in the evening. He usually found himself by the Union Canal and would walk up from Stockbridge, through the botanical gardens and on to the park where he would pause at a bench and light up his pipe. On the walks he made complex mental notes for the morning's assault and perhaps because he was so occupied he was not prepared for the physical assault when it came.

He had a vague sense that there were two burly gentlemen standing in front of him. He had no knowledge that they were proxy representatives of one of Farantino's less reputable business firms because he had no idea that such firms existed. They carried bin bags and one of them asked him for a light while the other took the opportunity to hit him on the head with a heavy object.

When he came to, his first sensation was the dull pain in his head. He experienced a terrible shortness of breath. The air was stale, almost unbreathable, his nostrils twitched to the smell of camphor and laudanum and it was pitch black. He could see absolutely nothing. He moved his arms and his sore wrist struck something hollow and dead.

Wood.

MacVicars cried out with the pain and his voice sounded close and muffled – unnaturally so.

It took his mercurial mind a matter of seconds to jump to a stunning if implausible conclusion; a conclusion which proved disappointingly accurate. Still, in those immanent and awful seconds he chose to disbelieve such a preposterous eventuality. With trembling fingers he managed to find the lighter in his jacket pocket. With trepidation and mounting terror he ignited the flame.

MacVicars had *almost* been prepared intellectually to see the inner surface of the coffin lid but was astonished to witness, directly before his eyes, words inscribed on the silk funereal padding in a neat and all too familiar script.

Reor te propensionem Poe indicavisse.

As the flame flickered and died it was small consolation that through his recent practice MacVicars was able to immediately construe the Latin as 'I believe you expressed a preference for Poe.'

GERTRUDE

Gertrude was a cow. Really, a cow. She had been a cow as a young girl but that was only a useful metaphor. Cheat, bitch, liar, tease, ghoul, parasite, sloth, vampire, slut – every possible term of approbation had fallen from the lips of her peers but 'cow' was top of the list. Her parents, shielded by a web of intrigue and deception, had only become partially aware of the extent of her iniquity when the police arrived at their door to inform them that Gertrude had been found dead of a drug overdose in the school toilets, her nylons stuffed with stolen money, illegal substances and a suicide note that they had been forced to destroy from the conviction that the catalogue of sick confessions and accusations would only shame the community and probably annihilate what little solace was left to her distraught mother and father.

'What a nasty piece of work,' said the young officer as they got back to the car.

'I don't know,' said the senior officer looking dismally at the towering obscenity that was Bellport High School. 'The one thing that struck me about that girl - she took the easy route with everything. Lazy cow.'

'If there's an afterlife she'll pay for it big time.' said the young officer.

'Hope they give her a job there. Lazy good for nothing cow.'

There was an afterlife and Gertrude had arrived at the next juncture - Farmer Brown's farm - where to her surprise karma had enacted a singular joke by transmigrating her soul into a cow's body. The mechanics of her transmigration were beyond her understanding (which had been fairly limited as a girl in any case). As a cow she had clear recollections of her shady past and her initial reaction, following a period of despair and disbelief, was to alert farmer Brown to her circumstances - She was a human trapped in a cow's body.

This presented a problem. Farmer Brown entered the cowshed every morning without fail, squatted down, patted her on the haunch, milked her bursting udders and soothed her mooing with a bit of offhand chat. Then he took her out into the fields where she would spend endless hours eating and dozing before he led her back to the stalls in the early evening. This was an unvarying routine and for the first week, Gertrude had a stab at informing him that she was a girl in a cow's body. But the apparatus of a cow's body was not quite up to conveying the message and Farmer Brown was not too clever in any case.

After a bit Gertrude realised she was on to a good thing. She had been a lazy cow as a girl and she enjoyed being simply a lazy cow. She stopped trying to tell farmer Brown and got on with being a cow.

The quiet bucolic days continued with only the seasons marking time. It was a pleasant life.

Until the economic crisis.

Farmer Brown always talked to Gertrude about everything. It was part of the unvarying routine; the quiet old man would unburden the day's events, tell of his petty troubles, keep up with the local gossip and generally provide an insight into the outside world. Gertrude liked chewing the cud, being milked, sleeping: Farmer Brown's monologue was a reminder that human life could be a bit of a pain in the ass. It was better being a cow.

But all good things come to an end and when the economy went pear-shaped Farmer Brown was not left unscathed. Like every other piece of news, Gertrude was the first to be told.

'Not sure if we'll make it through the winter, Gertrude.' Farmer Brown leant on the rickety wooden fence. He chewed on a stick of grass in painful imitation of Gertrude who had picked that moment to deliver a fresh cowpat in the mudhole. 'We're in big trouble. I think we can keep the farm but…' he spat out over the fence '…it'll be touch and go.'

Gertrude couldn't care less. There was always talk. If it was soothing pleasantries, fine. If it was moans and grumps it went in one big flappy ear and out the other. That night, as with all other nights, she slept in sound comfort amidst the sweet smell of hay, quietly enjoying the life of a sloth.

But the next week on Friday in the early evening, events took on a dark turn.

Farmer Brown had taken up his accustomed position on the fence. He was carrying the morning newspaper under his arm and his old pipe was jammed in his mouth. He gave her a long thoughtful stare and then sighed. 'I never thought it would come to this Gertrude. I'm going to have to sell yer. Break my bloody heart it will.' He gripped the newspaper in his fist and punched at the headlines with a thick finger. 'Bloody crisis. No money anywhere. The farm will go unless you fetch enough to see us through the winter.'

Gertrude was singularly unimpressed. Perhaps some tremor in her lazy eyes struck an empathetic note in the normally insensitive Farmer Brown. He took up a more comfortable pose. Leant on the old wooden fence and started pensively out across the open fields to the white farmhouse.

'I'll tell yer one thing Gertrude…you're a better listener than the wife. If a man could make that sort of choice…' He smiled ruefully and then slowly shook his head in a gesture of resignation. 'Slaughter-house for yer come Saturday.'

There seemed to be little else to say. After a moments silence, unwillingly and uncomfortably, he left. Gertrude watched his huddled figure tramp awkwardly up the incline until he reached the farmhouse and she continued to stare long after the distant wooden door had closed.

Gertrude began to think; quite seriously, and for perhaps the first time in two short and insipid lifetimes. It was difficult initially, to correlate the necessary processes but with imminent demise looming, it was not an insurmountable difficulty. She had died of an overdose as a girl but that had been a terrible mistake. The whole plan to gain sympathy had backfired and it had been a horribly painful process. Now, as a cow they were going to top her. It was going to hurt.

Some three days later Farmer Brown remarked to his colleagues at the village pub that his cow was 'playing up with all sorts of marvellous antics' since being informed of the forthcoming extended sleep. The gruff stoic farmers had replied with grim conviction. 'They know. Aye they know,' and nodded their collective heads wisely.

Gertrude knew: The first stirrings of panic were tumbling in her several stomachs. The realization that morning would bring nothing more than a walk to the local market on a non-returnable basis was only now beginning to form. When Framer Brown had passed the gate earlier she had been expecting him to be unduly surprised at his previously apathetic cow, dancing round in circles and futilely attempting handstands. However she had failed to allow for the unresponsive nature of her body which simply failed to transmit the messages sent by her mind. At least, in an attempt to translate it, misinterpreted, and the dance which she had employed to alert farmer Brown to her intelligence had merely perplexed his. It left her waiting, breathless and desperately planning.

When Farmer Brown returned home in the last fading hours of daylight his anticipation of a relaxing evening in front of a roaring fire with little to do but absorb the evening's news and chew on his pipe was somehow marred by the impending execution of Gertrude. After all, she had been his mainstay through numerous hard times. Somehow the inevitability of her presence in the small field had provided reassurance. She had always been there; existing not only as a provider of milk but as a confidant, priest-like, his private psychoanalyst who listened and never told. It came to him that, after all these years, he had actually become very fond of old Gertrude, so it was with something approaching fully fledged grief and a little self conscious embarrassment that he left the farmhouse with its radio proclaiming economic doom and gloom and ambled down to the fields. He approached the familiar wooden gate, newspaper under his arms, bonnet on head and pipe in mouth. In his mind was the thought that, even now, Gertrude was providing for his needs – financially but soon no longer emotionally.

As always she was waiting. This time, though, there was a tense and unusual air of expectancy. It was almost as though she really did understand that this was the last time she would listen while he talked of his endless petty troubles. For once he did not lean on the gate. Both of his hands remained in his pockets, one arm supporting his paper. His pipe, although unlit, remained in his mouth.

There was nothing to say. Their eyes met. For an instant his squinting blue eyes were lost in the depths of her large deep brown eyes and then, from shame, he lowered his own to her hooves. As if this was prearranged signal she stamped her right forefoot on the ground like a bull. Once, twice, three times.

Framer Brown stared at the soft mud before her feet. There, printed as neatly as was possible under the circumstances, were the letters G E R T R U D E. Twilight was fading, but the moon, wan and pale, gave enough light to pick out the small puddles created by the impressions of Gertrude's hooves on the soil. The name was clearly visible - G E R T R U D E. And farmer Brown was staring hard at the letters, incredulous. With a stupefied look of amazement on his old face he turned quickly and walked up the incline to the little white Farmhouse.

Mrs. Brown was in the kitchen, radio blaring above the sound of pots hitting pans. 'Take off those mucky boots.' She yelled as she brought in the cutlery. 'What are ye doing gawping like a great bull?' Farmer Brown stared at the mud on his boots. Slowly, he unlaced them and left them at the door. Stocking-soled he picked up his newspaper and sat by the fire.

'We oughtn't to sell Gertrude,' he said as Mrs. Brown came back with a large saucepan.

'What?!!'

'We oughtn't to sell her.'

'You bloody old fool. What have been talking about for the last few days but that old cow?' She held the saucepan up menacingly. 'You know we need the money. What's got into you?'

'We need to keep her on…'

'Listen bonehead,' said Mrs. Brown in a tone he knew only too well. 'The farm will go if the cow doesn't. Now get that into your noggin. Sat there holding the bloody newspaper and thinking you're the bright spark. Not as if you can even bloody read.'

Farmer Brown stared disconsolately down at the newspaper. With a stoic shrug he began to rip it into pieces, his meaty hands clenching and unclenching like a mangler as he threw the crumpled incomprehensible pages onto the burning fire.

Far away across the fields he was vaguely aware of the miserable lowing of an unhappy cow.

NOT WAVING

Mulholland was dining with Charlotte Dursley, who you will recall from school was always called 'Lotte'.

A great difference and distance had been travelled between doe eyed, quiet 'sprite' Lotte and the elegant, cultured and well spoken woman who sat before him picking daintily at her salmon in the Oyster Bar of the Café Royal. Lotte had really flowered into bloom and Mulholland had begun to inject a little more enthusiasm into his chat than he might have anticipated before she sent her card. He had been moved to relate an anecdote about an argument between a waiter and an obnoxious customer, which he had always regarded as a winner with the ladies, when he noticed that Lotte's attention had become disengaged. Mildly annoyed, he was about to make a self-deprecating joke then realised it had not been boredom but distraction which had diverted her.

Mulholland followed Lotte's eyes to the family group at the next table - grandparents, parents and a little girl about six years old. The grandparents were leaving and there was much thanking, and many expressions of love and endearment. For a moment he sat in silence as the party made their way to the restaurant door, the parents and child standing at the open door while the grandparents left to get in their car.

Lotte shuddered.

Mulholland, always sensitive, glanced over to see that the child stood with her mother, waving goodbye to her grandparents, an innocent, full smile animating her face. The grandparents returned the wave, their faces growing younger and Mulholland caught a glimpse of the child in the smile of the grandmother. The old folks creaked down into their car, and with further waves, they were off. The child, father and mother returned in to the dining area, and resumed their seats.

'Why did that bother you?' he asked when it became apparent that Lotte was considerably moved. 'The saying of goodbyes?'

'Oh, nothing,' Lotte said. She shook her head to emphasise the topic was closed but Mulholland was not so easily put off and eventually over a glass of red, she was persuaded.

'I can never see a child wave goodbye,' Lotte said, 'especially to an adult, without thinking of the summer of 1973, and a French holiday in a small village in the Cote D'Or. I was seven then, and the child at the next table reminded me so much of myself that it brought my memories to the surface so I saw and felt them clearly again - too clearly.

My parents had taken me there, with my mother's parents, as a break from the drudgery of their work. It was a much a convalescence for my grandmother - who I now realise was suffering from a blood disorder - as a final holiday in school term-time before primary school became too demanding, after which they would be tied to the crowded school holiday periods.

So this was a quiet time, and it was a quiet place. A little village of less than two hundred inhabitants, boasting nevertheless a *Mairie*, a Post Office, a café and a *charcuterie*, which my father subsequently told me was run by one lady pig farmer who kept and slaughtered and sold the stock of the shop. I still recoil from pork laid out in butchers till this day, having a distant memory of standing at a counter scattered with the bloody debris of what had once been a pig, and my disbelief that this could be related in any way to the 'Three Little Pigs'.

I have few memories of the village, though I do recall the glorious vision of a kingfisher as we looked down from a bridge; my mother exhorting me to keep perfectly still – 'don't move an inch!'; its silent swoop into the placid water and the glint of a small fish as its tail beat in a vain attempt to reclaim its freedom. Like childhood, all over in a flash.

The house we stayed in was called 'Le Manoir'. I recall my mother and father's mixture of pleasure and horror at its rudimentary comforts. No electricity, but gauze-covered flickering gas lamps. No modern cooker but a range stove of complexity and formidable heat that cooked bread, casseroles meats and cakes and seemed to cram the flavour back into the dish.

We were not alone. Next to our house, which was the larger 'Manoir' - and easily accommodated our triple generation family - were two further cottages and a small converted dove-cot where the owners lived.

We had communicated with these owners, a Mrs. and Mrs. Edward Bloomsbury, at first through an address found in one of the more aspirational women's magazines that my mother used to get passed down from an elderly and genteel aunt.

I can remember father grumbling as the weeks went by between letter and response and my anxiety that the exciting 'French holiday' might be endangered. But a letter finally arrived, with a romantic picture of a woman warrior on the stamp, and old fashioned dark ink in longhand to confirm the reservation. I now suppose that it gave instructions for payment and how to get to the place.

Our journey there was full of adventure for me, but was probably a trial to my parents as we stifled and sweated in our car down strange French roads. I remember my father being hooted at by a lorry and heated words being exchanged with the driver. I also remember the shocked revelation that my father was not the strongest man in the world after all, when he declined the French driver's invitation to stop and settle the argument.

Our neighbours at the Manoir were lodged in two smaller cottages. They were a Dutch couple and an English couple. The Dutch had one child - a son of five or so called Rins, who neatly became my prince. Not only was his name perfect but he had a malleable personality and played the prince to my queen with an eagerness that suited me perfectly. The English couple, whose interminable arguments kept me awake, had two children. They were much older, or seemed to be much older. Looking back the gap was probably only three or four years, but it was that unbridgeable time between innocence and nascent adulthood. So, they scarcely deigned to notice my presence and after following them around like an unwanted pet for a while, I gave up the chase and settled on my own pet, the remarkable Rins, to act out my games and fantasies.

And le Manoir was a perfect setting for these fantasies. The house itself was three stories high, but seemed like a castle with its high ceilings and stone staircases, tall wardrobes built in to the walls, all to a far bigger scale than the cramped London houses I was used to.

My mother and father slept downstairs and I had a room to myself on the second floor, with my grandparents in a room on the same floor but separated by what seemed like a mile of space at the stairwell between the two rooms. The floor above was not in use. This deserted area had only one large low ceilinged attic where the linen was once stored. Apparently, in former times two maids had slept there, kept away from both their master and mistress and the luxuries of fireplace, hot water, toilets and kitchen range. The attic room was now unused and the door to it from the first floor landing was locked (of course both mother and father, and later myself checked, but it remained locked, even to those who tried the handle). There was no sign of the key and we soon forgot about it. Or at least we forgot it as a room habitable by other people.

I spent some restless nights below that floor. Daytime excitement; strange beds and strange night time sounds keeping me awake and awakening me from my fitful light sleep. The background drone of urban life was replaced with the blood hunt cries of night time animals, the creak of the eaves of the old house and the flutter of the bats above. It was these bats which really worried me, and caused me to sleep so badly. I became so hyper-sensitive to the thought, let alone the noise, of the bats that for the first two nights I was woken repeatedly in the night by the scraping and rustling and movement above. I rushed through to my grandmother and grandfather's room so many times that they must have put their collective feet down and insisted on me being downgraded to a bunk in my parent's room. This probably destroyed any private moments planned by them, but it led to a more settled sleep pattern for me.

The garden and grounds were the perfect complement. Le Manoir was set in an acre and a half of land around a river and separate channels in a small forest. There were tunnels through the trees, creaky old wooden bridges and fish that lurked deep in weedy pools. My mother followed us around obsessively for the first week warning us to keep off bridges, stay away from the river and remain in sight - and most importantly that I ensure little Rins was okay. I began to feel slightly jealous of Rins, whose safety seemed more important than mine.

By the end of the first week maternal control had become very lax, and after another couple of days we were on our own, free to roam, and only reminded of the warnings when our mothers called us back for lunch or dinner.

And so the days passed in blissful enjoyment of all that is best of France - the weather, serene and colourful - the people, surly and gruff but warm to the joys of childhood - the food, high flavoured, loved and tarried over. Above all a sense that life was not to be rushed; a calm serenity which Le Manoir seemed to epitomise.

Our hosts were also in tune with this slow paced bliss. They were a kindly, elderly English couple. Alice Bloomsbury busy pruning and buzzing around the garden on a small electric lawnmower which I longed to pounce on but knew was out of bounds. Edward Bloomsbury tall and frail, with light dun slacks and knitted jumpers but always looking cool even under the hottest midday sun, his glasses slightly forward on his nose and a slightly querulous look when at rest, as though you had just asked him a very difficult question and he had to withdraw into his brain to seek the answer. They spoke when spoken to, but always with the greatest of attention even to a child's endless and often pointless questions.

My father of course, always gregarious, and able to persuade others to at least be forthcoming, gently pried open their reticence and extracted the story of how they came to be here, and their backgrounds.

It transpired that she was the daughter of a writer of some repute, Cardus Lyndon (though not such reputation that even my erudite father could drop a book name or two into the conversation to keep that thread alive). Her first husband too, had been quite literary but had sadly passed away. Despite my father's probing, he could get little more out about this first husband, who seemed to have drifted off and out of her life quite quickly, so settled was Edward Bloomsbury. Her tone when speaking of the first husband was that he had been a mistake, and had not fitted the pattern, whereas Edward was very much in the right mould. My father and mother speculated that the first husband may have just cleared off, unable to stand the quiet, idyllic, but stifling atmosphere of Le Manoir or perhaps unkindly, his over-particular wife.

The house was filled from top to bottom with books, but books which looked very old and smelled like damp clothes which have been left overnight in a bag. My father, who was something of a bibliophile , and occasionally bought and sold second-hand books, explained to me that they were 'literary' books and as I did not understand that term said 'serious books' and in a whisper 'boring books.' I heard mother say to him one night in a lowered tone, which indicated I should not listen, (but made me listen even harder) 'I think they're just for show - none of them seem to have been read, at least not recently'. My parents were of the opinion that Edward Bloomsbury was purely ornamental or as they said a 'hanger on'. He was referred to by Alice as a poet and an author but there was no evidence of publications or income.

One day Rins and I discovered behind one of the doors on the first floor, a set of bookshelves with detective stories and science fiction novels from top to bottom. These appeared well read, as my mother triumphantly pointed out. Her pleasure was doubled as she loved mystery stories and she declared that we had 'discovered treasure' much to our joy.

Edward Bloomsbury or his wife took turns about to clean our rooms every day, and we had to leave the house for an hour while they carried out their chores. My parents speculated about them being too poor to employ a cleaner, and how long they could keep this routine up 'at their age'. Usually, Edward or Alice would come to us before the cleaning with some ideas of what to do during the day - visiting a nice village restaurant or a cave where my father could taste some wine.

One afternoon, Edward Bloomsbury came across to discuss walking routes with my father, who was keen on getting us 'into the fresh air' as he put it. My mother demurred but I could tell that she would have preferred to sit and read as she overlooked the beautiful tree-filled garden, river and orchard. Bloomsbury saw the book my mother was reading (a detective novel) and started backwards – an involuntary reflex. My mother expressed concern, and he said something about a heart murmur. But I remember thinking it was something about the book, and I remembered the book cover in consequence – Christopher Cardax: Hunted to Death.

Twenty years later, my memory of that holiday was jogged by seeing a child waving to a friend (I'll tell you why later) and the memory of that cover came back to me, and I checked up the author on the internet. On a database of detective fiction I found a few well regarded 'whodunits' reviewed, and a birth date of 1925, but few details other than that he was born in a small village in Sussex, an old publisher's picture, and described himself as 'a man who likes his own company, good French wine and in consequence lives in a small village in France' on the back of a pictured dust jacket. No death date was given. I checked around a little more and found he had written five novels and a few short stories. I found a detective fiction collectors' website with a forum and discovered that his novels were still well-regarded and collectable, but no more. Later, when the dread in me had begun to grow, I wrote to his publisher. They could only tell me that no more manuscripts had come through and that his wife had written to them in the early 1960s telling them he was ill and had stopped writing. They had continued to send her the royalties, and had negotiated quite substantial rights with her when one of his novels was made into a successful film. A French friend tried to find a death certificate but no joy. I tried a little genealogical research but again nothing came of it.

Finally, I got lucky and found on microfilm in the University Library in a local Sussex newspaper a picture of Cardax's wedding. I stared hard at the smiling wife. There was no doubt about it – it was Alice Bloomsbury, only she was Alice Miller, becoming Mrs. Cardax, or if you like, Cardax was Alice Bloomsbury's husband number one.'

Lotte paused, made to lift her wine glass but replaced it. She swallowed heavily and breathed slowly out. She glanced back at the small family at the next table and lowered her voice.

'Then came that last day.

Now I'm older I usually find the end of holidays a mixture of sadness at the leaving, and pleasure at the thought of returning to the comfort of my own home. But as a seven year old it was just miserable. I cried as I hugged little Rins and his family, who had to leave early in the morning for a long drive back to Holland. We were leaving after lunch, and so I was left alone as my parents took a last walk round the garden after breakfast.

I decided to go back up to the first floor and play with some wooden puppet toys my mother had bought me to keep me amused. I played with the toys up and down the detective fiction bookshelves in the upstairs landing beside my parent's room. There was a gap where I assume Cardax's book had come from. I used that as a place to sit the granddad puppet. When I pulled him out the little belt on his trousers which was undone snagged against something and I saw something metal behind the books. I pulled them out and saw it was a key.

I remember I stood there for a while, mentally stuck between curiosity and a realisation that I was about to step into forbidden territory. But the magnetism of not knowing and wanting to know drew me towards the door that I knew would lead up to the attic floor above.

The key turned easily in the lock. I kept looking behind in case my parents would come but there was no sign of them and soon I was at the head of the stairs. I pushed open the door and it swung in.

At first I couldn't understand the scene in front of me. The room was completely empty, except that against the wall furthest from the window was a large home-made wheelchair. I say home-made because it was plainly put together with bolts and protruding wooden joints and had been repaired and repaired until I doubt there was much of the original left. It was larger and wider than the average wheel chair and it had pram like wheels so it was raised higher. Underneath it was a flat shelf on which there rested a large metal pot. And across the arm rests a tea tray was nailed, stained and old.

And on the chair itself was what I at first took to be an old woman but realised quickly was a man. His hair was lank and long and across his mouth he had what I took to be a mask but what I now realise was a gag. It was old and worn with bite marks.

The old man was sleeping when I walked in, but raised his head at first slowly but then stark upright, eyes staring straight at me. I took a step back, but he flung his head backwards plainly calling me towards him. I was scared, but I was also old enough to understand an adult was ordering me and too young to refuse, so I came towards him, but not so close that he could surprise me with a sudden movement forward. As I got to a foot away, I realised he couldn't do that, because his arms were strapped to the armrests of the chair, and his legs were strapped underneath. He smelled foul and I realised the pot beneath him was his toilet (a potty, I would have called it then) and that he must be naked beneath the tea tray.

He signalled with his head behind him and I saw that the wheelchair was attached to the wall by two pieces of wood. There were clips at the top and, keeping my hands as far as possible from his head I unclipped him. He nodded furiously then gestured towards the door and window with his head (I couldn't make out which). I got behind him, relieved not to have to face those commanding eyes. I pushed him towards the window. As we got there he let out a kind of sigh and I could see him relax. I went round for a side view and saw to my surprise he was crying. I was getting less scared of him now. He made a gesture at his neck and I understood he was asking me to untie him. In his eyes I could see both intelligence and kindness so my fear just melted away.

As I stepped towards him I heard my mother calling, at first distantly then closer, on the ground floor. I turned to go. He rocked the wheel chair violently from side to side and strained at the arm straps. He pointed his head at the strap on the left which was nearest to me. I hesitated but by some primitive and intuitive mental arithmetic my child brain told me there was enough time so I quickly undid the strap. His arm came up quickly and he pointed to the other one and to the gag and then down in the direction of my mother's voice. But I was more scared of my mother now and I ran, I ran down the stairs, without looking back.

I ran right into my mother's arms.

Without a word she hustled me to the car which was in front of the house. While I was upstairs they must have been packing and I guess they didn't want me to make a fuss so they were making a quick getaway before I started to protest. The Bloomsburys were standing beside the car and they smiled at me serenely and said 'she's been so sweet'.

I was bundled into the back of the car without ceremony and the car began to pull away on the gravel. I looked around and the Bloomsburys were waving, but I looked behind them, and up.

At the upper floor of the house, at the window, I saw the old man's face, a white oval framed in the dirty glass, mouth gagged and head bobbing. His left arm gestured to me.

At the time I thought he was simply waving goodbye. But now of course I know that he was gesturing and beckoning me to return, or to tell my parents – to act – to save him. He was gesturing, calling me. Not waving. Not waving at all.'

Lotte looked out of the window, at the place where the car and the little girl had been, the tears trickling down her once girlish face.

SPANISH SUITE

Paul Brown, late of Bellport High, Edinburgh, had grabbed the chance of the job. He'd always liked sweets as a kid; had warm memories of staring in at the old newsagent window on the edge of Mountcastle Crescent – rows of boiled sweets in big glass jars; the colours and textures so much treasure in the Aladdin's cave of childhood. The little shop had long gone but the pleasant memory remained.

Now, all his pals were returning home from their first year at university but Paul had topped their cosmopolitan talk with something unexpected. 'International confectionary,' he had said with a large smile. 'Essentially, an executive salesman, but Mr. Cameron has all sorts of plans to involve me in the full business- chance of a directorship. Loads of readies but perhaps more importantly, my first few months are to be spent in European travel.'

Paul had exaggerated: Europe could be shrunk to a single trip across France with a short sojourn in Northern Spain where Mr. Cameron, a portly man with thinning hair, had connections with a string of small shops, franchises and concessions and was trying to establish a few more. Mr. Cameron's wife had insisted that Paul took on the trip. Paul had heard on the shop floor that she was suspicious of her husband's foreign excursions. Perhaps the old geezer had a few mistresses tucked away in the little villages *en route*. And, in some silly way, Mr. Cameron's furtive allusions to the business trip reminded Paul of the time he had been caught stealing sweets from the little shop on Mountcastle Crescent. It had only been a single toffee but he'd had his hand smacked for it.

In any case, he had landed the job.

Paul had an aptitude for language and, although his French and Spanish were only B grades, he was a quick learner. With the old mp3 player and a bunch of books the trip through France was a roaring success. Not only did he consolidate the concessions in Brittany - boiled sweets and the new line in liquorice - but an excursion to Auxerre gained three more shops willing to take on the old-fashioned Scottish Caramels and Peppermints. The towns of Lyon, Orange and Perpignan all fell under his magic spell. It seemed he could do no wrong.

From each hotel and Pension, Paul managed to convey some of this excitement back to Mr. Cameron. He sensed that his boss was jealous but he knew well that greed was his ultimate master. Paul also renewed an earlier intuition that the wife was in the driving seat and Mr. Cameron had to pull punches. At one point Mr. Cameron relented a little. 'It's very good young Brown,' he said in his nasal whine,' but really it's Spain that counts and these Catalan's can be very stiff. I'm absolutely depending on you to crack Spain.'

Of course, Mr. Cameron was merely setting Paul up for a fall. Doubtless he'd be at home mollycoddling the wife and harping on about his past successes in France and how Paul was just a new face and the real test of ability was to come. But even so, if Northern Spain *was* cracked then this could be an annual jaunt regardless of the number of Mr. Cameron's hypothetical mistresses or his attempts to subvert Paul's success.

But somehow, it fell apart in Spain. Perhaps it was the language. Spanish wasn't easy but of course, to really get in you probably had to speak Catalan. The Catalan's were a fiercely independent crowd, somewhat taciturn and reserved and they didn't much Like Paul's attempts at Castilian Spanish. There was also something about the country. The dry, baking streets of the villages, flaking plaster on crumbling walls, dark shops with cheap furnishings. The sun blazing down, over-bright and glaring; sweat, heat and a perpetual thirst barely quenched with iced lemon.

The tourist and beach areas were an utter contrast to the poverty and bleakness of the villages. They had both style and commercial possibility but Paul didn't like those sorts of places *per se* and made no effort to sell there.

Truth be told, he didn't much like to see the women and girls baring themselves so shamelessly. There was something unutterably lewd about the oiled bodies like so many boiled lobsters disporting themselves on the beach although – and here he suppressed a shudder – there was something compelling about the nudity, a kind of surreal and abstract reminder of the sweets of childhood. He would find himself fingering the pockets of his shorts in search of an illusory brown paper bag. There was a visceral smell around the promenade, the smell of salt air and rotten seaweed, a perversely erotic aroma.

At night, in the bay of Roses, Paul strolled along the promenade under pale Daliesque skies, observing sand sculptures – enigmatic dragons, fishermen and Neptunes, some spectacularly creative, others with the desperate touch of the impoverished dullard. The beach bums with their long hair and marihuana-bruised eyes seemed to reflect an absorption he hardly recognised.

Paul watched with a critical eye, the silent and dignified black women weave fake pearls and glittering beads into the hair of young Dutch girls. He sneered at the antics of the British tourists although they were no more crass than any of the other nationals. On the beach, young Moroccans sold cans of ice-cool cola and split coconuts. The sand sculptors lit little votive candles and entrenched themselves for the evening as the little house lights appeared in their thousands along the curve of the bay.

After midnight Paul ate the house *paella* in a small but select restaurant on the promenade. He ordered a good Chablis and, in a veritable haven of isolation, listened to the great rolling waves of the Costa Brava crash on the shore. The wind, which had driven Dali's father mad, began to kick up and Paul began thinking of this kind of life. If only he could crack Spain he would be made. It all rested on Spain.

At this point, he caught the eyes of the waiter. He'd already established that the waiter was Belgian, and in one of these rare moments of indulgence had offered a bit of a tip. The Belgian was much in sympathy with the outsider view and already intimate with Paul's related profession. He brought out an aperitif and responded to Paul's invitation by drawing up a chair.

'The wind is up,' said Paul. He'd discovered that the Belgian was fluent in several languages.

'Yes,' said the Belgian. 'This is the wild coast. It's always best to expect extremes; the Costa Brava has a way of testing a man.'

'Those girls had better wrap up.' Paul indicated a bunch of Spanish teenagers grasping at their belongings. They giggled like school children as the wind swept them off their feet and scattered their parasols.

For a second the Belgian looked reflective then he spoke: 'I had a niece once, as pretty as those young things.' He raised his aperitif and took a sip.

Paul sensed a story. He was not by nature an inquisitive man but for a moment he felt the need of companionship.

'Let's drink to your beautiful niece then?'

The Belgian's eyes grew hard. 'I won't drink to her. She ran off two years ago with a Dutch waiter from the *Chiringuito*. Little slut.'

'Sorry to hear it.'

'Shamed the entire family – my brother-in-law is town mayor - He had a terrible time of it. Now he's very ill. All down to that little slut.

The venom in the Belgian's voice was unmistakable. Paul, who could rival Kissinger with diplomatic platitudes, ventured a sympathetic grunt.

'They say she became a prostitute. They say she didn't even have the decency to hide herself in a *whiskería*, Instead, she ended up on the road to France, in La Jonquera, selling her body to those perverted kerb crawlers. That's where my brother-in-law saw her. Or so *his* sister says. Poor Henri, who had so much to offer, saw that tramp disport herself on the road like a piece of shit and the sight of it caused his health to break down.'

The Belgian's eyes had glazed and his lips were pursed in an ugly scowl. Paul knew about the prostitutes on the road to La Jonquera. He'd seen some of the poor girls standing at the roadside on the way down. He raised his glass, desperately trying to think of something.

'Perhaps we should drink then to you brother in law, the Mayor…'

The Belgian looked up, regaining his composure. 'My apologies, my friend. It was deeply personal thing. She was so beautiful. Perhaps the beauty was her curse. In any case, I will drink to my brother-in-law, Henri Matini, a man of irreproachable character who stands before his maker, a victim of a broken heart. God grant him a peaceful passing for they say he will never recover.'

Paul raised his glass. 'To Henri Matini.'

The wind still thrashed the air when Paul rose from his bed in the morning. The high window of his hotel apartment gave a good view of the beach where the distant waves rose and fell fiercely on the windswept shore. The sand spun up in spirals and the puppet figures of the waiters and beach bums scurried to secure parasols, wind-breaks and deck chairs. The sand sculptures were crumbling in the wind like melting post-Christmas snowmen.

In a rare moment of indulgence, Paul ordered a strong black coffee. His head was still beating from a bad hangover. What a night! Images came sneaking in on his mind like clown robbers, over-lit and faintly absurd.

It had been a strange and marvellous evening. After the kitchen was cleared, the Belgian escorted Paul to a small *tabern*; a local place, not frequented by tourists and through until the late hours Paul had drunk red wine, enjoyed regional *tapas* and revelled in the company of the 'real' people. There had been dancing and melodic Catalan tunes from a small *cobla*. The musicians accompanied the dancers with a selection of brass instruments led by a flamboyant flaviol player. A young girl sang; apparently a distant cousin of the Belgian's in-laws, whose ravishing beauty he had confessed in a moment of weakness, was a mere shadow of the fallen relation. If the dead girl was half as beautiful as the singer, Paul would be surprised.

The vaguely sing-song mix of French and Spanish had seemed almost intelligible the night before. Now, he only had memories of the swirling dancers, the staccato of maracas and the roaring crowd. Above all this patina of images, the young Catalan woman had risen like a forbidden sweet before his eyes. Through the long night he had seen her pink lips and tongue, her dark, velvet skin, liquorice-black hair, her colourful sweet-wrap dress of silk and cotton. He had heard the soft tones of her melodic voice and once, when she brushed past, the cinnamon smell of her caused him to flush with embarrassment. It was like being a child again, looking through a glass window at a land composed of unobtainable confectionary.

It had been a perfect evening marred only by an ugly scene outside. The locals were linking arms for the *Sardana* when a boy had burst in the worse for drink. There was some altercation between this young drunk and some older men. The boy appeared to be trying to remonstrate with the girl singer in the *colba*. Paul had risen to his feet but the boy had been hustled out by lads not much older than himself. Apparently, he had made some vulgar sexual imputations but Paul had been unable to follow the dialect.

Hours later, head spinning from the strong red wine, he left

Paul could still not establish whether he had really seen a pair of black clad legs sticking out from behind a bin when he had gone. There was a vague reek of faecal matter, vomit and rotten vegetables and his head had spun with nausea. The image haunted him – the smell seemed to linger about him - but he had no idea if it were a figment of his imagination or even if it were not, whether the legs belonged to the boy he had seen earlier or some discarded, shop mannequin. Some deep instinct told him that something unpleasant had happened outside the *taberna*. These Catalans seemed frightfully insular when it came to their women. He shook his head in an attempt to dispel the images and at that point, when he was still battling with his hangover, there was a knock on the door.

A porter handed him a letter and he opened it

Dear Paul,

I hope I can call you a friend. Firstly, I must apologise for the scenes at the club last night. It was boy from a local village. He has something of as reputation and has been pestering my niece for some time. I hope his intrusions did not mar your evening.

I took the liberty of making some inquiries about franchises. I have many connections and I attach here a list of shops including the main market hall in Roses who will be delighted to take on your range of confectionary.

Regrettably, I cannot come in person to say goodbye as my Brother in Law passed away in the night. The family must make many preparations for the funeral tomorrow which will be attended by thousands from the whole region of Catalan. Henri was much loved and respected, a moral giant in this age of corruption and like you a good and honest man.

Your Belgian friend

Paul jumped on to the bed and did a victory dance, bouncing up and down like a kid on a trampoline. This was it! This was it! He would be made for life. The commission alone would be in thousands, the connection itself would pay dividends and he would be jaunting across Europe living like a lord for as long as he liked. What a stroke of unbelievable luck.

As if it sensed his new optimism the wind died to nothing. In its place the tremulous heat of afternoon began to bake the air. The reception chamber of the hotel was stuffy and close when Paul made last minute preparations for his return journey: A nice condolence note to the family, some tasteful flowers to be sent direct and a discrete invitation to Edinburgh for his Belgian friend. But of course, he must be allowed to grieve for a decent interval. Pompous crap but it would serve his purpose admirably.

All the way along the road towards Perpingnan, Paul conducted an imaginary troupe of gypsy guitars as Gasper Sanz's 'Spanish Suite' filled the Ford estate with its heady music. He imagined that his little Ford was an open top BMW and he knew that next year would see him in dark glasses and silk shirts; he would gain an intimate knowledge of fine wines, become a connoisseur of exotic sea foods. He was shaking with excitement.

Perhaps because he was so distracted, he failed to notice the girl until he was almost upon her. It was somewhere just within the notorious La Jonquera, in a deserted section of the road below the sweep of the distant mountains.

He pulled up sharply. The loud, baroque guitars swirled round his head and confused him. For a second he struggled with the car stereo but failed to find the volume control. He wound down the window.

'Can I help!' he shouted.

She was clad in a traditional Flamenco dress with flouncing ruffles, trimmed with piping, and a lined figure-hugging bodice. The dress was a vivid scarlet, spotted with white polka dots and Paul was vaguely reminded of the excitement he had felt long ago by the newsagent window in Mountcastle Crescent.

She was very young and intensely beautiful. Her eyes, a deep brown, held the kind of sadness Paul had seen on the stylised beggars in Roses. It was look of humble appeal and incalculable sorrow. Paul felt his lips grow dry. He realised that she had not replied and some madness took him. He opened the door of the car and stood beside her. The heat hit him like a force, the blinding light of the sun forced him to shade his eyes and his throat felt terribly dry. She shrank back a little and dropped her head.

'Can I help' he repeated in Spanish. She did not reply. Only backed a little away to where Paul could see a rough path marked by white stones that led through a field of olive trees. Her feet were bare.

Deep inside, Paul knew that she was a prostitute dumped on the road by some cynical pimp to wait for customers. This was the fate of his Belgian friend's niece: To cater to the perversions of lonely men on lonely roads. He felt a kind of disgust, a blackening of his heart. And then the curves of her body through the dress, the pale, soft skin on her arms, the sudden feminine toss of her hair sent a bruising desire through his entrails.

He took a step towards her. She bore an uncanny resemblance to the girl singer in the *Taberna*. A clamjafrae of doubts assailed him. He was already kidding himself that he would rescue her. A jumble of thoughts, responses, excuses came bursting into his head: *I tried to take her off the street, she looked ill, I sent for help*…but in reality his trousers were already tightening.

Then she motioned to him, still in silence, and began to walk through the olive field.

Quickly, Paul looked around. The long road was eerily deserted. There was no one about; the only sign of human habitation a high wall some thirty meters away. He hesitated, struggling with his conscience. But she came swiftly back – childlike - held his arms and led him slowly through the olive trees to the wall. The touch of her body was like a magnet, he felt the slow graceful clasp of her arm, her warm thigh against his.

In the field of olive trees he was hidden from the road. The wall approached. He scanned it quickly to determine if it were part of an occupied building. He saw behind its bleak white surface a cross, apparently the spire of a church or chapel; the head and wing of a statue. It looked deserted. *Where was his wallet*? He had left it in the car. *Was the door shut*? Questions thrust for attention in his mind but they were all dispelled when she turned to face him. She placed her back towards the wall, stared with a half smile and slipped her fingers into his belt to disengage the buckle. Then with a languorous movement she unzipped his fly. His trousers dropped to his ankles. She hoisted her dress to her stomach.

Paul had always intended his virginity for his future wife. That quaint hope was dashed. With an explosive grunt he pushed the girl against the wall. As she gripped him in her arms, her lips met his; teeth grinding, tongue searching and he was in her. Paul began to buck in uncontrollable spasms. He shut his eyes, blinded by overpowering lust, as the heat beat through his head and the insane strumming of gypsy guitars floated from his distant and unseen car stereo.

Her body went rigid in his arms. Her arms strong against his neck, her legs in a vice-like embrace.

It was the smell that first alerted Paul.

It was a smell of something very old, rotten, like the dead fish in the bay of Roses. It was a frightful smell. No less frightful the thing he saw when he opened his eyes.

She was dead; had died a long time ago. The sallow face of a reeking corpse was pressed against his cheek. The rotten hole of a mouth and the vacant, purulent sockets where eyes had been were juxtaposed to his own.

Teetering on madness, Paul thrust back from the wall to disengage himself. Then there was a moment of pure insanity as he backed away from the wall, unable to free his writhing torso from her corpse and alternately gibbering to himself and shrieking in terror. He became instantly aware that he was next to a Spanish cemetery and some tiny part of his mind, which still functioned in a semi-rational manner, knew incontrovertibly, that this was the mayor of Roses' daughter; her ghost, her resurrected corpse, spirit or whatever, that had managed to rise up from a shallow grave to wreak some unknowable revenge.

He staggered backward away from the wall, unable to tear his eyes from the corrupt and rotten face. Screams tore from his throat, spraying her putrefying lips with spittle but he was unable to disengage the rotted thing from his grasp. Her clammy body clung to his, decomposing as it did, the spider arms wrapped in a fixed embrace, the stick legs holding firm, the rotten guts weeping foul liquid over his shrinking flesh.

As Paul battled to both free himself and to retain his sanity, he tripped over his pants and dashed his head on the white stones of the path that led to the cemetery gate. Descending into unconsciousness, he was appalled to feel the putrefying lips fall against his own in some dreadful parody of a kiss.

On Sunday morning, still locked in this unfortunate posture, Paul regained consciousness. The funeral cortege of the Mayor had just arrived.

CRAIG HERBERTSON

THE ANNINGLEY SUNDIAL

UNAM TIME [3]

I think I may have mentioned Mulholland's abiding interest in *objets d'art*, antiquarianism and anything quaint and old. As a member of the Order these kinds of pursuit fall almost as a natural progression but there was one incident that occurred not long after he'd joined Edinburgh University as a young student; an incident that perhaps sparked off this consuming passion; although other less durable souls may well have been put off.

Mulholland was fairly well known to the local antique dealers in Stockbridge and the Pleasance as a collector and his rooms at the halls of residence were a virtual labyrinth of quaint curios, catalogues, old prints, conversation pieces and manuscripts. Mulholland, being at once a secretive sort but open and engaging on first acquaintance, had made a few close intimates and very many professional contacts. One of these latter, Hawkins of Broughton Street, who had no shop and worked from a series of limited edition catalogues, had dropped in on a Saturday evening to test Mulholland's recent acquisition of Islay Malts, special reserve. It was a more or less informal call if such things exist between collectors, and Hawkins had brought a few pieces to muse over whilst imbibing the *uisge beatha* and positing the relative merits of Ardbeg and Bowmore

Anyone who knows whisky aficionados will grasp that Hawkins delayed the production of his collectable pieces until the two men had reached the cigar stage. There is no need to adumbrate the general conversation before that point as it consisted mainly of a series of superlatives and an itinerary of distilleries, their owners and their foibles. Eventually, however, Hawkins pulled out his magic box. Amongst the collectables therein - a miniature of an unknown Scottish mercenary, a

---

[3] - **Fear one hour**

Napoleonic bottled ship and a complete set of tin soldiers of the Boer war - Hawkins also had on his person a small portfolio of mezzotints, comfortably small enough to fit in a leather briefcase. He had no intention of revealing these to Mulholland whose basic philosophy on engravings was that they were generally dull and unmarketable; he had no interest in owning them and no prospect of passing them on. However, Hawkins had been unable to tempt Mulholland with the militaria and the prospect of extending the evening a little longer – and the hint that Mulholland had reserved something special in the decanter on his desk led him to produce the portfolio. More by way of politeness than interest, Mulholland had cleared a deal table of cards and permitted Hawkins to place a number of mezzotints on its surface.

I'm sure you are familiar with the type of mezzotint – they flourished in the mid-eighteenth century in England and provide some interesting enough portraits and landscapes. Old encyclopaedias are rife with quaint studies by Bronlow and Tompson of painfully earnest aristocracy and haughty landed gentry, their landscapes and their country gardens. This lot contained no portraits but instead a pretty dull set of mansions and follies, fountains, gardens and sculpture and some old country manors.

The malt whisky was being introduced with the usual blandishments that accompany an especially good cask. The mezzotints were laid out with perhaps less neatness than entirely sober company might have allowed. So it was that with one eye on the decanter, Hawkins failed to observe Mulholland suddenly stand up with a start. As he stared at them on the table for a few seconds and frowned Hawkins finally asked if he was troubled but Mulholland merely poured out a smallish malt into the antiquarian's glass and after a few moments contemplation asked if he might keep the mezzotints over Sunday. Hawkins could collect them on Monday morning if he chose. After a few skirmishes around the arena of 'any particular one of interest to you?' and the like, which were hastily rebuffed as Mulholland gathered his wits, Hawkins departed with not a little curiosity as to the younger man's sudden interest in a topic with which he had hitherto displayed a remarkable disinterest. It was only on his return to Broughton Street that the wise old antiquarian realised that contrary to procedure, Mulholland had even failed to ask for an approximate price on the mezzotints.

We must leave Hawkins to his puzzlement and take a walk with Mulholland on Sunday afternoon down to Leith links where a cricket match was in its penultimate innings. Mulholland had enjoyed a good breakfast of bacon, eggs and black pudding after which he had made a number of tentative inquiries concerning the mezzotints before setting out for the links. It was a fine September afternoon and the breeze off the firth had spent its force. The sun was shining through tattered clouds and a small crowd had gathered round the clubhouse to watch the last game of the season. The match, between Bellport High and a makeshift team from Watson's old boys, was what they called then a 'blinder' but the results, though fascinating to those involved and much disputed for some years after, are now a matter of historical record and do not concern this tale. Mulholland drew up just in time to watch an acquaintance, one Norton who had been in the year below him at Bellport, being caught out by a ferocious 'bouncer' the result of which was that he narrowly failed to make a hundred. Naturally disappointed, Norton neglected to observe Mulholland - who had taken up a position on the clubhouse veranda - until he had changed out of his whites and was about to console himself with a dark beer.

'Rather bad luck,' said Mulholland joining him at the counter. 'Here let me get that beer.' 'Damned leg side trap,' said Norton. 'Unmercifully bad hook though.'

There was more talk of the 'deep square' and 'backward square leg' type which need not trouble the reader and the game would certainly not have been conceded by Bellport if the practice had matched the theory. Norton advanced another pint of 80 shilling beer to Mulholland just as the Watsons' innings concluded. The somewhat disconsolate Bellport team trouped into the clubhouse in a subdued silence while the Old Boys rather ebulliently started to order celebratory drinks.

Norton was not too unhappy to sit with Mulholland on the veranda and avoid the ribaldry that occurs after these matches. He was a quiet sort - chess player, mathematician and his acquaintance with Mulholland was based more on a series of mutually shared brown studies than conversation. Their acquaintance had been somewhat formalized by a chance meeting at his older cousin's wedding some six months before. The two youngest members of a sumptuous wedding party, they had throw in together and had found enough common ground in an appreciation of the architecture, art and sculpture of the great hall at the reception party to keep them both amused. Nevertheless, there seemed to be no particular reason why Mulholland would seek Norton out on a Sunday afternoon as Mulholland was not a keen cricketer and had never appeared at a match before. Norton brought this up in a tactful manner.

At this point Mulholland looked somewhat uncomfortable. With a trace of hesitance he brought forth that same portfolio that Hawkins had produced the night before. He laid it on the table and began pensively stroking his cheek.

'Cricket's not really my game, Norton. I'm a sportsman as you know but I'm not one for team games. I enjoy shooting. If you recall, that's how I gained the acquaintance of your cousin, George, on that less than Glorious Twelfth last year. Probably why I was invited to the wedding. Certainly the invitation came to me as something of a surprise.'

'Yes. George often mentions that rather nasty incident.' Norton cradled his pint mug in his hand and shook his head absently. 'You'd been up for the grouse and ended up saving his life as I recall.'

Mulholland had saved Cousin George by the judicious action of pushing that venerable chap out of the way of a stray bullet but that is another story which sounds far more exciting than it actually was. The consequence of it all was that Mulholland, who had simply been earning some extra summer swag as a ghillie, was immediately adopted by Cousin George and his young fiancée as something of a lucky mascot and invited to an aristocratic wedding. Mulholland, ever self effacing, shrugged and looked again at the leather portfolio on the table. 'He's plenty of acres to cultivate some birds of his own and speaking of which how is Lady Norton?'

'Doing grand I believe. In the third month of pregnancy or so. You know how it is with the newly wed. Faster off the traps than a greyhound. Expect the halls will be full of pattering feet in no time.'

In actuality, neither Mulholland nor Norton knew the first thing about the patter of tiny feet, partly through youth but mostly through inclination. Both were still in their morning glory but there was already the suggestion that they might see out the sunset of their days in the quiet torpor of bachelorhood. As if to emphasise this sobering fact Mulholland drew out a cigar and offered one to Norton. The younger man declined and leaned back in his chair with a wry smile. 'Cousin George, He does like his follies. At the moment he's obsessed with Victorian sundials of all things; reminds me occasionally of Toad of Toad Hall.'

'He's certainly a very rich man,' replied Mulholland. 'And his hall is very much as grandiose as Mr. Toad's.' Again Mulholland glanced at his leather portfolio.

Now Mulholland was not much given to hesitation but less to making an ass of himself. His acquaintance with Norton was only slight but he liked the man and felt a natural instinct towards him which under normal circumstances would have led him to cultivate his company. He knew Norton was a mathematician of some capacity and nothing in the young man's makeup suggested credulity. For these reasons he decided to forbear from his original intentions whose embodiment lay firmly ensconced in the leather pouch of the portfolio but fortunately thought of an alternative on the spot.

After a few more general remarks about Cousin George and his foibles, interrupted at several points by congratulatory remarks from Norton's team mates - only now recovering from the defeat and able to acknowledge one or two pieces of virtuosity that had nearly turned the game - Mulholland was able to persuade Norton to drop in to his rooms for a cup of tea around supper: This on the pretext that he had discovered something that might be suitable as a belated wedding present for Cousin George.

This small deception enacted, Mulholland walked from the links as the late afternoon sun dyed the Edinburgh skyline in jacinthe and saffron light. Grey serried clouds seemed to buffet the old town tenements with a Turnerian majesty as the wind from the Firth of Forth caught at Mulholland's jacket. It was the usual Edinburgh weather, full of paradox and vim, and it seemed to reflect his inner state to a nicety. The architecture which fell to his view might also be regarded as a neat parallel: The contradiction of the old town's charm and the gentile Georgian beauty of the new town had always fascinated Mulholland and no less now when architecture was very much at the forefront of his mind.

All the way along Leith Walk and the South Bridge Mulholland was in deep concentration. So much so that he almost forgot to visit the Sunday flea market in the University precincts. As finds at the flea market provided a large part of his student income you can imagine how distracted he had become. Needless to say the market was bustling with activity but rather less well served for bargains. One did fall to his predatory hand though: A rather tatty first edition of 'Ghost Stories of an Antiquary' by M.R. James published in 1904 and well thumbed since then by a number of careless owners. Mulholland flicked through the pages for a private confirmation. It seemed rather too coincidental. And it was at this juncture that a fellow collector from the Arts department was on hand to verify one or two particulars about the mezzotints, the main particular being that they were indeed genuine though not particularly valuable and that they had come from a collection from the now defunct Ashleian Museum. It was a much perturbed Mulholland who arrived back at his apartments clutching a leather briefcase in one hand and his collection of ghost stories in the other.

It's a well known commonplace about young men that they are easily led astray and prone to long bouts of dissolute behaviour. This latter most predominately measured by the judgment of their elders and betters. While neither Mulholland nor Norton could be judged moral lepers both were prone to the lesser sins of procrastination and distraction and I regret to say that Norton failed to turn up for supper and Mulholland, who had been genuinely discomfited by certain aspects of his recent discoveries was somewhat diverted from his course by amongst other things, a billiards tournament, a bottle of Laphroaig and the arrival of and old school chum from abroad. This initial delay was extended by a variety of circumstance that afflict the young and it was not until the end of the following month when the Michaelmas Term was in full swing that a phone call from Hawkins disturbed the tranquillity of Mulholland's temporary calm. He had entirely forgotten about the mezzotints and his unfounded fears, a circumstance that afforded Hawkins another opportunity to sample some select malt over supper on the Sunday. Mulholland duly purchased the single mezzotint that interested him – a rather innocuous view of a manor-house from the early part of the century. It was an unremarkable piece, 15 by 10 inches enclosed in a black frame with the producer of the work unknown.

Hawkins could not conceive of any reason that Mulholland should want the piece (and was rather surprised when Mulholland met his slightly inflated price). It showed a full-face view of an insubstantial manor-house, with three rows of plain sashed windows each rather shabbily decorated with rusticated masonry. There was a parapet with what might be balls or vases at the angles, and a small portico directly in the centre of the building. The unremarkable Manor was graced with a comfortable looking expanse of lawn and an avenue of trees that extended towards the viewer in two stately lines. A name had at one time been inscribed in the margins but this for some unaccountable reason had been defaced and was no longer legible. It was in short, an anonymous piece of arcana that one's eyes might glide over without substantial loss in any number of pubs or wayside inns through southern and middle England. Having procured the mezzotint, Mulholland saw Hawkins to the door as soon as he might be drawn away from the decanter of Bowmore – a process that took longer than you might imagine.

As he turned from his door a rather peculiar thing happened. He had left the mezzotint face up on his deal table during the transaction. Perhaps it was simply a trick of the lights but it seemed for a second that something ran swiftly across its surface. Nobody is really fond of insects on their table and Mulholland was hardly an exception; but his impression when he reflected on it was that the thing he had seen was not after all an insect but something that bore an uncanny resemblance to a tiny shambling figure; a figure of disturbing appearance that one might observe in the sequence of frames in a creaky old silent film. A quick inspection of the table and the area immediately below it gave no clue. Mulholland advanced back and forward in a kind of pantomime in an attempt to repeat the play of lights on the mezzotint's surface. The remarkable sequence was not repeated. He was rather pleased that it was not, but its occurrence reminded Mulholland somewhat urgently of a bit of reading he had forgotten to pursue. He advanced to his librarium with a troubled frown.

He found what he was after on the shelves of his recent acquisitions, settled himself into his favourite chair and began to browse the pages of the M.R. James collection that he had purchased at the Sunday flea market at the end of September. He had hardly begun his inspection of the story that had provoked his attention when the phone rang and who should it be but Norton.

Now coincidence is a remarkable thing and young men are apt to set a lot of store by events that the older and wiser put down to simple circumstance. Younger fellows might gasp in amazement that they have just encountered a school friend on the way to the cricket or chanced upon a group of friends in a local café where the cynic need only point to the proximity of their friends in the neighbourhood and the habitual paths that they follow. On this occasion it would be fair to say that Norton's apology and request that Mulholland should take up an invitation to lunch was something rather more substantial and it sent a strange foreboding through his normally imperturbable mind. With no difficulty, he persuaded Norton to pop over that evening and we must join them both in Mulholland's rooms where a neat silver teapot, some blue china cups and the aroma of Earl Gray and lemon will give us a clue to the activities.

'How is Cousin George,' said Mulholland after the usual preamble.

'George is in remarkably good spirits as always,' replied Norton. 'Having a fair job trying to keep up appearances at the Hall of course and he's had to employ a new gardener. He's a very old fellow – one of those venerable chaps who speaks little and looks a lot - but fortuitously he comes with an able bodied son. It's all hunky-dory down at the Manor.'

'Jolly good,' said Mulholland. 'And Lady Norton; everything shipshape there?'

'She, I am advised, is as beautiful as ever. Positively radiant and doing all that post conception stuff. Sorting out rooms, spending impossible amounts of plunder on baby clothes and all the paraphernalia that goes along with that.'

'It's a bit like blue-tits and nests I believe,' said Mulholland wisely. 'Ladies always seem to get het up and work rather too hard at the spit and polish while husbands stand in the background trying to be useful while fretting over much.'

'Yes,' replied Norton knowledgably (although of course his knowledge of this could be written on a scrap of paper). 'George bewails the fact that she overdoes it and can't sleep at the end of the day.'

Mulholland could not help but betray a slight inflection in his voice.

'Not sleeping well. That's tiresome.'

'Up all night, I believe,' said Norton with considerable lack of sympathy. 'Think it's fairly typical.'

The conversation had extended as far as two young men could reasonably be expected to dally over the perils of childbearing but Mulholland fought hard to suppress a growing concern. He shook his head and invited Norton to his desk where he had laid out the nigh forgotten mezzotint.

'Have a look at this and tell me what you think.'

'My, my,' said Norton. 'The trees are larger and older and I think there's been an extension to the west wing but that's surely Anningley Hall.'

(At this juncture I must advise that, as a convenient fiction, I have retained the names given by the redoubtable James)

There were a few moments of silence while Norton and Mulholland stared at the picture. It had gained nothing in charm or aesthetic beauty. It was simply a rather dull mezzotint of a rather dull manor house bathed in moonlight. Mulholland had been certain from the first moment that the picture was indeed a fair facsimile of Cousin George's residence. Norton's confirmation had not informed him of anything new. He realised in that moment that he had been rather hoping that Norton would not recognize the place at all. The foreboding that had crept up stealthily in his subconscious over the last months now seemed rather more concrete.

Norton picked up the mezzotint and scrutinized it carefully.

'You know, despite it being the Manor house there's something about the picture that gives one a rather bad feeling. I'm not sure George would fancy it on his wall despite it being apposite.'

'My feelings exactly,' replied Mulholland. 'Something of a curiosity but perhaps I'll stick it in a drawer for another day.'

A few acquaintances of Mulholland popped in at that moment with a speculative inquiry about tea and biscuits - the student mind being generally geared around mealtimes - and Mulholland took the opportunity to see Norton to the door. As the younger man was fetching his coat Mulholland made a single tentative inquiry before saying goodbye. When he returned to protect his biscuit tin he was armed with the comfortless knowledge that Norton had never heard of M.R. James or his ghost stories. He reflected a moment longer and decided that that might be just as well.

I'm sorry to relate that more frivolous topics engaged Mulholland's attention for the next few months although his tutors might have had a word to say in respect of the various academic disciplines that vied for attention with the young man's variety of pastoral pursuits. In this time he heard nothing from Norton with the exception of a postcard from down south indicating that the budding mathematician was off to attend the Oxford Science Christmas lectures at the University Museum of Natural History on the fifteenth. Norton appeared to be excelling all expectations in Mathematics, was corresponding with some German Academic in Leipzig and generally displaying the kind of rational mind that dazzles others with its remarkable perspicacity while perhaps sacrificing a little of the spiritual qualities others come to cherish. There was no mention of Cousin George except a cryptic line possibly in reference to coming examination results – '…as my cousin George says, UNAM TIME, or in the vernacular 'fear one hour'. For some scarcely definable reason this apparently bland statement sent a chill along Mulholland's spine.

Troubled in a way that he could hardly summarise, Mulholland penned an invitation to Norton to come over to his rooms for Christmas. This was by way of a ploy as anyone with parents or even a distant and much maligned uncle would find more Christmas cheer at home with family than the dubious comfort of a virtually empty student residence. The ploy had the desired result. Norton rose to the bait and wrote back reciprocating the invitation. He himself was going down to Cousin George's and was entirely certain that Mulholland would be a most welcome visitor. Norton's family was extensive and it was the habit of the rich cousin to throw a bash at the manor. Mulholland would be welcomed both as a friend of Norton and the saviour of Cousin George; any awkwardness in Mulholland's mind could be happily forgotten as there would be so many guests that another would be small potatoes.

Feeling mildly guilty and making effusive but unconvincing arguments about intrusion and disturbance, Mulholland finally accepted the invitation and looked forward to the event with mixed feelings.

A week later, two days before Christmas, Mulholland packed his valise for the train journey. It seemed the best part of frugality to take a small hamper for the journey. As he constructed some cheese and pickle sandwiches, he conducted an inner debate on whether to take the mezzotint down to Anningley and with this purpose in mind he had placed it on his deal table. For the first time he noticed that the surface of the mezzotint displayed some flecking or foxing. Tentatively he rubbed a corner of it lightly with a damp cloth but it did not respond. The flecking gave the moonlight tableaux the uncanny impression that it had begun to snow. Mulholland stared at the picture for a space of time, his expression inscrutable. With some qualms he replaced it in the drawer and added an extra bottle of Laphroaig to the hamper.

The journey was mercifully uneventful although the weather may have been kinder. Relentless rain in the borders of Scotland gave way to hail. Then the hail made way for heavy snow. Fortunately, as Mulholland had packed his valise with more optimism than commonsense, the snow let up by early evening just within the county of Essex. Mulholland was given to understand by the newspapers that Essex had seen an uncommon lot of snow over the last few weeks and such appeared to be the case. On a desolate platform, decorated with the footprints of a few fellow travellers, Mulholland picked up the local service. The old train armed with two rattling carriages weaved through hamlets and farms tucked in hollows of the hills, lonely moats, footpaths, fords with irregularly shaped groves banked by thick hedges, maple, spindle and dogwood all sleeping under white blankets of fallen snow. A beautiful calm descended on the world and Mulholland nodded off to the rhythmic rumble of the train.

The calm was disturbed somewhat by one of these awful dreams that seem to always occur during the day. The snow covered fields changed into shrouds, the trees to gaunt creatures - burdened with some invisible bundle - stalking grimly on the periphery of his vision. An elderly conductor woke him from this galling dream some minutes before they approached Anningley; and here the conductor was kind enough to supply Mulholland not only with a number of tips and observations on the failings of the modern world, the youth of today and the moral turpitude of the current government but also some information about the locality.

Still disturbed by the dream, Mulholland learned that the village of Anningley had been blessed with a Norman church (sadly ill attended) where the ancestors of the family of Francis lay buried. They had been the previous owners of Anningley Hall which stood nearby. It was a Queen Anne house with extensive grounds – although these had been reduced by the introduction of a small estate full (according to the conductor) of miscreants, vagabonds and newcomers from the city. The new owner – this was George Norton's father who was still regarded as a foreigner despite forty years of residence - had made an unfavourable impression when he sold the farmlands to create the estate but his ingenuous son appeared to be restoring the balance. George's young wife had been a great help at the church socials and the conductor's wife was very taken with her.

At this juncture, Mulholland who had tried but failed to interject a few supportive comments managed to make a polite remark about the coming child.

The conductor stared at him very darkly for a few moments and then said in a muted tone. 'I wouldn't be bringing a wee baby into them Halls. Oh, no. The wife's most upset, I'll tell ye.'

I'm sure that venerable gentleman would have told Mulholland of his particular concerns - and much more besides of a general nature - if the train had not pulled into the station.

The spire of the Norman church was just visible over the roofs of some small cottages but it seemed to offer little in the way of spiritual comfort to Mulholland who rather welcomed the sight of young Norton on the platform. Norton had apparently borrowed a motorcar whose capabilities he was anxious to demonstrate. Quickly, as is the way with youth, the nightmare was forgotten in general banter as Mulholland packed his gear and the two set off towards the Manor chatting volubly about nothing much.

At last we come to the scene of the crime so to speak. The sun had just set as the two arrived and the afterglow muted the light and shade of the landscape. The mezzotint of Anningley Hall succeeded in every particular to present a credible picture of the place. The snow had lent the mundane architecture an almost fairytale charm, the stately snow-clad trees lining the long avenue, the distant church, the expansive fields all conspiring to afford an image of tranquil splendour; the image enhanced by a series of lamps and candles which had been laid at strategic places to produce a festive spirit.

I will not bore you with the various introductions that were made or detail the variety of personages, exalted and humble, who were celebrating the festive season at the Hall. The Nortons were an extensive family: numerous grandparents, aunts, uncles, cousins, distant cousins and the like as well as servants, gardeners and cooks were all bustling about or relaxing according to their mood or conception of duty. Mulholland was sufficiently bewildered to recognize a few faces and forget as many names. One thing was perhaps worthy of note. There were no infants, babies or toddlers in the family; Cousin George being a very late youngest son and, although a number of teenage nephews and nieces were around somewhere, their whereabouts were mostly a mystery to their elders.

Mulholland was treated to a bite of creamed turnips in the dining room. It was not a terribly formal bite - various members of the family were occupied here and there with decoration, discussion or preparations of some sort. Cousin George dropped down from his private chambers to shake Mulholland's hand. He was a tall, spare chap with a sincere and affable nature. It has been unkindly said that he was not the sharpest weapon in a family armoury that boasted the mathematical genius of his younger cousin and a fair number of wizards in the financial sector but there was no doubt that he was a genuine and caring man who was much loved by his family and even tolerated by those members of his wife's kith and kin. He advised Mulholland that he was rather pushed out what with the festivities and the good lady being with child and this gave Mulholland an opportunity for polite inquiry.

'I do hope Lady Norton is in fine health' he said dutifully.

For a second, Cousin George's face took on a sombre aspect. 'Well, it's her first child and I suppose it's the same with all women. Off her fodder and not sleeping at all well. She's gone for a lie down.' He stared up at the ceiling as if it might be seen through and just at that point a stifled cry was heard from above. Cousin George muttered 'Damn. The midwife is up there now, thank goodness.' He took his leave as two spinster aunts entered and began to fuss about as ladies of this kind are wont to do.

'She's plagued with nightmares,' said Norton casually.

'Do you know what form the nightmares take?' replied Mulholland.

Norton gave him a strange look.

'It's not idle curiosity, I assure you.'

At this juncture Mulholland began to have an experience that you may have encountered yourself. While Norton with some reticence began to explain what little he knew of the nightmares, a conversation between the two spinster aunts became rather heated and he could not help but overhear its contents. The aunts were apparently discussing the pros and cons of birth at home, something that lady Norton had insisted on. It transpired that the young lady had fallen in with new fangled theories on childbirth. Apparently, she was now reliant on muesli, yoga, acupuncture and a whole host of other debatable foreign intrusions that seemed, according to the unsolicited opinion of the aunts, to be unwise and detrimental to a successful birth. The midwife in attendance now was some German girl come armed with homeopathic books and a range of peculiar glass bottles. The older aunts put a great faith in the local hospital, with all its tried and tested amenities but their opinions on this – and it seemed on a wide range of more general things – were being largely ignored. The effect of this dual conversation was that Mulholland felt somewhat dislocated mentally and could not take all the facts in.

Norton had something he wished to show Mulholland and before he knew it he was out on the lawns muffled up in a coat and borrowed scarf. Only when they had drawn near to the object of Norton's interest in a grove some distant from the west wing of Anningley hall, did the full import of both conversations rise to the surface of his mind.

'Lady Norton's having the baby at home?'

'Yes,' said Norton. They're preparing a birthing room

downstairs. I meant to tell you. No one's allowed in – don't for God's sake enter it by mistake bringing your repellent Scottish germs – something of a sanctuary. It's over there.' Mulholland looked back, following the direction of Norton's hand and saw a dim lit room. For a second, and he could never really be sure about this – a shadow flitted across the room. It was only a fleeting glance but in that single vision he seemed to catch sight of a hunched shape which jerked across the empty room with the distorted animation of a black rag caught by the wind on a washing line. He drew his hand across his face and looked again with some trepidation but the shadow did not reappear.

'And this nightmare,' said Mulholland with his breath icing in the air. 'It recurs you say? Someone creeps up on her and tries to steal the baby?'

'Not tries, old man. Steals the little beggar and runs off. I expect it's fairly common – some psychological root to it I dare say.'

'I dare say,' replied Mulholland. But his words echoed somewhat hollowly.

Norton continued blithely. 'You're full of questions recently old man. So, I'm here to answer another. Now look at this. Cousin George's pride and joy.' They had drawn up to what looked like a small pedestal raised up on a series of low steps enclosed by a bower of ash trees. It was covered in snow, almost as though a waiter had laid a tablecloth over the surface. Perhaps it was his unsettled state of mind, but something in Mulholland felt a creeping dread, a kind of preternatural cold that bit at his innards. His legs did not want to approach the thing but Norton had already marched forward.

'You were asking about my cryptic Latin and the exams. Well, look at this. Beauty, isn't it?' With a sweep of his hands Norton cast the snow from the top of a surface inclined like a church lectern. Perhaps Mulholland was reeling from successive worrying revelations but he almost jumped backwards in shock. In the instant where the snow sprayed to left and right Norton's moving hand gave an illusory movement to the carved surface of the podium. What he saw was a large Pholcus phalangioides, known by children the world over as the 'daddy-long-legs spider'. As a child he had never been terribly frightened of this ungainly creature with its long fragile legs. As an adult he had become aware that this was the spider that ate other spiders. Not a pleasant thought; and in that second the grotesque thing had seemed to move. In the half shadow Mulholland leapt back and then almost in reaction, craned his head forward and saw how much he was mistaken.

He saw before him, the surface of a sundial; the 'spider' merely the long radial lines and crabbed markings of the hours. There, beneath these functionary embellishments, a motto was inscribed with the sententious words 'UNAM TIME'.

'There you go,' said Norton enthusiastically.' 'Fear one hour'. Usual morbid sentiments of the Victorian age to which I am fairly certain it belongs.' Mulholland, having craned forward, drew back. He hardly heard Norton who had become voluble about the sundial's discovery by his cousin and how that harassed gentleman was continually using the phrase in the least appropriate moments. A kind of sickening of spirit had overwhelmed him. Almost a tactile sense of fear and loathing, all of which was directed forcibly towards the sundial. It seemed to Mulholland that something like a miasmic shadow emanated from the dial, as though the hours it foretold were somehow contained and rotten as a corpse embalmed and deteriorating within a casket. He backed off, face pale.

'Let's go in Norton,' he said hoarsely. 'I have something I wish to discuss.'

I regret to say that the discussion did not immediately take place. Mulholland could hardly be blamed, nor Norton for that matter. The two men on entering the door were immediately roped into a series of furniture rearrangements by an octogenarian aunt who had assessed the capacity of their youthful strength and decided that they were expending it needlessly on frivolity. There followed a good two hours where they must demonstrate their abilities to move this cupboard here and this oaken table there. After which sherry and brandy were produced, Mulholland remembered his bottle of Laphroaig, a late supper intervened and the two young men collapsed in bed at a very late hour. Again Mulholland had a restless night. I need not tell you of what he dreamt. It was not pleasant. The next two days being Christmas Eve and Christmas itself, seemed utterly inappropriate for Mulholland's topic of discussion. Mulholland was alone only for a few moments and in that time he managed to have a quiet word with the gardener as he prepared some table wreathes.

I would love to tell you of how pleasant that Christmas was. It was conducted something in the old fashion manner: mince pies, hemlock, cinnamon, cranberry, and apple; mistletoe, endless games of charades, dressing up, an extempore Punch an Judy show, goose and trimmings, a Norwegian fir tree decked with candles and all manner of fruits, nuts and homemade biscuits. Sadly, the pleasanter aspects of a tale tend to make somewhat duller reading than the morbid. There is one thing I had better mention. Lady Norton only came down for the Christmas dinner. Mulholland was shocked to see the poor woman, once a picture of glowing health, wracked with misery. Her wan, pinched face once so beautiful seemed cast like a death mask. Where she should have been blooming she was in fact withering. Her hands shook, she stuttered and she seemed utterly distracted. She did not stay long, ate very little and was shuffled off to bed by her German midwife. Mulholland's last memory of her was enlivened by the two elderly aunts nodding in secret agreement; for once he felt an almost total identification with their viewpoint.

But the opportunity came after the festivities. Norton reluctantly gave back the motorcar and they must both take the train back to Edinburgh. It seemed appropriate that the boundaries of Essex had been left behind them and they had joined the main line. A good few hours lay before them and it would have been fairly normal practice to dispose of a fair length of the laphroaig (and, in those more relaxed days, enjoy a cigar) before snoozing off for the remainder of the journey. If Norton had this in mind he was sadly mistaken. Mulholland reminded him of the mezzotint and took a deep breath before making the plunge.

'You're a bit of a wizard at Maths, Norton and I noticed recently you've been imbibing rather a lot of Russell and Nietzsche and Mill as a bit of a distraction I presume from your studies.'

'Philosophy is intriguing, old man. Spinoza has rather impressed me recently with his views on rationalism and mathematics.'

'Do I strike you as someone who holds irrational opinions?'

'Far from it. I know you've been dabbling in those occult books and your excuse for an academic discipline must tend a man towards some irrational spirituality…'

Norton, of course was about to launch into one of those conversations that can hardly be avoided if you frequent enough student cafes or are unlucky enough to be crammed between two freshers on an omnibus. But here Mulholland raised his hand and began to slowly explain the basis of his recent strange behaviour.

He began with the mezzotint of Anningley Hall, (he did not mention the coincidences) he brought up Lady Norton's apparent ailments, he mentioned the birthing room on the ground floor and he spoke of the shadow he had seen in that room and his strange feelings on approaching the sundial.

Norton was quite shocked. He looked at Mulholland as one might look at a friend who, after years of expressing profound atheistic beliefs, kneels on the floor and begins to pray for one's soul. It took some time for Mulholland to persuade him to spend the next half hour in examination of 'The Mezzotint' in 'Ghost Stories of an Antiquary'. You will recall the story of the awful revenge wreaked by some nebulous apparition on the last heir of Anningley Hall. Norton finished it in silence and shook his head. 'This story's set you off. It's a piece of fiction Mulholland. I'm rather surprised-'

Mulholland held up his hand. 'I researched the events Norton. The tale as such is certainly fiction but you have seen the mezzotint at my rooms. After much searching I managed to establish a few more particulars.' Mulholland drew a packet of yellowed papers from his pocket and laid them carefully on the table. 'In here there are a few accounts of local history, names, death dates and a couple of relevant notes and addendums. The tale was certainly based on your cousin's hall. There were unpleasant people there at one time, dark deeds were done and the newborn infant of the last heir was kidnapped and never found.'

Norton shook his head. Mulholland pressed on hastily:

'I had a word with your cousin's gardener. Lovely chap. I managed to draw him out on the local gossip. It's all anecdotal, folk tale and the like but there is a disturbing history and some of the older generation do talk about these events, if only amongst themselves.'

Norton remained entirely unconvinced and it was some feeling of regrets and not a little strain that they that they took leave of each other at Waverly Station. Mulholland felt he had ruined a promising friendship and all perhaps for nothing.

It would difficult to describe the somewhat ambiguous emotions that tried to gain ascendancy in his mind when he received an agitated phone call from Norton near the end of the second semester. It had been a deep dark winter and the inclement weather had left the greater part of Edinburgh in enforced hibernation. But the rains had finally come. Auld Reekie was being sluiced like a drain and from what he had read in the newspapers, England had endured some dreadful experiences of unprecedented flooding. Mulholland could make little of the call, except that Norton had 'seen it; he was terrified and he would be much obliged if Mulholland could forgive his earlier scepticism and come down to have a word with Cousin George on a matter of life and death.

Naturally, Mulholland obliged. What he found I would rather not describe in full detail and I regret, sincerely regret, that your imagination will have to provide the rest. Lady Norton was in a frightful condition, very nearly 'due' and still insistent on having the baby in the ground floor room which had been so carefully prepared by her German midwife. In the security of the smoking room, far from his wife's ears or that of the entourage of helpful aunts, Cousin George explained to Mulholland that the nightmares had increased in duration and intensity. The particulars were ghastly. Some kind of lurching figure would shamble into the moonlit room and tear her new born baby from her paralysed arms. Everything had been tried by way of medicament, advice and expertise and he would now listen to a Shaman's least favoured apprentice if by listening he could help his wife. He understood that Norton had discovered something and that Mulholland had some wild speculations. Regardless of their improbability he must offer them up for consideration

Mulholland felt in that moment like a fresh faced schoolboy caught in flagrante delico by the intimidating stare of the Head Prefect. Carefully he placed a leather brief case on the table before him. From it he withdrew the parish records, the book and the mezzotint, neatly wrapped in a silk cloth. On its unwrapping he was startled to observe that the flecking and foxing on its surface seemed to have changed. Its surface no longer gave the tableaux the impression of falling snow but instead offered a distinct impression that the moonlight hall was being drenched in a downpour – a deluge that even now was echoed by the heavy fall of rain on the windows, casements and guttering of Anningley hall.

Of course, Cousin George had never seen the mezzotint or the apparent change and after some minutes in which he examined the objects, read the story and the relevant addendums and notes in the papers he looked up with a hopeless and cruel disappointment. He was, if anything, far more sceptical than his younger cousin and perhaps the story would have played out in an entirely different and grisly manner if Norton had not played the trump card. Immediately, on observing his cousin's hopeless expression, he demanded that the company move outside to see what he had found. Here they were joined by the gardener and his son (who it transpired later, were privy to the plan). The weather was foul; rain battered from the roofs and rafters and Anningley had taken on the appearance of a galleon beset by stormy seas. Nevertheless, Norton, with assurances that he would be borne out by his evidence, led them all past the west wing to the ash bower where the lonely sundial stood. UNAM TIME it read and it was long before any of the men were able to forget that particular hour.

 The rain had swept the quicklime and gravel from the lower steps of the sundial's pedestal, the grey sand of this part of the foundation was bare and the tiles had cracked. It was apparent that they had been rested on ancient wooden joists and the deluge of water had caused a partial collapse. Just visible in a hollowed chamber…

 Well, I will go no further. I can only relate that the horrific contents of that secret place; the fragile yellowed remains, the loathsome desiccated rags, the other things, were enough to persuade Cousin George to instant and formidable action. By the following morning the weakly protesting Lady Norton had been transferred to the local hospital. The baby I believe was born a trifle prematurely but remained safely within that good lady's protective arms. The nightmares disappeared forthwith and Mulholland found out sometime later in correspondence with his good friend that on her return to the hall Lady Norton had been most surprised to find that Cousin George had had the men remove the Victorian sundial and all its surrounds including the foundations and the bower of ash trees which surrounded it.

It transpired that she had never much liked it in any case.

SOUP

Peters stared upwards and observed, with detached serenity, the slow drip from the central rose of the sagging ceiling. The white plaster bulged in a sweeping concave that resembled nothing less than the belly of a long dead whale. The mottled patches of moss-green dissolution festered like archipelagos across the pale surface, affording the quiet mathematician uneasy images of rotting flesh.

When the lights dimmed at indeterminate times, Peters would picture the bulge as the swollen breast of a cold, dead giantess, its protuberant nipple dripping foul milk directly into the slop bucket.

They had got used to *that* smell.

But sometimes, as the mind is wont to dwell on trivia under extreme duress, Peters wondered why their host had neglected to fix the broken pipe that produced the effulgence. It seemed…untidy, especially given their otherwise sumptuous and bizarre treatment.

There were low points in the whole affair of course; extremely low points, but Peters still liked the highs. As a bachelor past middle age, he lived a solitary and uneventful existence. He possessed, of course, a few like-minded friends and could point to certain bearable colleagues, but his true companions were mostly mathematical conundrums and Occidental poetry. While he recognized the perversity of his response, he had to admit that he appreciated the attention even if Jennifer Dunning did not.

She didn't look well. The simple wrought iron bench and the white chess table obscured her elegant legs and the ugly manacle around her ankle. The beautiful face that had adorned high fashion magazines was marred somewhat by puffy eyes and the tracks of last night's tears. Her husband, Captain Dunning, was gone. He had looked queasy when they had taken him.

It was probably the screams.

The screams, prolonged, ululating and piteous had impressed themselves in the small room much like the cacophony of a hidden tape recorder: Faraway, extending through the night: background noise, but not noise that sent one off to the land of nod. In fact, from their brief conversation this morning, Peters understood that he was the only one who had caught a few winks of sleep.

Farantino's sense of humour, no doubt. The reason they were all here. He had been a wit at Bellport High among his other talents. Bit of a joker. He always had style of course, something that Peters saw and admired without owning himself, but Farantino's jokes had a predisposition towards sadism. Like his introduction of the chess table in the centre of the room, apparently placed there for them to while away the long hours. But only apparently: As with the pack of cards, the crime and horror anthologies, the kaleidoscope and the set of Ludo, each distraction had an amusing catch.

The Queens in the chess set were glued irremovably to their squares rendering the game useless. The crime novels all had the dénouement removed. Nobody, of course, had so much as opened a page of the horror anthologies for obvious reasons. The kaleidoscope, when shaken, revealed various pictures of Farantino's smiling face and the little men in the Ludo set were smeared with a hot paste that irritated the skin for days after their handling. All in all, Farantino had excelled himself in creating a nervous atmosphere full of minor irritants.

Couple this with a sumptuous meal each night, clearly prepared by Farantino, a small carafe of Domaine de la Romanée-Conti, arguably one of the finest wines ever made; add the string quartet, virtuosos every one, who arrived promptly every third evening, set out their musical stands in the hallway, and performed Beethoven's String Quartet No. 10, Op. 74, in C minor for the benefit of the imprisoned. (After three nights Peters had noticed they had dropped a tone to B minor;

something he found more irritating than the fixed queens on the chess board.)

Then there was the Thai masseur who worked tirelessly on the aches and pains engendered by their confinement but who, at irregular intervals, simply came in and watched them in utter silence.

It was difficult for victims of pained and cramped muscles to imagine anything more hellish than the reluctant masseur: Except perhaps the pursed lipped whistler who rendered a series of bird songs and wouldn't depart until they guessed one correctly or, perhaps, the naked lap top dancer who left the men in ball aching agony to stare at poor Jennifer Dunning; the Captain with a look of melancholy betrayal and Peters with shamefaced lust.

The expert mime, who had been regaling them with silent versions of Broadway films, seemed almost a treat.

This recipe of minor irritants had been balanced then, by Farantino, the maestro, with a mix of exquisite or bizarre entertainment. The resultant emotions of the entertained: a cocktail of confusion, wonder and fear. It was a conundrum of course, and Peters had spent most of the weary months trying to solve it.

Perhaps that constant dripping tap was not some negligence on the part of Farantino, because, all in all, the treatment was driving them slowly insane. Peter's suspected that that was the intention. He also suspected that they would be not quite insane before the finale. Close, but not quite close enough.

And it *was* slowly building to some kind of crescendo.

There had been six captives, initially: a software programmer fresh from college, some Bulgarian athlete and a young female soprano. For a time they had been separated, the others placed in a cell some distance up the corridor. Captain Dunning had tapped out messages to the Bulgarian on the stone walls for the period of their mutual incarceration. Basically, it had achieved nothing but the solace that they were not utterly alone. Then, five days ago, the three had disappeared.

Not long after that the screams had begun.

How long was it since they had stopped? Perhaps three days? In that time the men's diet had been changed to a kind of sweet smelling clove, a peculiar mushroom and a sage-like paste, all unfamiliar even to the Captain, and both men had suffered an undignified regime of forcible enemas and regular emetics. Even though Mrs. Dunning had been spared this indignity, Peters suspected that the end was in sight. He had no doubts the end was something awful but, after the long confinement and the refinements of Farantino's mental torture, he had managed to accept this prospect with something like a stoic calm. Not so the others. Perhaps they had more to lose: Youth, Beauty, strength…each other.

They had been newly weds for only a matter of a weeks; the disparity in their ages clearly not an impediment to their love. Jennifer was twenty years old – a perfect object, as far as Peters was concerned, of unobtainable desire. The Captain was some fifteen years her senior. He was utterly besotted with her as, in fact, anyone would be. Yes, Captain Dunning and his lovely wife were certainly suffering.

And yet the whole farce had all begun with such promise. To put it bluntly, when the invitation had presented itself, Peters had nearly come in his pants. No doubt, with all its immense social implications, the newly weds had felt much the same

Peters reached forward and picked up the black king on the chessboard. Jennifer Dunning started like a deer at his sudden movement, stared at him with wild eyes and then dropped her head. He guessed she felt less than comfortable with her husband gone. The screams too: Unnerving, and they had gone on and on. It could have been two or three days. They only stopped about three hours after Captain Dunning had been escorted from the cell. About lunchtime. Unhappy coincidence? Thought Peters.

Jennifer had begun to weep again in her quiet way. His

experience of consoling her had proven ineffectual on previous occasions so Peters returned to an examination of the chess man. He hadn't noticed it before, but the King's head was a small gnome-like Farantino. In its hand there was a letter and yes, the tiny symbol of that soup tureen.

Farantino? He was famous beyond mere celebrity: A legend, a myth, a living testament to the possibilities inherent in the human race. To come from a relatively humble background, son of a vicar and an Italian parishioner, and end up as the wealthiest, most sought after man, nay genius, in the twentieth century was incredible. That he should have remembered Peters, the humble math's pupil who had sat behind him in Year 7 at Bellport High, was unthinkable. To get an invitation from Farantino was the catholic equivalent of the pope begging to be best man at your wedding.

Even the invitations had that special magic. Farantino was principally known as the greatest chef on the planet. His various explorations of the lonely planet, his ballooning exploits, the numerous follies, his privately financed trip into space, the ownership of six islands, his legendary poker skills, the voice that had graced the Royal Opera and the seventeen languages with which he was familiar were all peanuts compared to his ability to cook. It was notorious that kings and queens, Prime Ministers and Heads' of State, celebrities, everyone who was anyone, had been snubbed by Farantino, that it was impossible to buy his services.

Farantino invited you to a banquet and whoever you were you dropped whatever you had planned and went along for the meal of your life.

The pattern of the invitation was not widely known except in a kind of inner circle. Of course, many of those who had attended Bellport High knew of it because Farantino was their most famous son. And word did get around, even to non-entities. But it was only spoken about in the in-crowd or amongst those, like Peters, who were simply in the right place at the right time. *His* knowledge was a bit like that of a villager, who never discusses the indiscretions of a local politician outside of his own village.

Still, for all his unworldliness, Peters had known exactly what was happening the instant he had opened the door three months before.

It was two in the morning, streets silent and eerie, a little light rain. Peters had been up late, toying with puzzles in Cheiro's book of numbers, when he heard a light rap on the door.

There, in the dim-lit entrance of his suburban home, were two masked, dwarf harlequins framing, like bookends, a small golden-haired boy who bore a silver tray. On the street behind the silent tableaux, an antique silver Mercedes stood poised like a predator, white-gloved chauffeur beckoning. Peters had hardly seen the letter on the tray. He had barely observed the single silver line-drawn picture of a faience *saucière* in Rococo taste: Farantino's famous soup tureen.

The picture was the key; Farantino was known to have a 'thing' about soup. The tableaux, the timing, were irrelevant: The invitation could have come with a parachute drop in the morning, a Christmas card sent in spring, a newspaper advert, a cryptic, signed Ace of Spades delivered by a croupier at a late night casino. The variety of the invitation and the quixotic nature of its delivery were the stuff of legend. The drawing of the soup tureen was the thing. Anyone not recognizing that symbol would simply not have been invited.

Peter's hadn't even taken his hat and coat. Whisked away into the night, he had almost welcomed the blindfold because it had some effect in calming his nervous excitement. He had to bite his tongue to stop repeating Farantino's name out loud. He was still rehearsing the story he would tell his friends and colleagues, trying to impress every detail on his mind, when the car had stopped. Escorted blindfold by the dwarves, they forged a path through long grass.

With the succubus brush of grass on his trouser legs and the chill on his naked arms, Peters strode blind through the still, graveyard world. He projected these mild discomforts into a distant land. Soon, in a matter of hours, at most a day, he would be sitting at a table of the great and the good. There would be displays of ostentation, creative acts, farragoes, heavenly meat and drink, wild extravagances: the lot. And Peters, the humble mathematics graduate employed for thirty years at Wellber and Sons CA, would be there amongst it all.

Even now he could only recall two or three people from Bellport High who had been to a Farantino feast. There was the deputy head master, Mr. MacAteer, an amateur expert in Egyptology who had taken Farantino under his wing when he was only sixteen. MacAteer had helped with some extracurricular work on embalming techniques. It was said that MacAteer had once taken Farantino on a dig in the summer holidays but he always denied it. The two had been quite close and it was a fair few years later that MacAteer had been rewarded for his kindness. Peters could dimly recall MacAteer afterwards in a brief discussion with a gaggle of masters. He had simply repeated 'Doves in pies, Doves in pies' to the others' insistent requests

Then there was the Head boy of the year above, John Palmer, who had gone on to win Olympic bronze in the triathlon before he disappeared some years later in an avalanche on a British expedition to the Virunga mountain range.

Shortly after Palmer's legendary invitation, and many years before his loss, Peters had been in the common room tidying up. Palmer was lounging on the battered sofa; feet up in a state of euphoric bliss. The older boys had been chivvying him endlessly about Farantino. Eventually, Palmer had replied in a dazed voice. 'It's not something you can talk about. It was simply spectacular. But I can tell you that I will still see mental images of that naked, dancing girl on my death bed.' Palmer had slouched back further into the couch, a vacuous smile on his handsome face as he left the others scrunched up like insects.

'Naked,' he repeated. 'Naked…' That was how it was always described. One ingredient in the whole soup, one epiphanal moment, one slice of the cake that summarized the taste of the whole. And Peters was already savouring the *hors d'œuvre*.

A rocking motion, a tang of dampness and the feel of hollow, wooden boards beneath his feet suggested some kind of boat. Minutes later, with the blindfold removed, Peters' assumption was proven correct. A narrowboat: All the curtains drawn and only a dim glimpse through mirrors of the prow. Here Peters could discern the back of some phlegmatic giant who wielded a long oar and propelled the narrowboat silently through an unseen canal.

It was a scene he quickly dismissed in favour of the geisha girls, dressed *hanfu* style, lit by perfumed candles, who were preparing a green tee and some light wafers. Soon, one of the girls had taken up the *pipa*, and a volume of *Chu Ci* poetry was intoned in quaint English as the strings of the Chinese lute wove their magic spell. Qu Yuan was Peters' favourite poet and the Songs of Chu melted through his mind - like the vaguely recognized incense - in tones as smooth as the wooden belly of the pear shaped *pipa*.

Peters was aware then, that Farantino knew his intimate soul. For a second he doubted if he was even alive. Somewhere in the recesses of his mind this particular fantasy was etched on a blind wall. What else would happen, what *could* happen to improve on perfection? The music drifted on, the girl's lilting voice, the incense and the light from the perfumed candles touching, with the delicacy of moth wing, the wooden slats of the interior.

The image of the wooden bellied *pipa* brought Peters back to the cell, the lute-like shape echoing the bulge of the ceiling. It was always thus. The reveries and then the stark horror of the reality. He had drifted off again; lulled by Jennifer Dunning's weeping and the survival instinct, no doubt, of his own mind;

the mind that Farantino was trying to unravel with the skill of a seamstress, and which now protected itself by focusing on better things.

The present was pretty awful and the future didn't look much good but at least Jennifer Dunning was silent: Probably exhausted. Peters put down the chessman with its little Farantino face, shut his eyes and tried to drift back in time again. He noticed with little interest that his manacle had been removed. For all he knew it could be another hallucination. There were plenty of those around.

The memory of the screams intruded for a while until he dozed into a fitful sleep.

Again he felt the rush of wind on his face as the carriage left the narrowboat behind and swept up the driveway between the sentries of oaks. Time had been suspended. Peters knew that he had slept at some point on the boat, but not until he had experienced things he had only distantly read of in exotic books, and now his skin prickled with the *hanfu* style dress. His mind still lingered on the geisha girls and their flickering hands as they had first undressed and then clad him in their traditional costume. But for the moment there was only the wind and the beat of horses' hooves.

From all directions they came, white stallions forming a *cavalcade* before him. To the North and West along the other approaches individual set outs, teams of horses, carriages, glittering attendants scattered across the lawns as far as his eye could see. He was aware of faces that peered from the recesses of the coaches, some as bewildered as his own. Others regal; all masked like himself.

Then he saw the mansion house rearing up against the blackened sky: A huge palatial affair. Peters had heard rumours that Farantino had erected a secret country house in the North of England, somewhat on the scale of the Caprarolain Palazzo Farnese in Italy.

Here was the evidence. Lit by flambeaus and hosts of imported glowworms, apparently imprisoned by gossamer nets, the red-gold walls of the buttress supported a gracious *piano nobile*. The huge, lit windows, open to the night sky, were darkened only by the flitting shadows of dancers. Venting forth from their capacious depths, some Wagnerian piece by a full orchestra sweetened the air with dark, melancholic chords.

Above this middle terrace, decorated with gargoyles and projecting bastions, two more floors of the central villa seemed to climb to the moon. The Villa rooms above the *piano nobile* were eerily silent. They appeared to be not so much asleep as brooding. At the time, Peters had dismissed this intrusive thought as morbid speculation. He was simply speechless with admiration. Later he was to remember.

He tried not to run up the wide marble steps. He even managed not to gasp when thousands of red admiral butterflies and Death's head moths burst from the opening of the huge doorways like thrown rose petals - to the delight of those who stood by the balustrade. He contained his eagerness, attempting like a few other guests, a stately walk. It wasn't working. He was simply overwhelmed. As the huge entrance hall widened before his eyes with its massed velvet curtains, Steiner grand piano, dwarfed by huge monolithic Egyptian kas, obelisks and enigmatic koras, culled from unknown Greek and Egyptian hoards, Peters felt himself on the edge of swooning. In a minute he would start to gibber like a five year old.

Chinese acrobats swung from the vaulted ceilings, silent flunkies glided with silver trays, elegant men and women, all masked, all clad in theatrical costume, drank fine wine, danced or idled by the Steiner. Some sat, bare feet dangling in the vast goldfish ponds. A festive atmosphere prevailed. No one seemed silent unless imbued with awe, no one who spoke could conceal their delight. As he wandered enthralled through the crowd, Peters became aware that all were apparently strangers to each other. This would be a one time invitation, an unforgettable experience. There could be no social dimension to this moment; the individual must simply live, for the first and only time, in a dream wrought by genius.

There was one name on everyone's lips. The Maestro, the impresario, *the* genius: Farantino!

Everything ever said about the man seemed now to be an inadequate description. Someone remarked that they thought his covert space trip had been faked at the time. Now they knew that there was more possibility that the Americans had faked the Eagle landing and that Farantino was probably having diplomatic discussions with Martians. Farantino had no need to fake a damn thing.

Another guest with a heavy accent had listened to one of Farantino's recordings of the nigh impossible Percaro language. 'Word perfect' he said in adulation and he shook his head in disbelief. Peters paused half listening to the exotic tones. 'My tribe neighboured theirs, if the vast lands of the American basin can be talked of in such terms. The Percaro occupied a hidden valley in the foothills of the Acarai Mountains. Somehow, no one knows how, Farantino managed to infiltrate their village, notorious cannibals. To have survived such a thing. To have become fluent…'

Another was comparing Farantino's majestic tenor to old recordings of Caruso. Farantino wasn't losing there either. Everywhere the talk rose and fell from cultured, erudite lips and everywhere it returned to the same focus: Farantino!

It was here, immersed in euphoria at the foot of the stairs, that Peters had first encountered Captain Dunning. Peters hadn't known at the time, of course, because Dunning was masked and clad in a Jaeger rifleman's uniform from the Napoleonic wars – green fabric like pea soup, and neat little epaulettes - very dignified with the grey hose. But he recognized the military type by the stance, the erect head and the eyes searching the hall. It had to be the military or the police. Peter favoured the military. The man had a certain quality about him.

His was the carriage of an officer; a man who commanded the utter obedience of elite soldiers.

Captain Dunning's wife wasn't beside him, of course. One of Farantino's jokes to have them come separately and incognito. When you were incarcerated for months with a person, you got to know their body; their movements, their carriage; even their smell and Peters remembered all these things a long time afterwards and related them to this meeting. But for the moment, Captain Dunning was some stranger in an entrance hallway.

At the time, Peters was impelled by greater needs. He looked at the vast series of steps leading to the *piano noble*, to the dancers, to mysteries beyond his ken. He actually trembled as he walked up the main stairway. The golden balustrade was about the only thing that kept him on his feet. Part of him wanted to simply remain in the entrance hall because, when he analysed his feelings, he had never been happier than now. But another part drove him to explore. Was there any limit to this?

A man of medium height stood alone at the well. He was masked and clad in a jet black Imperial Chef's coat with silver buttons. He sported checked pants and dark chef's shoes. It was almost as though the man's very presence, somewhat death-like, had cleared an avenue of space: The space that emerges when a way is open. One can walk there, but it is empty. To fill the space is sometimes to invite other energies. It is not always wise to walk paths others avoid.

The man stood at the centre of the stairs where they split like red Spanish fans, ascending to left and right. Peters walked up. He intended to slip past but the man smiled and said quietly.

'Peters.' How nice to see you after all these years. How's the old counting coming along?'

Farantino! Even now Peters had no idea what he said in reply. Another of Farantino's jokes – to simply turn up in his work clothes, spectacular though they might be.

Beyond speech, Peters was aware of his elbow being taken.

He was escorted up the stairs as Farantino pointed out this and that painting, all immeasurably valuable or more or less priceless. The Persian rugs, golden filigree on the wallpaper - the holders for the lamps would have cost Peters his house – But it was all so tasteful…Then as an afterthought Farantino had turned and caught Captain Dunning's eye. He waved him up and the Captain began to follow.

The next moments were a blur. Peters had a vague, single vision of an immense ballroom, colours blazoning out into the starless night, buddhistic sculpture that towered monumentally to vaulting heights, the great sweep of the string section as the orchestra proclaimed the opening movement of *Thus Spoke Zarathustra*. Beauteous dancers, whose elegant movements merged like wave and strand as they struck up a pavanne to echo the symphony.

But it was only a tableau, a single, glorious moment before they were escorted to a small ante room. The world stilled and Peters and twenty-four masked guests stood in audience to Farantino.

The simple dignity of his costume, his unremarkable height and quaintly staged movements were the antithesis of his voice. Farantino spoke quietly, without emphasis but every word struck the core of their being. It seemed they were to be his special guests for the evening. They would taste delights that others had only heard of. Even throughout these hallowed halls, few had gained the inner sanctum. Peters felt it in his soul; a kind of rush of warmth, like the first sip of laphroaig. And then, something of the alien in Farantino seemed to reach out like a silk glove. He began to speak in tones that caressed Peters' heart like a dead monkey's paw. This time there was no blurring of his mind. Peters was good at counting, to some extent his memory was almost photographic. He could remember Farantino's speech word for word…

But for the moment the vision fled. The chill words retreated to the recesses of Peters' brain. He coughed, his bleared eyes opening on the familiar claustrophobia of the cell. Jennifer Dunning's head lolled across her breast; asleep at last. She snored quietly. Peters shook his head, tasted his dry lips. He could see the faint pulse of the great arteries in Jennifer's elegant neck, the faint traced, blue veins.

Despite the dark circles around her eyes she was still very beautiful, beautiful like Praxiteles' Aphrodite. Even Farantino had been stirred by her great beauty, visible even while masked. Almost like a predator, the chef had circled her as he made his one, great speech. At the time Peters had got a faint echo that Captain Dunning had changed his stance. Now, on reflection, he realized that, at that moment, Dunning had doubtless recognized his wife through the mask and she him; an irony that had not escaped Farantino as he began to intone to a stupefied audience in words that had etched themselves on Peters' memory…

'Welcome,' he had said. 'Welcome to my life such as it is. All lives are short. We have an obligation to make of them something wondrous. You have enjoyed yourselves? Was it not beautiful?'

A murmur of assent spilled from those gathered.

'There is more to come,' said Farantino, 'but before the sugar, you must try a little salt. How can I express it?'

Here Farantino had paused. He seemed to struggle for words. In that instant, Peters got an inkling of the essence of the man. Like Buster Keaton, like all great comedians, Farantino existed only in the present. He had no past, no future, only an interminable 'now'. His uncontainable emotions, torn living from his soul, were manifestly visible in his tortured eyes. With a violent movement Farantino had beckoned to the opposing doors.

Slowly, at his gesture, the doors began to open on a vast dark chamber. In stark contrast to the perfumes of before, a dank smell wafted from the exposed room like old bandages and dark, dead things. Somewhere, far away, something moaned.

Farantino ushered them through the doors. There was a faint gasp from a woman, probably Jennifer Dunning, in retrospect - she was fairly fragile - But others were not immune to the chill.

At first, Peters saw only the pedestal at the centre of the room and the quaint statue of a goblin creature perched there, lit by hidden lights. He had a sensation of vast depths, unseen passages beyond. Then, he saw the iron chair and Peters knew that they had entered a room quite different in character from the others. The chair was large, laced with spikes to penetrate flesh, sporting ancient metal bands to crush the feet and hands. He felt a shudder race through his frame.

'A German Inquisitorial chair,' said Farantino, 'last used in 1800.'

Beyond the chair, awakening in the dim lights, a wall of shrunken heads gazed sightlessly upon three maidens of Nuremburg, the sarcophagi open to display cruel spikes stained rust-brown; bleak interiors that seemed to scream in shocking silence. Beside the sarcophagi, a garrotte. In dim, shadowed alcoves great wheels, Judas cradles, racks and strappados lurking like huge skeletal insects. A variety of smaller instruments, no less threatening for their size, were suspended from the ceiling: the branks, with its distinctive ass's ears; head crushers, cats paws, pears and spiders to rip and split the intestines.

Farantino paused then he deliberately picked up a fiendish metal cross, spiked at two ends and bearing a metal collar.

'The heretic's fork,' Captain Dunning said quietly. 'Place the collar around the victim's neck, one point in the breast and the other under the chin. The victim's head cannot move without intolerable pain -'

'-Yes, Captain. You know about these things. The British army trains well.'

'The captain nodded,' I'm not sure the ladies *should* though.' His eyes, suspicious now, behind the mask.

'But why have this ugly room?' said a voice, 'amidst so much beauty.'

Farantino placed the fork under his chin and then smiled. 'You may well ask,' he said. 'But then why have soup when one can eat meat? They all say it do they not? Farantino and his soup. I will tell you why.' Farantino peeled off his mask. His bright, ferret eyes steeped in intelligence, his narrow chin thrust forward. 'Because nothing in life is alone. All things have a doppelganger, an accompaniment, an animus. There is nothing fine and wonderful that does not have its visceral root. You have heard of the term *Duende*?'

'*Duende*' said Peters, surprised to hear his own voice. 'A Spanish concept. The demon within the angel, perhaps: Emotion, expression, authenticity. They use it about dance.'

'Yes,' said Farantino, 'but it is more than a description of dance. The artist's Muse gifts inspiration, *Duende* gifts blood. The Muse gives life, *Duende* death and the struggle of knowing that death is imminent; the knowledge that death waits and the despair of that knowledge. The dancer, *tenere Duende,* expresses the entire gamut of the human condition.'

Farantino paused. 'My life's work is only authentic because it surges up, inside, from the soles of my feet. My living flesh needs to interpret the voice of *Duende*. I like fine meat but meat is nothing without the basic simplicity of soup.' Farantino gave an oddly sexual gesture towards a cracked and rusted wheel.

'Look carefully on that instrument. Imagine the broken shambles of a human being strapped upon that wheel, writhing in the splintered chamber of its own bones; a huge rag doll, screaming, slimed with blood and gore. And there, the cauldrons with which the Percaro cook their victims – a process lasting three days, three days of excruciating agony. And there just beyond. A favourite of mine…'

Reluctantly the little group advanced further into the room, impelled by the hypotonic voice. Dunning hesitated. He was looking with concern at his wife. A huge copper basin stood just beyond the pedestal. It was concave, about the size of a paddling pool. A tracery of metal bars formed an inescapable cage above the basin. The whole appearance of the contraption was suggestive of a vast, oval bird cage.

'The slave griddle', said Farantino: 'You lock the doors such. Then light the coals so. The screaming victim springs around like a March hare-'

'-This is enough, Farantino,' said Captain Dunning. 'The ladies…'

'My apologies,' Farantino smiled. 'I will desist.' He took one look at the revolting apparatus and then said quietly. 'A musician once told me that good cannot be trusted unless it has breathed the same air as evil. Perhaps later you will understand.'

Farantino smiled again made a mock bow. The doors at the further end of the room opened. Glowing lights showed beyond. The torture chamber dimmed. Peters last saw the grinning face of the gnome like some twisted Cheshire cat above the pedestal.

As the lights died, he realized that the face was uncannily like that of his host.

Again Peters found himself fully awake. He stared at the chess man. Farantino and his jokes. His smiling visage on every artefact. But he had been right. After the glimpse of the torture chamber, the banquet was beyond words. Faced with images of horrific death and pain, the palate reacted with gusto to the superlative food. The conversation sparkled with innuendo, wit, laughter. Each guest had appeared more animated and alive. Each moment had seemed eternal. Farantino, noticeable by his absence, had forged god-like ambrosia from the smithy of his kitchen; each course a new wonder. It was only now, many months after, that Peters realized with a sudden jar, that despite all the talk of Farantino's obsession, there had been no soup.

'No soup,' he said out loud and he began to laugh.

Awakened, Jennifer Dunning stared at him. Peters lapsed back into silence and continued his contemplation of the ceiling.

The concave, white expanse glistened with moisture that spread from the central rose. He realized that the ceiling looked uncannily like the rust spotted underbelly of a faience *saucière*, Farantino's famed soup tureen. The laughter simmered at the edge of his consciousness. Peters was unsure whether it had a voice outside his own head.

The end approached. His fine mathematical mind was unhinging.

After an indeterminable time, the door opened slowly. Captain Dunning stood in the opening. He was naked and he didn't look good. The heretic's fork jutted from his sternum and poked under his chin, held by the metal collar. A rivulet of blood ran freely between his chiselled pectoral muscles and spread like a gory marsh among the hairs on his belly. His head was forced back by the fork so that he could only speak through gritted teeth. In his hand he held a second fork. With great difficulty he spoke.

'Don't struggle Peters. I wouldn't like to hurt you. You'd better strip.'

Peters was beyond struggling. He removed his clothes, looking with some regret on the soiled Chinese *hanfu*.

Passively, he waited as Captain Dunning fixed the collar around his neck. The biting pain of the fork brought a fresh awareness.

'You too, Jenny. Clothes off. You're not to be hurt. Trust me.'

She stripped, unseen by Peters, who now observed the world in agony, his head thrust upwards to stare at the ceiling. With care he could look through slanted eyes at the top of Captain Dunning head. Any sudden movement dug the prongs of the fork into his chin and sternum.

'We're all to be spared Jenny. Everything will be fine. Farantino wants to play a silly game. The man's a sadist but he won't murder us. He won't hurt you at all - gave me his word. He's going to humiliate me and Peters but he's taken a shine to you.' Peters could vaguely see Captain Dunning attempt to caress his wife. 'You just have to dance for him love, play his silly game. Whatever he asks just go along with it and we'll be allowed home. It won't change anything between us, I swear…'

Peters was almost glad of the fork, he could only hear the dreadful sobbing, the whispered endearments.

After a time he felt Captain Dunning take his hand.

'Right Peters, we walk on now. Jenny will follow.'

Each step was painful; each tiny jar on the stone floor sent an involuntary shudder through his frame. The fork dug in. Itching, scratching. It had only been minutes but the strictures on his neck were already agony.

They got some distance down the corridor when Captain Dunning gripped his arm and leaned in close to whisper.

'There's no way out Peters. I know my job and Farantino has every angle covered. The bastard's making soup out of us. I know you're a man and won't let the side down so I'll give it direct. Farantino explained how he does it – part of his warped pleasure, I believe - and it's far from pleasant - a long, slow process learned from that bloody Percaro tribe. I saw the remains of the others. Not nice. We'll be off our trolley before the end, hopefully, and none the wiser. Damn that sadistic bastard!'

Peters grinned like a puppet. There was nothing to say.

'For Jenny's sake we have to carry on.' Captain Dunning gripped Peters' arm tighter to emphasize his lack of alternatives. 'Farantino's really taken with her,' he continued. 'He'll let her live, I'm just praying he won't let her witness what happens to us. I made a deal. We cause no trouble, make it easy for him and…well, you understand.'

Peters said nothing. They had come to the door. Beyond, he could vaguely discern a large room. A murmur of conversation, hushed by their arrival. His arms were taken. Led step by step to a large metal basin sunk into the floor, he felt leather chords tighten behind his back. Captain Dunning mirrored his every action with stoic calm, holding out his wrists passively as two robed men imprisoned his arms. Then they were up to their shoulders in warm water. Peters felt bubbles rising between his toes, a barely perceptible increase in the temperature of the water.

His head locked at its unnatural angle, Peters was only able look comfortably up to the tiers above where he could see seated guests, their faces unmasked, their mouths red and their eyes glinting with anticipation in the flickering lights. He was only vaguely aware that he, and Captain Dunning, were at the centre of an amphitheatre A huge velvet curtain suspended by a rope, shrouded some vast object placed beside their basin. Then Peters saw Farantino, clad in his black Imperial Chef's coat. He made a great flourish with his meaty hands. The crowd murmured. Farantino began to pull the rope

Captain Dunning opposite stared at the crowded tiers. No anger or resentment registered on his impassive face, not even the disgust that he must have felt. Already the soldier had taken over. He was lapsing into a state of catatonia, dropping into defenses as he prepared for a long and terrible death.

'And now the dancing,' It was Farantino, his voice imbued with peculiar relish.

The curtains flew upwards exposing the huge, copper-plated griddle and the open doors of its cage. Peters noticed with a gritty smile that the lower half of the contraption was remarkably like a giant soup tureen.

With the last vestiges of his rational mind, he concluded that Captain Dunning would certainly have died like a soldier if he had not seen the heated coals flare up beneath the griddle and heard the first of his poor wife's pitiful screams.

A GAME OF BILLIARDS

'Not your kind of place then,' Mulholland rested his cigar on the edge of the windowsill and we both looked out over the splendid Georgian new town to its tough cousin, the port of Leith.

'Apparently the only gaff, though, where a chap can have a smoke in peace.'

The Club - it had no other name - was a relic of some distant age. Mulholland, who seemed to spend each day constructing a new surprise for me, had his valet deliver an invitation.

I was almost becoming accustomed to largesse: The formal hallway with its grand front entrance led to a short lobby. Beyond that, the stair hall, where the reception desk was manned by a gentleman whose manners had apparently been cultivated in some Noel Coward drama. On finding me alone, and obviously socially incompetent, the gentleman had divested me of my coat, escorted me to the back drawing room, and laid out some tea and scones.

After an interval of contemplation, Mulholland put me out of misery: The production of Glenlivet and cigars a prelude to a long evening of dissolute bachelorhood.

'Fancy a game of billiards?' said Mulholland.' The table's just been revamped.'

'More of a snooker man but I'll give it a go.'

'Don't think my one eye will give you any advantage.' Mulholland tipped his eye patch. 'Billiards, like chess, is the sport of kings and depends as much on strategic genius as aerobic skill.'

We were on the third game and the third Glenlivet. Mulholland had pasted me in the first two contests but this last had become a bit more of a tussle – a thing Mulholland seemed to relish. He paused for a second and chalked his cue. 'My Grandfather was a sergeant out in India in the first world war,' he said with a grin. 'Told me a bit of a tale about billiards.'

I smiled. Mulholland knew my profession. Since our meeting at the school reunion, he had supplied me with a fair number of suitable shockers.

'Seems,' said Mulholland stretching across the table, 'there were two officers vying for the same lady. This was in the days when holding hands with the fair sex was a major erotic triumph. Rivals spent most of their time not saying what they wanted and not telling anyone what they felt. Well, I'm not sure you would know, but the Indian campaign was fairly much polo, evening concerts, curry and of course, billiards. Everyone had a manservant and a superiority complex the size of a house. Captain Petronius was no exception. In fact, he was the *par exemplar* of the jumped up ass who would later slaughter his men on the Somme. But of course, not all the officers were such buffoons, particularly those who had just seen a bit of action at Ypres.'

Mulholland struck the white ball. Like a ballet dancer, it glanced off the red and both balls came back neatly to rest on the baulk cushion. I looked on in dismay, visualising grand disappointments on the horizon of the green baize. Mulholland tinkled a small bell and we took a high stool next to the table. Mulholland continued.

'Well, one such officer, who became quite a pal of Granddad, was Captain Boyd. The men worshipped him. Word had sneaked back from Flanders that Boyd had done quite a bit of legwork in the trenches. In point of fact, he led a counter charge against a rather strong Bavarian regiment simply in order to rescue three wounded men. Wouldn't have been quite so remarkable in these awful times if it hadn't transpired that he'd been ordered specifically not to, but went ahead off his own bat. There were other stories which backed up my Granddad's impression, First thing Boyd had done for example, was to consult him on how things stood with the battalion you see. Granddad, who could be somewhat taciturn, was very impressed.'

A couple of Glenlivets arrived and Mulholland relit his cigar.

'Not so impressed were those measly Indian officers whose only idea of a struggle was the gait of a polo horse and the odd squabble at poker. The worst of the bunch was this Petronius. He took an instant dislike to Boyd.

Captain Petronius was a large man, very well made and athletic you see, and Boyd was not only a small man but he'd picked up shrapnel in the right leg at the First Battle of Ypres, and cut a bit of a sad figure. Petronius, whose father was some bigwig, used every opportunity to belittle Boyd. Captain Boyd said nothing in reply, partly because he couldn't, and partly because he wasn't the type. He managed somehow to convey his utter contempt of Petronius though, and the rivalry became the talk of the camp. Everyone felt sorry for Boyd except those stuck up idiots and it all looked a bit sad.

Then, a couple of nurses were seconded from Jubblepore Army Station and one, I'll call her Anne, was from a very well known family. This Anne was one of those self-sacrificing wonders who brave all sorts of dangers and diseases just to help out. She was beautiful to boot. You won't be surprised to hear that the entire camp, man and boy, couldn't sleep from dreaming rather fanciful dreams about her, or that both Captain Petronius and Boyd fell instantly in love with the girl. The incidence of sickness was quadrupled in a matter of days until they put a notice about that the sergeants would be administering medicine, not the nurses.

Of course, what with circumstances being what they were, and the girl being what she was, she fell in love with Boyd. Apparently, she couldn't bear the pompous and arrogant Petronius but of course, he wouldn't have that. Petronius had everything on his side: money, looks, family but he didn't have decency and that of course, is what she was after.

To cut a long story short, Petronius took the huff. He made life a misery for Boyd; cut him at every opportunity, got his cronies to do the same. Nothing made a difference. Boyd would still be the one chatting outside her window or pottering in her little garden on the few chances he got, while Petronius made do with billiards, whisky and hitting sepoys, which as you will come to understand, was not very clever of him.

You see, what Petronius hadn't quite grasped is that there were a fair number of the Indian Corp amidst the native contingent, They were just servants and coolies to him but there were some damned brave men amongst them, and class and creed aside, these men had seen action in the front line. War is a great leveller and of course, in contrast to that ass, Boyd respected the sepoys and they he.'

I sipped a bit of the Glenlivet and had a look at my possibilities on the green baize. Perhaps Mulholland's story fired me up a bit, because I managed a cannon off the far cushion and followed it through with two more before I was forced to attempt a long red. Mulholland made mince of my subsequent miss and after a few more gaffes, the third game was slipping away before my eyes as he continued.

'Anne's birthday came up and it all went a bit Mad Carew. Her father, a doctor had wangled a trip over with his wife and the meal seemed to consist of mother, father, Anne and Boyd. In those days, as you well know, a sure recipe for wedding bells.

Petronius couldn't bear this. Shortly afterward, there was an appalling incident in the billiard room. No one could quite get to the bottom of it. Petronius had somehow managed to insinuate into the higher echelons that Boyd was playing about with the Indian boys – a thing so far from the truth that it probably wouldn't have borne weight even with those donkeys at Staff HQ. In any case, it was honour or bust for Boyd. It started with an open challenge at billiards. Boyd of course had been virtually excluded from the billiard room and was at a complete disadvantage. That was where Petronius and all his cronies held out. Petronius was a dab hand at the game and of course, no one knew if Boyd could even play. Well, he could. The game, as everyone knew, was simply a warm-up for the fisticuffs to come but even so, Boyd apparently played like the devil and trounced Petronius. The arrogant ass snapped and there was a brutal altercation.

In short, he beat Boyd senseless and managed to convey the impression that the injuries were all a bit of bad luck. One of Petronius's side-kicks took the blame for the blows to keep Petronius name out of it – Boyd' leg was broken and a rib crushed – supposedly in an accidental fall. Officer and a gentleman, he never blamed Petronius but he didn't survive the summer. The girl went shortly after him. Diphtheria or something of the sort but of course they all said it was a broken heart.'

Mulholland made an uncharacteristic miss. I capitalised on the opportunity and found a string of remarkable shots. If I could just touch the white I might have an in off in the side pocket and an easy red.

'Think I might have you here Mulholland.' I raised my Glenlivet in a toast and Mulholland smiled wryly. I raised my cue. 'It's a horrible story but not horrific if you know what I mean.'

'Yes, I know what you mean. I find those tales of snobbery and misplaced authority most horrific but I suppose your readership might fall for the closing incidents.'

I paused mid-shot. 'And these closing incidents?'

'Well, Petronius kept quiet for a bit. He was upset when the girl fell ill. He waited what *he* thought was a decent interval and then kept pressing his suit like the fool he was. Some say that's why the girl succumbed so quickly. He got in the habit of proclaiming his love for her in a fairly public fashion and the sepoys must have picked up on something he said about love itself.'

'Yes, Mulholland?'

'Well, one night they found Captain Petronius laid out on the billiard table, the baize no longer green but stained with blood and gore. There had been a bit of a struggle and his hands and feet were bound to the pockets of the table.'

'Dead?'

'No, he wasn't *dead*,' Mulholland said soberly. 'But no one *quite* knows how they managed to insert the red and the white billiard ball where his eyes had been.'

I fluffed the shot.

It looked like the third game was about to go the way of the other two.

THE NAVIGATOR

'At the end of the road turn left.'

'Left,' said Dermott. 'Doesn't feel left?'

'It's dark; we've no idea where we are. It says left.' Jane curled up in the front passenger seat and tugged at the tartan blanket. Her feet were cold; Dermot was being the usual indecisive ass. The female voice of the navigator was irritating but at least it saved her poring over a map. Better still, it eliminated the need for another serious argument with the driver.

'That looks like the lights from Athens airport. Remember we were there last year.'

Jane kept silent. Was it worth remarking that Dermott had made a single previous trip to Greece? That one trip did not necessarily gift the traveller with omniscient instinct for direction? She pulled up her knees.

The car slowed up to the junction. Dermot tapped on the steering wheel. 'Can't see any street signs. Bloody Greeks. Never any signs when you need them.'

'Turn left.' The navigator's insistent monotone interrupted Jane's attempted reply.

Dermot turned right. His lips, faintly visible in the mirror set in a grim line. Jane said nothing. The navigator began to set a new course, the wheels of its invisible computer doubtless turning in a rush of disbelief. The road was dark, sheer cliffs supporting the night and tipping away to invisible depths.

'Turn around when possible,' the navigator intoned.

Dermott's lips set in a thinner line. He pushed his foot down on the accelerator. Then he flicked the headlamps on. 'Bloody mist,' said Dermott. 'Greece doesn't have mists. We should be able to plot stars like Phoenicians here.' He punched a switch, sending a bright lighthouse-beam into the gloom.

Had it always been like this? thought Jane. *Perhaps lives are predestined, the mapped lines marking the set course.*

She had met Dermot by accident in a small bar in Whitby. His indecision then had seemed cute. His hair, now thin, had been full; he had affected a pipe, which made him look older. She had been fascinated by the tang of his accent. Even the strange name of his comprehensive school, Bellport, had been made exotic by his Scottish burr. All of these things with time had become ugly mannerisms and social failings that aroused simple contempt.

But the first days in Whitby where they had walked arm in arm around the museum together, Dermott intoning the bright litany, the very voice of history; his voice strident, eyes shining. 'The siege of Quebec,' he had shouted. 'The plains of Abraham. Oh to have been there, then, when the world was younger. The maps, Jane, the great circumnavigation of the globe, the uncharted waters made malleable to human vision.'

Over fish, chips and mushy peas, Dermott had outlined his plans to travel the paths of the greats. He speculated an audacious attempt on the Polynesian journey in a small craft. His febrile excitement conveying the storm-lashed seas, the isolation and the womb like world of the loner. He poked his fork at the Antarctic and invented incredible engines that would open up the frozen south. Sucked in by his wild enthusiasms she quickly envisaged a role as the explorer's muse: Tea in billycans, servile porters, gruff sailors, makeshift fires on deserted beaches; editing the scribbled notes; the brave wife and companion of the visionary adventurer!

At the time, it had seemed like the world was as open to them as it had been to those mythic navigators: Columbus, Franklin, Armstrong: the globe walkers, making footprints in the sands of time.

But now it seemed like a blind alley, a maze with no exit. They had somehow adopted banal schedules, uninteresting paths. Dermot had procrastinated. Money had been tight, pressures of work intervened, practical plans became idle speculation. Slowly, they settled into routine; a week's holiday in Whitby to revisit the locale of their first meeting. Christmas spent at alternate families, she to his father and he to her mother. In both cases, they found an almost positive release in familial boredom. They drank coffee for breakfast, tea at teatime and shared a sherry for supper. One trip to the continent every two years from which Dermott derived an appalling misplaced sense of grandeur and became the self styled expert geographer and naturalist. With the passage of time, he had managed to consign their exploration to the realm of the imagination and the occasional jaunt like this tiresome 'long weekend' in Greece.

Jane had suffered the embarrassment of weekly bridge parties. Dermot would invite his friends; uniformly garnered from tedious Bellport school reunions. They were all of a type: Earnest, dull, unimaginative, aspiring working class boys. Dermot would never fail to astound them with descriptions of Flemish musical instruments, photos of Spanish beach sculpture and collections of attic pottery shards. The worst torture he reserved for his 'mountains of Europe' slide show, so carefully catalogued that Jane spent each evening, while Dermott snored, fighting the desire to nip downstairs and mix up a few slides.

'Junction ahead,' the navigator intoned. Dermott grunted in satisfaction. 'See eight kilometres ahead and we have a better alternative. I was right.'

Right? Couldn't he see the navigator was full of electronic maps? Who could be lost in a virtual universe?

All these years ago. It had been a mistake to go with him on the subsequent archaeology digs; it had been a greater mistake to accept his offer of engagement. She should have run when she met the best man, the obsequious best pal, Harry from Bellport Comprehensive, who failed narrowly in second year at Birmingham but settled nicely into Banking. That dreadful young man with the opinions of a pensioner was a clear sign of duller things to come.

But perhaps all life was like that? A series of tiny accidents all impelling one down a predetermined path?

Now they were reduced to middle aged bickering or unhappy silence: the sorry end of romance. No children, no cats even, just two lonely people trying to make holidays appear like adventures, neither with the imagination to initiate an affair.

The olive trees shuddered in the rising wind, the over-packed car tugged by invisible hands. Dermott slowed down as distant car lamps appeared on the horizon. Jane gripped the edge of her seat. Night journeys, Dermott's incredible sense of invincibility, as though he had never crashed the car. He was not a good driver but good at blaming others for the numerous bumps.

The car approached and passed. Darkness seemed to well up around them. There were no lights here. Only silence.

'Radio,' said Dermott.

'No. I want to sleep.' Not true, but it prevented his out-of-tune accompaniment to the choruses.

Dermott grunted. Another kilometre. The navigator intoned, 'at the next junction turn left.'

Dermot pursed his lips.

Carefully he swung into the bend, the narrow mountain road.

'That's the nice thing about navigators' Dermott said in the face of impenetrable darkness. 'You get to see parts of the country you would never see for fear of being lost.'

This, in spite of the oblivion around them.

'We can't see the country.' She said quietly under her breath. 'We never see anything.' In her head, she said. *We're lost. We always were lost, even before we met.*

Dermott said nothing.

They hit the barrier with a whiplash smack. In that awful second, the jar of the vehicle and the instant report like a gun,

Jane's whole life flashed before her eyes. The final vision of the car teetering on the brink of a cliff sprayed across her retina. Dermott screamed. The windscreen shattered inexplicably, the whole face of glass torn away like broken ice.

Dermott stamped on the brake. The car bumped and shuddered down. The wind thrashed their faces and finally died as they came slowly to a halt.

It was little like that cove on the outskirts of Whitby where Dermott had first popped the question; the gentle slope down to where the cliffs shadowed the sea. Through the gathering mist, they could faintly see where the cliff edge must begin; the immense drop to the sea, thankfully hidden. Jane whimpered quietly, the stink of Dermot's bowels gagging her breath. For want of a few yards, the car would have taken them over the precipice. She would have died screaming.

Dermott was breathing heavily. He pulled up the handbrake, stared dumbfounded as it came away in his hand. He stabbed again on the brake pedal. The sound of its hollow lifeless clunk was masked by the neutral voice of the navigator as the car began to slowly roll down the slope. 'Straight on' chirped the navigator

Dermott caught on the door. Scrabbled with his seat belt. 'Help me', she screamed. But he was rolling out of the moving vehicle on to the grass. In those last moments, the rear mirror revealed his face, splashed with relief, a man pulled from the brink of the grave.

Incredibly, the car stopped. Hands shaking, Jane pulled open the door and crawled from the vehicle. She dropped trembling to the grass.

There was a sound of footsteps. 'Lucky,' gasped Dermott from above. Lying face up on the ground, Jane could see only the paunch of his belly.

'You bastard,' she said finally. 'You fucking bastard'

Dermott said nothing. He knelt down on the grass and spewed. For a while they lay. The sky deepened. The mist became bizarre, almost tangible as though somehow sentient. Jane stretched out her hand into the black. Shrouded by the deepening gloom it grew faint and ugly like the hand of a wounded doll. The sound of the sea, at first throaty and hollow seemed to swamp all other sounds. After a time it was lost. All sound receded. The smell of Dermott's vomit paled. The pain in her head declined like a fading torch. She could no longer see her hand.

'My God,' said Dermott in a small voice. 'There's nothing here,'

'Nothing?' said Jane.

Faintly, from invisible depths, the navigator replied 'You have reached your destination.'

THE TASTING

'The water of life; honey dew that drips gold from the glass like nectar from the bowl of an ancient god: The amber glow of sweet, translucent waves cascading in the topazian cavern of the mouth. Each trembling moment a cacophony of impressions, the overture to a composition that will play in your innards and explode into majestic life in the amphitheatre of your head, drawing you ever closer to, but never reaching, the unspoken symphony of eternal verity. Gentlemen, I give you whisky: Good Scotch whisky.' Campbell raised his glass. '*Slàinte mhath*'.

There was a moment's silence. The American tourists, millionaires to a man, had barely understood a word of the preceding hour, and none of the closing speech, but their palates and their heads had been impressed by the smooth Scotch dialect and the smoother Scotch whisky. Each dram of several priceless bottles had been downed to the last drop. A litter of lesser bottles and tumblers, half full or untouched, decked the tables like flotsam and jetsam from a shipwreck as, in the ensuing moment, Campbell, the whisky taster, smiled and drained his glass and the barriers of decorum broke and gave way to a spatter of applause that sounded, from the comfort of the Balmoral Room, like dry sticks cracking.

Bannerman downed his laphroaig. 'Right! Let's get rid of those lightweights and we can enjoy a serious drink.' He rose from our table with a curt nod to the company. The 'big man' strode across the room, launched a quick '*Do dheagh shlàinte*' to the whisky taster, and began to harass the bemused guests.

Bannerman's restaurant was a legend in the Highlands; Bannerman, owner of the caboodle, was a chef who had made his name across Europe as the inspirational maestro of several select restaurants. His name had been good, his food legendary but that elusive beast, money, only finally fell into his lap with a shrewd bet on the Musselburgh races. An insider tip and the unholy risk of a three way tote had gained him the several millions a man requires to make life complete. Some might have thought of instant retirement and a life of aimless leisure. Bannerman had simply refurbished his golf clubs, his boat and his fishing tackle. He then closed up all his restaurants and bought a highland hotel, north east of Fort William.

Thousands of customers across the length of Europe were left with a hole in their culinary life and Bannerman was left to carry on the things he had always done – cultivating his own small vine, tending his simple allotment, cooking excellent food and drinking the same inordinate amounts of Laphroaig. The only difference in his lifestyle was that he now cooked whenever he liked and invited only those guests with whom he cared to spend an evening.

On this occasion, he seemed to have approached two whisky tasters from the town or perhaps they had simply turned up unannounced; not an unusual scenario as one could always pop into Bannerman's. The local villagers would often drop in for a pint –'We're all Jock Tamson's bairns', Bannerman was wont to say and he had no snobbery, rather preferring the simple wisdom and dark humour of the local Scots to the 'foreign' guests. He took every man for what he was. Indeed, on many occasions a rich and influential guest had found himself turfed out into the rain with a curse. Equally frequently, an impoverished crofter who had dropped in on the way to Glasgow might discover that his joke about sheep had gained him a full dinner and an endless train of expensive whisky as the chef fended off his money with a 'Stick a couple of bob in the charity box.'

It was a rare privilege for me to dine at Bannerman's; the place was a well kept secret, a secret that Mulholland had neatly discovered some years before through Campbell the whisky taster, an old climbing companion. Me? I was one Jock Tamson's bairns, somewhat down-at-heel, penniless and in need of a feed, so it was with a sense of baffled awe and unashamed gratitude that I watched Bannerman handle the rich Americans like a farmer shifting cows, smug in the knowledge that I had been invited by the 'big man' himself to stop over in comfort at the grand hotel.

Mulholland and I had come up on the train with the whisky taster, Campbell, a dignified man of around fifty clad in kilt and velvet Montrose. Campbell was now parrying requests and small talk like a doctor's receptionist. Finally, he shook off the last of his admirers - a fat New Yorker whose clothes would look excessive on a Woodstock poster - and spoke a quiet word with his fellow taster. After an interval, where he checked the odd bottle and exchanged a quiet joke with Bannerman, he strolled over to the bay window that overlooked Loch Craich. Mulholland and I joined him.

It was a magnificent view. A sheer drop of some two hundred feet, shaded by an erratic line of Scotch pine, revealed the dark, silent waters of Loch Craich, which spread before us like the blood of a dying Ossianic hero. Far across the loch, one could see the mare's tails of the twin Craich Falls known well only to experienced mountaineers; hardened men who had tired of the runs on Glencoe, the more difficult Munroe's and the subtle intricacies of the Cairngorm range; men who kept the mountain secrets close to their hearts and out of guidebooks.

The Falls glittered in the fading light; two ribbon tails of shimmering water that shone like the tracks of tears on a roughened cheek.

The three of us gazed out across the loch towards the glistening crags, each to our own thoughts. I couldn't speak for the others but mine, warmed by the comfort of whisky, were of the men who had tried and failed this grim buttress of the Craich Mountains. The crags themselves, diminished by distance, still bore the excessive grandeur of the highlands. Eerie, almost contemplative; peaked with late snow, I knew that they were a dangerous climb in winter. Mulholland and

Campbell had done it in the 1980's and Crowley also once long ago in his colourful youth; but several deaths had tended to dampen enthusiasm, an unusual occurrence among mountaineers whose normal response to the violent dismissal of one of their number is a devil-may-care nonchalance to the manner of their death and a questionable desire to imitate the circumstances.

There was talk of a curse. The climb hadn't been attempted in any season for more than ten years, the last summer mountaineer being dragged out of the Craich burn when the snow thawed in the spring of the millennium. The rescue team said his corpse was still holding the rock that had broken in his hand.

Campbell, who had been on that rescue team, seemed entranced by the view. He nursed his glass with the wistful far-off look of a man recalling his past.

'Sometimes,' he said after a moment, 'in the gloaming hour I think I can see Glencoe through the waters of the Falls of Craich. Impossible, of course, with the mountain range in between but still I seem to see it.'

'Wouldn't be terribly welcome there anyway.' said Mulholland with an irreverent grin. Campbell smiled sourly. 'Best join the ladies,' he said with a curt nod. He turned his back on the view and us and walked stiffly over to the table. Mulholland frowned. 'Not like Campbell,' he said, and then, cryptically, after a space 'Must be the anniversary.'

Mulholland drew out a cigarillo. His single good eye surveyed the grandeur below and beyond. Like myself, he appeared shy of company for the moment; content to immerse himself in that hour of twilight known in Scotland as the gloaming. It was a time was a time of contemplation; the grey space between light and dark, a time when ghosts flitted the landscape and memories and reveries became almost tangible.

It seemed a shame to break the mood but my curiosity had been piqued. After a space I said 'Anniversary? Did you mean the anniversary of the massacre of Glencoe?' I referred to the ancient feud that had long estranged the clans. Mulholland had certainly implied it in his failed attempt at humour. I continued: 'I know the MacDonalds and the Campbells have been stealing sheep from each other since they first discovered that sheep were edible, but surely that old nonsense wouldn't trouble him nowadays?'

Mulholland smiled. 'Well, the MacDonalds are all mad and the Campbells...well, they're just Campbells. But no. I'm referring to the anniversary of the disappearance of Jeanie Brown, Campbell's fiancée. I forgot about it.' Mulholland drew on his cigarillo and gave a penetrating stare out to the Craich Falls. 'Must apologise to Campbell, immediately.'

But despite his words, Mulholland seemed reluctant to move from the window. In the unfathomable waters of Loch Craich, drowned stars began to glitter like scattered confetti on new, black tarmac. The tiny shimmering points of light disturbed levels of the unconscious mind and in some sub-ethereal manner almost implored the imagination; as though the clammy hands of submerged sirens reached outwards from the depths of the loch; as though these subterranean creatures might draw you downwards towards a very cold oblivion. For a moment, charged with the inner light of the pearl moon, the strange afterglow of the highlands lingered in the air, glinting ephemerally on the now indiscernible Falls of Craich. Then a dark pall descended like the sweep of a cloak and the gloaming became suddenly night. Mulholland put his cigarillo out in the ash tray and shivered.

'Farantino's here,' he said tersely.

'How do you know?' I replied.

'I can smell the bastard,' said Mulholland through his teeth.

Bannerman's German wife had joined the throng behind us and I could see that the Laird of Maichvarness and his mistress had filched a few bottles of single malt from the Americans' tables. Two eminent Italian occultists were inspecting the

Jacobean portraits on the wall with a magnifying glass. Sir Delaney, the infamous ornithologist, was insisting that the bottles be shared among the musicians who were waiting for the Americans to leave before they debouched their fiddles and accordions. The rival whisky taster, a man of ages with Campbell, had escorted one of the young English waitresses to the floor and was demonstrating an extemporary version of the sword dance with some of Bannerman's silverware. In short, the *craic* was on.

I saw immediately that Mulholland had been correct. The last of the Americans had just departed and standing next to Bannerman by the door was the infamous and incredibly rich chef, Farantino who, for a reason never explained, provoked an uneasy antagonism in Mulholland.

Farantino, a man of medium height and dwarfed by Bannerman, was asking some intense questions. Doubtless it was about food – both were epicures and perfectionists, both rich and influential. Although Farantino's incredible wealth made Bannerman look a pauper, there was an obvious mutual respect between the men. Bannerman was the type who only came alive when a guest could truly appreciate the quality of his cuisine and Farantino was, of all men on earth, the one who could appreciate it most. After some minutes Bannerman left for the kitchen and Farantino came over to us. He shook both of our hands in a formal fashion. The fiddler began to play 'Farewell to Whisky' and together we joined the party.

Farantino took a seat with his back to the log fire, somewhat in the shade of the stag's head that rose splendidly over the great fireplace mantle and somewhat apart from the others. His eyes, partially in shadow, studied the antics of the late guests with an ambiguous expression.

There was something about Farantino that lent an aura of inapproachability. Occasionally, he glanced upwards, lizard-like in the light, to view the great painting of the Highland Charge at Culloden on the far wall or stare with a peculiar intensity at the younger waitresses. He would look sometimes with a somewhat supercilious smile at Campbell, which was more than enigmatic.

Mulholland and I pulled up beside the two whisky tasters. I warmed my hands in the glow of the flames of the oak fire as Mulholland made his apologies.

'I forgot: The anniversary,' he said simply.

Campbell looked gravely at his glass. 'Sorry, my fault. I can't expect everyone to share that burden. I was unpardonably rude.'

'Not everyone,' said the other whisky taster, 'but certainly me.'

'Again I must apologise,' said Campbell. 'This is my closest friend, Jamie MacDonald. We go back a long, long way.'

Macdonald had clearly given off teaching a sword dance to the waitress. He looked breathless after his exertions but nevertheless seemed an exceptionally fit man for his age with bright clear blue eyes and red hair. He was large, almost a colossus; broad shouldered, with a slightly florid complexion to his skin – probably unavoidable given his occupation – and a rakish twist to his full lips.

'Aye,' he said in that melodious west coast lilt, 'it's unusual for a Campbell and a MacDonald to be the best of friends but as the man says we are that; ever since that night.'

I was about to make some pleasantry about the clan feud, mostly to avoid discussing the subject of this enigmatic 'anniversary', which seemed to hover in an undercurrent behind the conversation. Fortunately, the accordionist took the moment to explode into a rendition of 'Lady Whisky'. Half of the company, now swollen by a couple of crofters and a travelling salesman, began to ring out the chorus. Laird Malcolm endorsing the peoples' choice, raised himself precariously to the table and let his baritone ring above the crowd

'Whisky, whisky I loved you so well
Promised me heaven with a wee kiss and tell

*You'll ay be the lady in good company
My lady whisky, whisky and me...'*

It looked like it was going to be a long evening.

We must have consumed half a bottle of Laphroaig each by the time Bannerman brought in his special supper.

Apparently, you could never rely on its appearance – sometimes he slipped off to bed, sometimes he might simply enjoy a drink – but it was clear that with Farantino in the company, Bannerman wanted to try something a bit different.

With the true genius of the great cook, different did not mean lavish. Bannerman bore in his own hands a large silver platter spilling over with fresh salads, wild rice and fruit, the centrepiece of which was a single rabbit discernable as such by one hind leg projecting from the carcase. The waitresses had already removed a reluctant Laird Malcolm from the table. They rushed to clear a space amidst the whisky tumblers and lay small plates and cutlery.

Some Tarja Bil Bajt, (those Maltese noodles), chutney butter and hobz were also laid out as side dishes. A bottle of Chianti was opened and as always Bannerman gave his toast to the ladies. For some reason, at that moment, I caught the eyes of Campbell. He seemed to hear nothing, see nothing as he stared into the burning embers of the logs behind me. This was almost a physical statement – his absence of participation. Then he recovered his poise and automatically raised his glass. With the toast to the ladies over we tucked in.

The rabbit was superb. The company was silenced for several minutes. The light clatter of cutlery, the clink of glasses, the wind soughing in the branches; then the travelling salesman, who had suddenly recognised Farantino's face from the newspapers, suddenly said 'What do you think of the food?' Bannerman, always unpredictable, laughed but inevitably eyes turned to the renowned chef.

Farantino's head slowly projected from the shades like a

turtle from a shell. His disingenuous face carried a slight smile that seemed to shimmer and change in the deceptive light of the fire; as always when he spoke it was with a compelling urgency that none could mistake.

'Bannerman's cuisine is quite brilliant of course.'

Bannerman laughed lightly.

'I can boil an egg.'

'It was a delightful rabbit, your own mustard sauce. Parsley grown in your garden: the Chianti a perfect accompaniment. All delightfully cooked. A delicate touch.'

'But what would you cook then? You're the genius?' The salesman had drunk beyond his depth. A few sharp looks fired in his direction but Farantino simply directed it to Bannerman.

'What is the ultimate recipe?'

Bannerman paused; the low flames of the fire caught the angles of his cheek and for a second seemed to transform the congenial face to a death mask. 'Human, of course,' he said lightly. 'It's like hunting. The greatest hunt is human game because of its intelligence, its ability to thwart the hunter and, not least of all, the taboo of its killing. The greatest dish would be man.'

The English waitresses and a few of the guests made a big show of emotion but the mistress of Lord Maichvarness, a classical beauty of French stock, said with conviction: 'You are right of course. It's reminiscent of the ancient cults of the fisher king. Human sacrifice may be abhorrent but it had its place in the growth of human awareness. Whoever eats a human must surely give the body the reverence it deserves and its preparation would be the ultimate challenge to a chef.'

Farantino, who had known the answer, smiled a peculiar smile and retreated back into the darkness.

Bannerman, seeing himself being forced to justify his position alone, pointed to the despoiled carcass of the rabbit.

'Don't all be so high and mighty,' he said. 'Cannibalism isn't so far away from us as you might think. Some of you might have noticed the leg on that rabbit -.'

'Why leave one leg on a rabbit?' said the salesman. 'I wondered about that.'

'I learned it in Malta a few years ago,' replied Bannerman. He slipped a cigarette out of his silver case and stabbed his palm with it. 'The island is full of cats. They leave a single leg on any meat so that you can identify the beast. I mean a rabbit is pretty similar to a cat. Very hard to tell them apart.'

'I hope that wasn't a fecking cat, Bannerman.' Laird Malcolm appeared to be regaining momentum after the meal.

'Only on your plate,' replied Bannerman with a sidelong glance. 'Instead of questioning your free grub why don't you do something useful and bring over another bottle of Laphroaig.'

As Laird Malcolm returned, Bannerman pointed his lighted cigarette at the rabbit. 'I personally think it was medieval custom, perhaps even earlier than that.'

'Of course,' whispered one of the occultists,' the crusaders ate the Mohammedans on regular occasion.'

'History is replete with examples,' said Mulholland airily, 'The Kolufo and the Kalingo are reputed to have practised cannibalism. Although everyone over the next hill was accused of cannibalism by their enemies, and most denied it, the eating of human flesh was probably far more prevalent than we imagine. New Guinea tribes I recall were reputedly very fond of 'Long Pig'.'

'The closest flesh to man,' said Bannerman with a grin.

'Thank feck it wasn't close to rabbit,' said Laird Malcolm.

Bannerman gave a knowing grin.

It must have been around the phantom hour of two or three in the morning when a tawny owl began to sound in the darkness. The conversation had ranged the length of the world and back and there was a kind of hushed expectancy gathering over the remaining guests. Farantino had long since left for Edinburgh. Bannerman was in a jolly mood because he had secured his permission to fish the Craich Burn and its environs, land owned by Farantino for the last few years. The salesmen's head had hit the table so we no longer had to suffer his gaucheries; the crofters were holding up but Laird Malcolm appeared to have run off with a young English waitress. The accordionist was asleep but the fiddler still toyed with the melody of 'Farewell to Whisky' in a thoughtful, self-immersed fashion.

The company had settled into that period of the evening when great truths and greater banalities emerge. The rational mind has long since given up the ghost and all conversations become a subliminal jigsaw of reaction and metaphor, gesture and symbolism, where the flick of a wrist, the twitch of a smile, the blink of an eye convey more than any words. One can nearly see the companion's soul through the bleary drunken eye. The whisky had given us breath and now it took us into the Low Road, the Hades of the Scottish collective consciousness; a dark underworld inhabited by the ghosts, fairies, sprites, silkies and bogies of myth and legend. The fiddler would find a tune in that maze and a hundred years from his finding it would be part of the woven tapestry of living traditional music; the whisky tasters would find some description for the fragrance of a new cask, the laird would sense a new wonder in his lady. We were, in short in the dream time.

It was thus that I almost gave a start when Macdonald stood clumsily to his feet. For a second I thought that one of the occultists was working the man like a puppet. He pulled a small bottle of whisky, unlabeled from his pocket and pushed two glasses into the centre of the table. Carefully he poured the entire contents of the small miniature into the glasses. He passed one to Campbell who looked at it with the absorption of the drunk

'To Jeanie,' he said. Campbell took the glass in hands and slowly stood to his feet. 'To Jeanie,' he replied and drained the glass. He sat down heavily; morose in his thoughts. Macdonald poured the remaining whisky on the floor.

I hardly need explain that Scottish hospitality demands that, if a bottle be opened, it must be shared. One or two of the guests stared aghast towards Bannerman to see his reaction. I almost spoke – it would have been the first time that evening – but Mulholland gave me a nudge. A lot of people had been thrown out of the hotel for a lot, lot less. Bannerman stared at the two men with an enigmatic eye. It was a blatant affront to him as a host. He rose stiffly to his feet. I fully expected him to explode in a rage.

'Time for bed,' he said quietly.

We rose early. It was bitterly cold and my head was thumping with toxins. Mulholland and I got kitted out in our fishing gear with heavy waders and waxed jackets provided by our host. When we stumbled outside, like a red nail clipping along the ridge of Ben Craich, the glimmer of the dawning sun was visible from the hotel; but 200 feet below at the small wharf the mist made it invisible.

In the shadow of the mountains, Bannerman had organised a party of three boats: Himself, Laird Malcolm, his butler and Laird Maichvarness in the largest four-oared Norwegian boat; MacDonald and Campbell made the next party in a smaller Whitehall. Mulholland and I settled for a tiny skiff that had seen better days.

The expressed plan was to fish the Western end of the loch near the peninsular waters of Craich Burn where a short passage of roiling water, overhung by cliffs, led to the smaller enclosed waters of lesser Loch Craich and here emerged a tributary of the Lochy Burn. By the afternoon we would move to the smaller section of Loch Craich and from there we would split again and try some fly fishing on the waters of the Lochy Burn till the gloaming hour when the trout would be rising again. There was a kind of informal competition but, as with all fishermen, about the last consideration was catching a fish. Bannerman had stocked each boat with bacon butties and flasks of coffee and a bottle of ten year old Laphroaig to keep us warm. There was a hamper with several iced beers, chicken legs, bread, pickles and cheeses under the seats.

We cast off the wharf; a swift dram for luck and the hangover and tiredness washed away. Mulholland took the oars and I felt a strange almost hallucinogenic exuberance.

All morning we fished the main body of water in stoic silence. The tiny flies rose around us, the fish began to rise, sending concentric ripples across the gleaming water. Once or twice we saw giant trout leap from the water like shining paladins. As the daylight progressed I dozed off for a while, lulled by the lap of water on the gunwales. Slowly, with a certain inevitability, the three boats drew nearer to the buttresses of the cliffs. The sun, late over the mountains, tipped the peaks and ascended the heavens the colour of a blood orange. Cloud banks embroidered with violent red began to disperse in a light breeze. The air grew warmer.

In the late afternoon, by some kind of mental osmosis all the boats gathered together at the Western end of the main loch and we sculled towards the gap between the cliffs. From here the tremendous heights of the Craich Falls could be fully appreciated. The cliff walls were clearly visible through the buttressed face like the shadow of a giantess viewed between a gap in enormous curtains. As the trains of a parted wedding dress reveal the thigh of the bride, the shining water spilled down the glistening rock walls.

We debouched into the lesser loch and the full grandeur of the enclosed space fell out before us. It had the air of a secret garden. Mist burgeoning up in ever moving clouds, the roar of the waterfalls, the thrumming air, dark pines marching down the northern slopes of Ben Craich, the vast skirt of the scree slope before it spilled into the waters; but, most splendid of all, the huge and indomitable cliff face between and surrounding the two waterfalls, glistening with damp and emerald with lichen; its ancient granite surface, formed by cataclysmic events lost in antiquity: The cragged overhangs where so many climbers had tried and failed; its feet a scatter of huge boulders and immense broken rocks.

We rounded away from the cliff and beached on an inlet opposing the Craich Falls. The scotch pines rose up here on a sharp slope above a natural shale beach where Bannerman had somehow carved a few wooden tables from dark wood. He had sent some waitresses and his junior chefs by the hidden paths and already deer roasted under an open fire. The ladies wrapped up in shawls sat on camp chairs drinking champagne. The mistress of Lord Maichvarness was posing in partial deshabillement for one of the occultists while the other spent an inordinate time apparently gathering mushrooms from the forest floor.

I couldn't quite participate in the revelries with any real enthusiasm and after a space Mulholland joined me as I contemplated the Falls from the shale beach.

'You're wondering about last night?' he said.

'Yes, the whisky. I'm still amazed that Bannerman didn't throw MacDonald out of the building.'

'It must have looked bad. I'd better tell you the story.'

Mulholland drew out a Havana, cut and lit it. After a space he said. 'It was thirty years ago. Macdonald was engaged to Jeanie Brown –'

'– But Campbell said that he was engaged to a Jeanie Brown?'

'Yes, he was, but only after Jeanie broke off with MacDonald.'

'Aha.'

'It was a *cause celebre* at the time. She had bridal nerves or whatever they call it. Campbell was the best man. She ran off with him on the night of the wedding.'

'And Macdonald calls the man his best friend?'

Mulholland laughed. 'Well they certainly weren't the best of friends for a bit.' Mulholland contemplated the burning end of his cigar. 'No, in fact Macdonald tried to kill Campbell a few days later. It was all very unpleasant. He would have killed him too but Jeanie stopped it in time. Jean was….well, she was an incredibly beautiful woman, fiery, red-haired a magnificent woman really. I'd have married her myself if she'd noticed me at all.'

'That's some admission.'

'You never saw her dance,' said Mulholland. His eyes drifted across visions of long ago. The cigar burned forgotten in his hand. Finally, he came back to me. 'Well, MacDonald left Scotland and became that sort of freebooter that men become when slighted in love. Took chances, risks, worked on the oil rigs in Norway, road-building out East, gambled in Ireland. I think he was a mercenary soldier for a bit. Made a fortune and lost it several times over.'

'There was obviously a reconciliation of some sort?' I glanced back at the fire where the two whisky tasters were laughing and joking over a leg of the wild deer.

'Yes, but not how you might imagine it though. About a year after the fiasco Campbell made an announcement in the times for his forthcoming wedding to Jeanie Brown and by private invitation a date for his stag night. As a bit of a joke it was to be done in the tiny bothy up from that hotel at Glencoe.'

'Stag night in one of these poky bothies. Must have been a bit of an enthusiast?'

'Well, we were all very young and hardy; boys from the rugby club, sportsmen climbers, and you can make those little mountain huts quite comfortable – a good fire, loads of whisky. I recall we had a big bonfire outside too and we'd erected some decent tents.'

'Sounds almost tolerable.'

'Almost,' grinned Mulholland. 'It was late September before that hard winter and there'd been a rush of early snow which persisted and then over the months gave us the worst conditions in living memory. Campbell being a great climber had organised a weeks climbing around Glencoe. The wives and girlfriends were all staying at the hotel down the hill but the stag night was clearly going to be an all male affair. It could have been a bit of a rum do because Jamie MacDonald arrived in the early hours sporting a gun and was quite obviously going to take the opportunity to murder his old friend.'

'Jesus, remind me not to mess with the MacDonalds!'

'Not where the heart is concerned,' said Mulholland with an ironic grin. 'What saved Campbell's life was something quite out of the ordinary. You see, the hen night was going on across the glen in the lounge room of the hotel. I can visualise it now even after all these years. It was faintly conceivable that the men could keep a covert eye on the girls and vice versa. The hills make distance deceptive. You could actually call out and be heard down below. An adventurous soul could be down the mountain and out the back with a lady or improvise a quick rendezvous outside somehow. I was frankly in a bit of a quandary myself because I was half thinking I might grab Jeanie and elope – she was really that beautiful and I was young and not a little drunk. She had been dancing all night to the local band - their accordionist was at Bannerman's last night - I'd seen Jeanie at intervals through the evening, through the big windows of the hotel and laughing with her friends and the local village lads outside in the snow. Some hours earlier, just before the men and women separated for the night, I'd even had a brief talk with her at the door of the hotel where I nearly spilled my heart out.

She seemed distracted somehow. Not just by my obvious difficulties – I don't think she even heard what I said. I think she may well have been having regrets about the whole marriage thing. It's hard to tell with a woman like that. She was flighty, overenthusiastic; glowing a little with the drink. It's difficult to remember after all these years. I do remember that she was dressed all in red. A beautiful silken shawl, ruby stilettos designed by that London fellow and a scarlet Parisian evening dress that made her look like something out of epic theatre: Utterly stunning.'

Mulholland drew on his cigarillo. When he spoke again it was almost as though it was only to himself.

'I must have been the last to see her later that night. The moon was up, a clear bright evening with the whole splendour of the heavens looking down. The air was brisk and cool with your breath condensing and your teeth on edge. I'd been drifting in and out of the stag night. Campbell was consuming whisky like water; everyone was tremendously drunk and singing rugby songs – not particularly my cup of tea even then - I wandered out a little into the snow and looked down across the deep spaces of Glen Craich. It's there that I saw her walk out towards the hills; a lonely little red figure making tiny tracks like a robin through the drifts. To this day I curse myself for not following her. I didn't really know what was happening, what she was doing; how could I know?'

'But...'

'She walked out into the snow,' said Mulholland quietly. 'Never came back.'

Bannerman shouted across in some unusual excitement. He wanted us all to come together for some sort of announcement. Mulholland picked up a stone and threw it into the water. For a few seconds he watched the ripples battle with the flurry. Then he turned round and we both made our way to the fire. Just before we reached it he stopped and said 'That's what the drink was about last night and why Bannerman said nothing. It's something they've been doing every year for the past twenty years, in remembrance of Jeanie. Many people here know about it.'

'Is Jeanie buried nearby?' I said.

'No.' said Mulholland. 'That was the reason that Campbell and MacDonald reconciled. Jean's body was never found. Campbell was in a state of shock. When the alarm was raised, MacDonald threw away his gun and took charge of the main search party – he was on the rescue team in his younger days - He spent three days awake on the mountains leading groups through some of the worst conditions imaginable. The weather turned really bad, gale force winds white-outs. Two men were killed in the rescue party. Campbell broke his leg in a fall but MacDonald ploughed on without sleep for days, searching, searching. We all tried of course, but MacDonald was driven. I'm no slouch but I collapsed of exhaustion; many of us did. The last one on the hill was MacDonald. They brought him down on a stretcher and then the weather turned so bad the search was called off. Everyone expected Jean's body to turn up with the thaw but she was never found. It was a terrible, terrible affair.' Mulholland peered at the end of his cigar and spoke with a noticeable tremor. 'About ten years after, MacDonald told a few of us that he'd distilled a special whisky in remembrance of Jeanie. He only ever shares it with Campbell.'

'Come on you two,' shouted Bannerman. 'There's venison on the go and announcements to be made.'

It was strange fact that, despite a promising look to the water, the only one who had caught a fish all morning was MacDonald. He stood holding up on the scales with the waitresses with an enormous grin on his florid face. Campbell was laughing at his friend's antics as he haphazardly gathered firewood from where he sat. The mistress of Maichvarness had wrapped up in a shawl and now examined her unfinished portrait with a critical eye. The other occultist offered some mushrooms to Bannerman but the 'big man' gave him a dark look.

Bannerman inspected his work. He had made a small pit and placed a young deer in it after stuffing the chest cavity full with the heart, liver, vegetables, butter, salt, pepper and various secrets of his trade. Then he had wrapped it heavily in foil and placed it down in the fire pit on the hot coals; after all this effort his boys had built a big fire on top of the deer. The flames of the fire were dying now and Bannerman began to unwrap the carcase exposing the single hind leg. The occultist was cleaning his paint brushes. He looked at Bannerman with a keen expression. 'You knew that custom of identifying meat was a secret among initiated highlanders?'

Bannerman shrugged. 'No one is making you eat it.'

The meat fell from the bones revealing the rib cage as he drew out portions with an expert hand. In a few moments we all found a seat on the camp chairs and tree stumps; the waitresses served us venison on china plates while Bannerman poured out the whisky.

MacDonald had given his fish to a waitress to try on the grill. The carcase of the deer seemed to mesmerise him. He sat vacantly holding a whisky glass for a moment, staring at Bannerman helplessly and then he came to his senses. He stood up.

'I've something to say,' he intoned heavily. 'As most of you know it's been thirty years since we lost Jeanie. Here's to her memory.' He took a sip from his glass and we joined him. 'Not long after she disappeared I founded a secret and entirely illegal distillery somewhere in the vicinity. Since that time I've allowed a bottle out every year and, on the anniversary of Jeanie's disappearance, I've shared it with my friend and fellow raconteur Mr. Campbell.' Campbell nodded in acknowledgement and looked soberly towards the fire and the stripped carcase of the deer. 'People have badgered me for years about a drink of the whisky but I've always reserved that for my friend. Those who know the story-' he nodded to Bannerman '– have respected my wishes. The location of the still is another matter entirely.'

A few heads looked up in wonder. MacDonald smiled. 'After thirty years I have decided to reveal the location and allow everyone who wants it a bottle of the whisky.'

'My, my,' said Mulholland. 'That's a very gracious offer.'

'Not quite as gracious as you might imagine,' replied Macdonald with a wry grin. 'There is a single condition. Those who want to see the distillery must climb the Craich Falls with me tomorrow morning.'

There was an astonished silence. The report of the cracking wood in the fire seemed to pierce the ubiquitous deluge of the Falls. A moorhen whirred up from the surface of the loch disturbed by some invisible predator.

Campbell was the first to speak. 'I'll give it another go,' he said quietly.

'My God,' said Lord Malcolm 'You nearly died on that climb thirty years ago.'

'But I didn't,' said Campbell with a twinkle in his eye.

'I have a hundred percent record on the Falls-' said Mulholland with a grin. '- having done it once thirty years ago and not fallen off. I'll have another go.'

'I'll have a crack at it,' I said - and as suddenly regretted it.

Bannerman shook his head. 'Bloody mad,' he said, 'the lot of you.' Then he grinned. 'Let's drink to bloody mad people.'

If I had any regrets about my decision that evening they were magnified a million times in the morning when I stared up from the boulder-strewn feet of the Craich Falls. Mulholland had tried to talk me out of it in the evening but had finally agreed to act as my lead. Macdonald was going to share the ascent with Campbell.

The three experienced climbers were dishing out the gear: chalk bags, kermantle ropes, hexes, carbines and the like. Every now and then MacDonald would laugh. 'You didn't have all this crap when we first took this wee climb,' he said to Campbell.

'No, but as I recall Jeanie and the girls were watching us at the time and we both decided to be ridiculously foolhardy.'

'Not even a rope,' said Mulholland to me. 'But then we were all in our twenties then. I'd settle for a circus safety net at the moment.'

After a few minutes they had organised the ropes. 'This chalk might be handy though, against the damp from the falls,' said Campbell reflectively.

'No doubt,' said MacDonald. 'Everyone set? I started this foolish affair so I suppose I'd better be first up.'

Without another word Macdonald began the ascent. Campbell waited a few moments and followed him on the rope.

There are moments when one reflects on decisions and one of the moments occurs when you stand at the bottom of a sheer cliff. I watched MacDonald move up the face with that peculiar undulating grace that marks the born mountaineer. He was a colossal man but on the mountain he looked like a ballet dancer. Campbell, thinner, more fragile but no less the climber, followed like a spider on a web. They both took a route slightly to the right of the cascading fountains and cataracts of the sister falls.

I looked away from the cliff face to the scree slopes, the scotch pines and the splendid waters of the loch. The dawn would break over the mountain tops in a few moments. It was late September and the winter would be coming on. We were quite alone.

Mulholland gave me a sharp look. 'Still time to call it off. We're experts even if we're no longer spring chickens. There's no shame in it. It's a risky climb'

I shook my head. Sometimes death seems, if not welcome, not an enemy. Mulholland shrugged, checked his rope and began the ascent.

Mulholland had told me that he was a better climber for having only one eye. He always insisted that the single eye kept him more focused than other climbers and gave a kind of two-dimensional security to his climbing, as though it were all some old-fashioned video game. Mulholland, like the others, was certainly a natural climber – he lacked the grace of MacDonald and was slightly heavier than Campbell but there was no doubting the aggressive strength in his hands.

Perhaps because of the risk, Mulholland elected to take a separate approach some three or four meters right from the drop of the others. I noticed as I began to scale the surface that Mulholland was leaving a wider gap between his belaying ropes than MacDonald. His strong hands spanned out like starfish on the green scale-moss; his legs taut in the moleskin britches hugged the cliff as his booted feet found slender purchase on the basalt. After some moments he fixed a static belay and I followed, mimicking his movements as far as I could.

I had once in my youth attempted the Medusa Wall in the Lake District but had been forced down by a turn in the weather. These Craich Falls were far more intimidating: The roar of the water that cascaded in leaping cataracts, the damp and lichened surface of the rocks, the constant spray, the paucity of holds and crevices, the treachery of the rock, the very steepness of the climb. I could never have been first on the rope and even second became an endless nightmare. Mulholland kept a constant running commentary as he advised of weakened stone, crumbling rock, special grips and holds that he had rehearsed with me in the wee hours, the night before. Minutes seemed like hours. My hands and legs were cramped with pain. Once and only once, I glanced downwards. The sudden shock of that immense fall sent vertigo to spin in my brain. For moments I clutched to the cliff-face frozen.

'Look up,' said Mulholland tersely. 'Look up!'

I pulled my face upwards. Mulholland gave me a grin. He belayed again. 'Safe as houses now. We've done half in. There's a ledge just up here where we can rest.'

I could just see the feet of Campbell and MacDonald dangling above the abyss. A few moments later and we joined them on the ledge. By unspoken agreement they allowed me to rest in the single deep cleft that traversed the ledge. I'm not embarrassed to admit that after a single glance across the unfolding spaces of the air I shut my eyes for the length of that stay. I could hear MacDonald and Campbell in voices raised above the deluge of the waterfall and the faint flickering breeze.

'I kept this cavern secret since I stumbled on it over thirty years ago,' said MacDonald. 'Just up there beside the bladder fern. Do you see it? Where the water leaps off that stone shaped like a face. It's behind there.'

'Under the waterfall?'

'Yes,' said MacDonald. 'A man can stand squarely in it. I think the reason it was never discovered is that you have to climb under the overhang; extremely difficult under the waterfall. It's completely masked on the other side but you can just about do it from here.'

'You old dog,' said Campbell affectionately. 'After all these years. How the hell did you get a still in there?'

'I've got a whole lot more in there than you would imagine. There's an easier route from the West. I lowered the stuff off the top on ropes and abseiled at night. After a while it was a piece of cake.'

'Piece of cake my ass,' said Campbell. 'I'll take the first look if you don't mind.'

'Not at all,' said MacDonald. 'You've waited long enough.'

A few seconds later, I opened my eyes. It was one of these moments that you might see in a film but you would never believe it possible. Mulholland was checking his belaying rope, MacDonald was just beyond him on the ledge and Campbell was about the height and length of man in a diagonal from the party. He was bent in a crouch like an overturned beetle, head masked by the crashing water beneath the overhang as he performed a classic three point move.

And then he slipped.

To this day I think it impossible. The belaying rope snapped on the rock and MacDonald lunged suddenly forward and, with one immensely powerful arm clutching the rock, caught Campbell by the leg as he fell. I can picture it now after all these years. Campbell's hoarse cry as he fell, his head striking the basalt as he tipped over upside-down, Mulholland turning, aghast, and the giant MacDonald grasping outwards to clutch into space. Somehow, beyond any sensible physics, MacDonald took the falling body in one hand and clung like a maniac to a crevice. Horrifically for us all, Mulholland in the same moment was hit on the shoulder by the loosened climbing anchor. He was already turning and the weight of it took him off the ledge.

Fortunately, his anchor held. I was stuck still in the cleft but could see that Mulholland, although unable to help immediately, was not about to fall. MacDonald shouted for assistance but could not see us. Instead, like some gargantuan, he drew Campbell up and managed somehow to make a fireman's lift. The thinner man had been struck but had not lost consciousness. He clung on as, step by gruelling step, MacDonald, unroped and prey at any moment to certain death, pressed upwards to the overhang. There were moments of sheer vicarious terror as he paused at the cascade of water, seemed to lose his grip, then plunged through the torrent and was gone.

Mulholland had got to his feet. He looked down and I realised that he had seen nothing of this impossible climb and thought they had both fallen.

'Up,' I said through gritted teeth. 'He went up.'

'With Campbell?'

'With Campbell on his back.'

'My God,' said Mulholland. 'My good God.'

In the next few moments Mulholland and I made up the ledge and under the overhang, where the cool, sharp waters thrashed at us like birches. I stumbled forward. My head still spun with the selfish reflection that I had nearly been left alone on the cliff with its hellish, vertiginous spaces, and suddenly we were all inside, soaked and exhilarated, in the comforting darkness of a hidden cave.

MacDonald had lit a couple of paraffin lamps. The constantly shifting curtain of the waterfall played on the interior of the cave like one of those magic lantern slides; a kaleidoscopic tapestry made eerie by the subdued partially-shuttered lights. In the background I could see through dim shadows, huge towering bell-like shapes, barrels, copper boilers and tubs. In the foreground a rusty bain-marie and a dust-clad beaker stood before rows of glass bottles. On the left, in a recess, a large chicken cage and beside that a bunk, two chairs and a small table with inlaid drawers covered in old tools of varying sorts.

Sitting on a blanket right before us, Campbell clutched his bruised head with one hand as MacDonald administered the last drops of whisky from a flask. Campbell shook his head after a few gulps.

'I thought that was me,' he said quietly.

'Never seen anything like it,' I said under my breath. 'Nothing short of a miracle.'

'My friend,' said Campbell thickly, suddenly gripping MacDonald's arm. 'Who's like you?'

'No many,' said MacDonald with a grin. He rubbed his shoulder. 'You're heavier than I reckoned.'

'Sorry.'

'Don't worry,' said MacDonald rising to his feet. 'I'm sure this'll be worth all the excitement.'

I saw now that there was a recess a little to the right festooned with woven furbishing and blankets and what appeared to be a plain woven canvas drape across the upper part of a large barrel. Mulholland and I walked a pace forward.

'How on Earth did you do all this?' said Mulholland.

'It was my all-consuming passion,' replied MacDonald his face wreathed with an absurd smile. 'It was all for the whisky, the Usquebaugh. That's the thing about whisky – it's the water of life. It's deeper than anything else we have. It provokes a mythic response from the deep places of the body and mind. It's greater than us all.'

He drew two glasses from a drawer and filled them from the exposed spigot of the huge whisky barrel. 'You don't mind do you?' he said to Mulholland. 'This is between MacDonald and me.' Mulholland shook his head. MacDonald walked back with the glasses to his friend. They stood framed in the curtain of falling water like two gentleman toasting in a chiaroscuro picture.

'I've waited thirty years for this,' said Campbell with a rueful smile. '*Slàinte mhath*' He drew a long dram from the glass, his face screwing up at the bitter taste.

MacDonald smiled 'And I've waited longer for this.' He flicked on a hidden switch. There was a peculiar sound like a small generator. A light shone behind the barrel.

The canvas that covered the upper half of the old whisky barrel suddenly revealed itself as a theatre scrim or gauze which, when lit from the back, exposed its hidden tableau.

From the top of the barrel a solitary human leg could now be discerned, extruding from the centre of the cask, in its way much like one of the exposed legs of the wicked witch in the Wizard of Oz, viewed not with an adult perspective but with the transfixed eyes of a terrified child. Rotted flesh, saponified in the red silk stockings, seemed to slowly ripple and move in the shimmering deceptive light. On the slender foot the exposed yellow bones spread like an ivory fan encased in a ruby red stiletto that shone with a macabre, museum glow.

It was as though the woman who had worn the shoe over thirty years before might suddenly ask her lover if it suited her.

At the same moment I observed with a sickening lunge that a long red hair clung to the lip of Campbell's glass. He looked back, with an expression of bewilderment, which I will never forget, to the shocking extrusion from the barrel and all that it implied. Somehow he tore his eyes from the sight of the mummified leg, the stockings, the stiletto, only to stare appalled at the familiar red hair curling wet from the lip of his whisky glass.

'*Do dheagh shlàinte,*' said Macdonald. 'Your very, *very* good health.' He licked his lips with a mocking smile and took a single sip from his glass. For a few moments he rolled the slug of whisky in his mouth, savouring the aromatics with all the élan of an experienced taster then, staring mercilessly at Campbell with an expression of gloating lust and grinning the grin of an exultant fiend, McDonald walked deliberately backwards through the curtain of water.

On the following evening, Mulholland I got back to Bannerman's Hotel. After long interviews and the inevitable red tape at the local police station, the tragic death of the two whisky tasters was already local gossip. Climbing accidents were not so common that the policemen who accompanied us didn't need a whisky. The dark humour of the highlands forced the older officer to express his opinion that the worst of it was that MacDonald hadn't mentioned the location of his illicit still before his tragic fall.

Mulholland agreed but for once declined Bannerman's Laphroaig in favour of a tepid glass of water.

STEEL WORKS

At night, after the massage session, Anne cycled back to her home on the hill. She always stopped for a few minutes on the metal bridge. The deep waters flowed beneath her and it was time to smoke a cigarette. She felt easier in her body; the drifting swans bundled up asleep were scattered like white blobs of clotted cream on the dark placid surface. The ripple of water snakes and rats, and the gentle sway of the bridge echoed the rhythms of her pumping heart. Sure, she shouldn't smoke but there was something easy about it. It felt just right, what with the hollow stars in the night sky and the light, chill air on the lungs.

The only thing that spoiled the effect was the vast steel works on the west bank still spewing out its vile smoke. The smoke itself was picturesque enough, tainted orange by the distant street lamps. In a way it echoed her own attacks on an otherwise healthy body: Her lungs the mirrored equivalent of the beautiful river and its accompanying polluter.

The colours and the flashing lights of the inner workings never really bothered Anne.

It was the noise.

After the massage, she liked to take the back ways towards home, avoiding the city centre to sweep down the cycle paths that skirted the big river. It was quiet; a time for those lonely thoughts and creative ideas that only come in silence. Then, when she hit the metal bridge the noise began to intrude on her.

The steel works always sounded as if some giant leviathan was tearing its cage apart. The shudder of steel on steel, grotesque bangings and clatterings as bits fell off or were thrown aside by God knows what kind of machines. It was a horrific sound, the exclamation of a giant devil locked in a struggle with unnatural elements. Why people should insist that the works were a twenty four hour affair baffled Anne. She had little idea about economics and cared less. The thing could be building cars or deconstructing empires for all she cared – as long as it did its stuff during the day.

At the edge of the metal bridge she leaned on the railing and took another drag on her cigarette. From the steel works a flurry of orange smoke spumed into the air. A burst of spray like a kid's firecracker followed. Anne observed the sparks hurtle skyward with the phlegmatic eye of a graphic designer. There was certainly something majestic about those awful construction grounds that sprawled for nearly a mile along the bank. Grim buildings and towers, metal shacks surrounded by barbed wire fences and all absurdly lit by thief lamps. During the day the factory had little to commend it aesthetically but at night it provided a fantastic spectacle; fantastic with the exception of the smog and that grotesque noise. Occasionally she even heard it, a distant cacophony, in her little apartment on the hill.

Anne examined the burning ember of her cigarette. The strange thing was that even during the day you never saw any people there. Of course, the great wagons rolled in and out but as a cyclist, or even come to think of it, on the rare occasions she had walked past on foot, she never recalled a driver. You would see the wagon roll in or out and then it was off to somewhere utterly unknown, its driver a vague puppet shadow behind the wheel. You couldn't see inside the works unless you went up close to one or two areas of fencing that exposed a flat plain or, as she remembered, on the south side a series of gantries and a huge pile of steel slag. There was one other break in the fence where you could see the top of a mound of wrecked cars; fuel for the perpetually burning ovens. Anne recalled stopping at these various points some years ago, before she had discovered the alternative quiet route but as far as she could remember she had never seen a person in the factory.

It was an odd thought. She tossed her spent cigarette on the bridge and carefully stubbed it out with her foot. The burning sparks drifted down towards the slow-moving river beneath her. The white swans remained huddled together and the water snake had gone under the banks. There were only the deep currents of the river making abstract art with the reflections of orange tinged smoke and some where, far away, the chirp of a moorhen.

Anne mounted her bicycle and idly pushed out over the bridge. Her tiny lamp sent a moth-wing flicker across the way like a failing spotlight in the large theatre of evening. It was a lonely little light. She was about half way across when she stopped and the dynamo ceased to power the battery.

As always, after the massage, she felt a heightened state of perception. The yoga in the morning was the prelude but the massage sessions, once a week affairs, really brought up her levels of awareness. She became suddenly aware of a desire to visit the factory – not to look at it in the cold light of day but to see it when it became truly alive, in the deep of night. It was a disturbing thought. She stopped at the far side of the bridge and leaned against the rails.

The desire, when she analysed it, was linked with memories of her father. He had been dead now for over two years but occasionally at moments of crisis she would dream of him. He'd usually be admonishing her for some wilfully dangerous behaviour – her habit of hitching lifts down South alone, not locking the apartment door and of course her solitary bicycle rides through the night. The aftermath of these actions, now that she was alone, would precipitate a nightmare but she always managed to control her emotional reaction.

She was nothing if not independent.

Now, however, she could picture his face, his pointing finger and the inevitable 'Come on girl, if you don't look after yourself who will?' She smiled gently and turned her wheels around. 'Sorry Dad. Here we go again.' The only response to her whisper was a sudden shriek from the distant steel works. The factory buildings seemed to shimmer in the air and a rocket-like flame burst into the heavens.

October nights, Halloween, fireworks, sparklers, burning the guy; Anne's father had loved Halloween and all its trimmings. Autumn had been his time. The time of falling leaves and cold winds with the log fire and the little ceremonies of tea, biscuits, charades and games of chance- just the two of them. It was strange how the massage sessions brought back all these deep memories. The memories were mostly happy. She had long since accepted his death. The wound wouldn't heal but it was no longer a thrusting stab of pain

With a little shake she mounted the bicycle. The lamp hesitated and came on full as the dynamo sent its little hamster-wheel voice out across the water. An owl swooped across the moon in a sudden silent glide and for a second Anne had a terrible vision of her old bedroom at night, the clawing fear of the shadow coat that hung on her door. The creaking as it opened to reveal her father coming to kiss her good night. She had cried then but he was there. Why should she remember that now? The bicycle left the bridge and found the path that led along the factory road. Trees whipped by, caught in the tiny lamp light. The roar of the steel works was muted by the wind in her ears and the rustling of the trees. Anne picked up speed. She didn't want to be too late home. Just one look and then off.

As she hit the long road it suddenly occurred to Anne that her father had driven trucks at the steel works when her mother was alive. It was so long ago. She must have been only five or so. He'd only worked there briefly, deliveries or something. Strange she should forget. The massage always did that – left her dreamy and prone to sudden flashes of insight. Perhaps it was the sight of the huge delivery wagons banked up on either side of the road; a peripheral vision seen through the trees.

The first fence was visible on her right hand side. Then she was alongside the wagons and the fence was obscured. As she passed each dark window she went through the usual zombie scares. It was easy to imagine the doors lurching open and grim bodies falling out.

But none did.

She turned on to the pavement, slowing down. The noise from the steel works reached a threshold. The smog had made everything a little fuzzy except for pools of light embossing the heavens in amber and teasing reflections from the puddles. There was no one around. The wagons were all at rest. Through the bars of the first fence she saw the huge gantries and lifting machines, the massive pile-drivers and bores; machines without end and without names. A little further along, half-covered by the main building, a towering heap of slag merged with the dark clouds. It was an awesome sight. So strange to think her father had been here years ago, perhaps taking orders from some big foreman, driving one of these trucks. God knows what he had done. He hadn't been very happy with it whatever it was.

Anne reached the first gate. There were a series of them in dwindling perspective but from memory this was the main one. It was open, presumably for night deliveries. But there was no one around. She dismounted from the bicycle and took a few tentative steps towards the works check-in hut. The hut was deserted. Slowly, she pushed her bicycle into the yard. She was already forming an explanation – it would be hard to make oneself heard with the racket but she was fairly sure a few shouted words about directions would save her face. Maybe she could just tell the truth, whatever that was. Her father used to work here – always wanted to have a little look. Who would care? But really, there was no one around. Just ahead was a long brick wall carrying a placard with some union rules and regulations, and a visitors' sign hanging crookedly from a steel pole. She strode forward with a bit more confidence. Just visiting… just visiting memories…

It was then that Anne saw the bicycle stands. There were a number of them just next to a small door dwarfed by a large forbidding entrance.

A huge clash of steel on steel clapped like thunder. She held here ears for a moment and hurriedly pushed her bicycle on to a stand. After a moment the reverberation of the steel died down to a familiar overpowering but almost bearable cacophony. With some curiosity Anne looked across to the visitors' office. She could see an open door next to it and rows upon rows of men's overalls: Still no one around. When she turned back to take off her helmet she was really struck by the number of bicycles: Hundreds of them; all neatly, stacked against the wall. Most with their owner's helmets hung on the frame. Some of them looked worth stealing and strangely she couldn't see a padlock on any of the ones nearby. The bicycles further away were older. Some of them even seemed rusty but it was difficult to tell in the smog. She placed her helmet on the frame. She couldn't imagine it would be stolen. She could just see her father shaking his head 'it only takes a moment, Anne-' But no one else had bothered and there must obviously be some workers around. They were hardly likely to steal a bike.

A strange almost bestial shout bellowed from the larger entrance. The grinding of steel on steel made Anne grit her teeth. It was like an enormous dentist drill gnawing on an open nerve. Still, she had come this far. She shook her hair and unzipped her coat. A light, brilliant in its intensity, played across the far wall of the revealed entrance. The ante room was basically empty – a few cans and drums, a stack of working boots and small tools on a series of palettes; and on the left hand side another smaller door. Still thinking of excuses, Anne advanced into the large entranceway. The noise here seemed suddenly subdued, contained, like the waters in a tank, at a consistent level. Through the door she could see a short corridor and another metal door firmly shut by what looked like a ship's central locking handle. Anne walked down the corridor and peered for some time at the metal door and the large handwheel, There was a metallic smell in the sweating air, tinged with a chemical odour of burning steel. For a full minute she stood hearing the pulsing throb of some great engine and the huge drill-like sound of some unknown machine. What would her father say now? What would she say the moment some safety-helmeted worker popped through the door; a young woman looking for directions? It seemed a bit silly. Hundreds of men could come pouring out of the door on the way home. She had no idea of the shifts or hours they would be working or what they were doing. She might even be arrested.

Behind the door the sounds suddenly began to diminish. A strange half-silence filled with tones of dripping water and erratic clicks. It was now or never. She gripped the hand wheel and turned it. The door swung inwards easily.

At first it was difficult to make anything out. Steam billowed outwards and twisted in curling wreathes. Anne peered forward, unwilling to cross the threshold. There was a sense of vast space and the noise changed exponentially as though her ears had popped with a drop in pressure. The chemical smell seemed intensified but somehow changed; a vague fishy odour, strangely musty yet perverse with male pungency. She took a step into the chamber.

She was next to a wall. On a rack at head height rows of clothes, shirts, scarves, jackets, endless clothes stretched until they disappeared into the mist. On the floor, boots and shoes lay in a neat row. The mists parted.

The chamber was immense with the proportions of an aircraft hanger. The metal roof soared above, obscured by gantries, steel ropes and huge metal beams that spread like the scaffolding of some manufactured parody of the Sistine Chapel,

But Anne saw none of this. Her consciousness had been heightened as always by her massage; the tactile feel of hands on her naked body. Dreams had been awakened. She now remembered with a terrible intensity the real reason that had promoted her father to come into her room so many years before. She saw now that the clothes, the boots and shoes, were as bizarrely organized as the rows of bicycles and even as she stared with growing realization she saw the children's shoes and girls dresses strewn pathetically among the rest. Those near were new. As her eyes travelled the endless line, the garments took on the appearance of an old thrift shop until they were nothing less than mouldering rags.

They were all female clothes

An orchestra of huge metal instruments screamed as though tortured by a giant leviathan Explosions like war cannonades battered Anne's mind and paralysed her thoughts as sparks of raw molten metal flew in burning sprays across the chamber. The shudder of steel on steel; grotesque matings of metal that rutted on metal. It was a horrific inhuman sound, the exclamation of some giant masculine monster locked in conflict with unnatural desire.

Slowly, mechanically, she began to strip.

LIEBNIZ'S LAST PUZZLE

Outside the dome restaurant, I paused on the steps; at my side, Mulholland. He rested his cane against the crisp leg of his plus fours then drew a cigarillo from a small silver case. Absently he offered one to me and on my refusal lit his own.

It was one of these moments that I believe only happen amongst men. The brisk, night air, the distant laughter and clinking glasses, the rain-washed, empty streets all offering a temptation to walk home in solitary contemplation. Yet we both paused in that masculine companionship, which neatly combines a mutual appreciation of the absurdity of the universe and an empathy with one other. Mulholland, smiling whimsically, tasted a breath of smoke and watched it curl out to meet the streetlamp glow.

'Fancy a pint?' he said finally.' Oxford bar is only across the way. Quiet. We can have a bit of a talk.'

I pondered Mulholland's transformation as we walked to the pub. Gone the weak and cowardly schoolboy with the skinny legs and the stutter: Gone the gawky clothes. Instead, here he paced up the street, a man approaching fifty with the step of a twenty year old, his clothes elegantly tailored, his voice assured and commanding. The only certain means to know that he was once that maligned boy – the lewd wound where his left eye had been.

Almost as though Mulholland sensed my gaze, he paused then drew a patch from his wallet and placed it over the missing eye. 'Bloody school reunions,' he said with a laugh. 'Still we saw off that bastard, Gray.'

I knew then that my tacit support of Mulholland at Bellport High, so long ago, had remained in his memory; and the farce of a reunion meal had cemented a newfound camaraderie.

'Bit of a puzzle that Gray,' I said as we walked.

'Yes, he is. Yet I suppose I have to thank his sadistic games for getting me out of Bellport.'

After losing his eye in the Gray escapade, Mulholland had moved to a public school. From there, Oxford to study Anthropology. Then, apparently on a whim, he had taken up Egyptology and had joined a couple of digs with our old deputy head. After a masters in Divinity, he became a missionary in the Far East.

'When that fell through,' he said blithely as we pushed open the bar door, 'I took up big game hunting.'

'Big game hunting,' I spluttered. 'Bit of a contrast from saving souls?'

'Oh, I wasn't quite the missionary you might imagine. I was dabbling in the black arts all through my education. I had my eye on something and the church seemed a dandy way of covering my tracks.'

I contemplated the occult as we settled into the snug of the Oxford. It seemed a far cry from the simple wooden chairs and unpretentious surroundings that momentarily lent Mulholland an archaic charm. I cradled my pint of 80 shilling. Mulholland made to light a second cigarillo, then remembering the proscription said, 'Writer now, Horror?' Plenty of preparation for that at Bellport High.' I laughed but then Mulholland's voice took on an earnest tone: 'You mentioned 'puzzle' earlier and that got me thinking. I have a little tale that you can perhaps use. Must do the usual; change a few names, tart it up, but I'll tell you it, if you like.'

I nodded and Mulholland began to unravel the tale that came to be known as 'Liebniz's Last Puzzle'

'We were in the year above Norton at Bellport. You remember Norton, the school chess champion? Prefect, cricketer, endearing fellow. You probably don't know that he had a German pen pal, something of a mathematical genius. His name crops up everywhere in chess circles, conundrum clubs and the like.

Norton and this fellow, Lubecker, met up at the Liebniz

Universität, in Hanover and became best of pals. They were working on some significant treatise in applied mathematics – mind bogglingly clever stuff; utterly beyond the likes of you or me, but for some reason it all fell through and the two of them left the University and came over to Blighty. Caused a sensation in academic circles – rumours of a homosexual affair, which in itself was nothing – but of course, giving up such promising careers on an apparent whim…

In any case, they left immediately for a camping trip; that much was known to their erstwhile colleagues. In fact, their destination was the North East Coast of England, specifically the Yorkshire Wolds. As far as the academic circles of Europe were concerned, they simply disappeared from the ken of man. But not, as it transpired, from the ken of good old D. Mulholland. It was late November- and here you have to ask yourself, whatever were two men doing out in tents in the deep of winter – when I received a letter from Norton. I was to come immediately. There would be expenses as an incentive but you know, I would have gone without any mention of money.

There was something in the tone of the letter. Can't quite describe it, but you could tell that Norton, normally fearless, was a bit on edge. And then, of course, he asked me to brush up my research on occultism and in particular the sixteenth to eighteenth century. There were more specifics – this was the time of the witchcraft madness and certainly, a bit later, the ghastly period when even the cathedrals came under threat. Norton was aware of my interest in the occult and I suppose he banked on me being anonymous enough, external to his academic penumbra and trustworthy. The specifics will become clear as we go.

Intrigued, I took a train down to the address he'd given. When I arrived, there was no one to meet me at the station, no taxicab, no village bus and the usual sense that one has entered an utterly foreign country. Fortunately, Norton had prepared me in advance with a small map and a picture.

Norton's pal, Lubecker - he seemed to be the one with the readies - had rented a cottage somewhere off the beaten track. It was apparently, one of those small places surrounded by nothing but dry stone dykes and bleak hills. As I began the long hike I could almost imagine lonely tribes of Brigantes out on the moors doing whatever unpleasantness Celtic tribes did back then. Parts of Yorkshire can be a bit eerie and this was living up to the image in style. A light snow wafted through the sky but it wasn't sufficiently strong enough to lie. It was damned chilly.

By dusk, I arrived at a small beck and perched on a low promontory, was the cottage. It was possibly bleaker in aspect than the surrounding hills.

Norton had warned me that he and Lubecker only occupied the place at odd intervals while the main work, whatever that might be, was going on some distance away in the hills – hence the tents. Whatever it was, they insisted on at least one of their little team being present on site. When I arrived, the cottage was empty. They were both out somewhere in the growing dark. The back door was open. I stumbled around a bit and found a candle.

It was a typical bachelor mess in dire need of a woman's hand: Dirty plates lying around on the floor of the kitchen, rubbish piled high in bags, empty whisky bottles, muddy boots and digging equipment in the hall. But equally typically, there was a wide open doorway that revealed a small room at the back, devoid of furniture with the exception of a very large oaken table. Placed on this table were neat diagrams and an ordered stack of books and papers. The walls of the room had a built-in bookshelf or two filled with a collector's bonanza and I reflected even then, that it was lucky that no one of significance knew where Lubecker and Norton were hiding or the whole library, lock stock and barrel, would be out gracing the tables of every dodgy book dealer.

Naturally, I looked first at the bookshelves. It was an eclectic mix but there were five clear strands- archaeological fieldwork, endless reams on games, puzzles and conundrums, a lot of German texts about the history of Hanover, some of the dullest mathematical books imaginable and a small section on concave and convex mirrors. In reference to the latter, there was an early edition of Ibn al-Haytham's 'Book of Optics', worth a small fortune. I had read it with interest at university.

After musing over the contents of Ibn al-Haytham's masterpiece, I turned to the desk. A cartographic board revealed a maze of scribbles, equations, lines and planes. Geometric devices of unfathomable variety set alongside some Tilly lamps. These quaint lamps were positioned around some small mirrors not unlike those described in the 'Book of Optics'. Under the flickering light of the candle the table looked a little like some awful dwarfish discothèque. This appearance was not unaided by an exquisite pocket chess set whose pieces seemed like so many tiny dancers. The reflections of the chessmen in the distorted mirrors lent a kind of surreal carnival atmosphere to the whole diorama.

I didn't like to fiddle with the antique lamps but I found a few more candles and set them about the place. Then I unearthed a clean glass and poured myself a Glenlivet from a half-full bottle. It was in that relaxed postured, with my boots off and my feet up on the table, that I suddenly saw the letter. I confess I took my feet off the table quick enough.

You see, I recognised the handwriting from my studies. It was that of Liebniz, the German philosopher; the chap who amongst many things, invented calculus. And it was either an extremely good fake or, quite unbelievably, an original. I rose to my feet in astonishment.

What with the flickering lights, the fatigue and the silence it would have been quite easy to assume that I was hallucinating, but you know me, I'm not the type. Still, even I had doubts. Problem was I couldn't even touch the thing because I had no gloves. I could only look at the two pages open before me. They were written in old French and *Fraktur* that pedantic German script, neither of which is much of a speciality of mine but there were all sorts of interpolations and comments in Latin, which is a nap, if I say so myself.

I had studied Liebniz at University, of course, and as chance would have it, was something of an expert. The thing that had so impressed me? The title on the letterhead: 'Episcopus'. I didn't recognise that title and I knew them all – curse of a photographic memory. I was staring at an unknown Liebniz, priceless not only in monetary terms but also in its possible enlargement of our understanding of history and philosophy and a lot more besides.

Carefully laid alongside the open page, a small notepad had the word 'bishop' written in various styles and languages and a little picture of the chessman clearly drawn from the set. Beside that there was a scrawl of translations. The more I looked at the open page, the more I thought the writing was genuine. And it wasn't *a* letter. It was a series of letters and presumably all in the same revered hand.

At that point a voice said 'Yes, it's the real thing,' and there was Norton behind me, clad in dungarees and heavy boots, his boyish face somewhat careworn. Nevertheless, he was smiling with genuine pleasure and he held out his hand.

'Liebniz?'

'Yes the great man himself and a reason we invited you to the party'

'I can't see why, Norton. Selling this would probably ensure you and your friend a wealthy retirement. That is, if it is yours to sell.'

'Doubting Thomas.' Norton filled a glass with the malt and took a sip. 'It's ours alright. I found it, of all places, in a Burgdorf flea market.'

'Lucky you. Don't suppose your old colleagues at Liebniz Universität know much about it?'

'Hardly. They will. But only when we're ready. In fact, as you have doubtless surmised, no one knows much about these notes except you, me and Lubecker.'

'Notes? I thought letters.'

'It's a mixed bag actually. Some correspondence, notes, other bits and pieces. In fact, that invaluable piece of parchment is the tip of a rather large iceberg.'

'Interesting. And it's just us three. Much as I value our friendship Norton I can't imagine a reason why you would let me in on one of the finds of the century.'

'Because,' said Norton – and here he looked distinctly weary, 'without you we can't crack it.'

No amount of badgering would make Norton come out with any more. He insisted that telling would do no good. He would simply show me in the morning. We finished off the whisky. Norton advised me there was room on the couch until they could fix something up.

After Norton retired, I stayed up for a good hour. At one point, I heard something; could have been a scream but I suspect it was a peacock or a dog. I opened the front door and had a look about. The air was chill. There was nothing but bleak hills, silence and the awe-filled sense of centuries unfolding like so many seconds. And then faintly, on the periphery of my senses I thought I heard a cathedral bell. Which was quite impossible, of course.

Lubecker never appeared. Presumably, he was up working in the hills.

Lubecker was still absent at five the next morning when I scrambled into my all weather gear. Norton had made Earl Grey tea with a dash of lemon and there was Alpen cheese and some of that hard German bread that lasts forever. I mentioned the scream, which Norton dismissed immediately as the peacocks who still inhabited the environs of a derelict mansion in the next valley. The cathedral bell made him stop. He looked up at me with those intense pale-blue eyes. 'Sound carries here,' he said finally, and gave a strange smile.

While he was off getting ready, I had another look at the table. I found some gloves and was able to handle the Liebniz notes. It is difficult to express the feelings that accompany this kind of exercise. Hernando Cortez might be able to tell you as he looked across vistas of unknown continents or perhaps that virgin boy unhooking a bra for the first time. There was no time, however, for me to indulge in bibliophilic fantasy. Norton was in the doorway with a walking stick and a rucksack.

'You can pore over that at your leisure Mulholland. But we best take a bit of breakfast to Carsten.'

Strange to hear his first name. Academia was gossiping like mad about the famed Herr Lubecker. I wondered what he was like.

We walked up the low valley in the morning mist; the sun just peeking over the hills behind a bank of clouds. It began to rain lightly almost as soon as we left and I was glad of the foresight to bring my wet weather gear. It took us just under an hour to walk up the hill; the last section a bit of a scramble that revealed a slight plateau before a steep crag and a deep cleft between two promontories. It was an unusual sight. Below us a deep wooded gully, less than a mile in dimension and this narrow rift bridging a tree-filled gap of perhaps seventy or eighty yards. Massive trees edged the ridge on either side and lent the secluded valley a certain wildness unusual in the Wolds. I would have called it beautiful but something intangible held me from saying that. Norton nodded. 'You felt it,' he said ominously.

We climbed down a rather steep slope, the last part a drop of some twenty feet, but easily negotiable. Then we walked a little further, hugging the cliff face, and here a low shelf appeared. It was very flat but felt as unnatural and misplaced as that racetrack at Mount Olympia. Though shrouded by trees and bushes, it was clearly manmade. I said as much to Norton.

'Yes,' he said. 'Another reason I wanted you in. You're sharp

Mulholland. Now what do you make of this?'

I have to stop here and say that much of what is termed 'The Occult' is a species of nonsense better left to melodrama and the funfair. Occult research is a highly practical affair to most of its credible aficionados. You won't often get an occultist saying 'I felt something strange' or the like. It's an experimental 'science' you see. However, on this occasion - as I looked at what appeared to be the ruins of a dry stone dyke or possibly an old sheep pen from the late eighteenth century – 'strange' is about the only epithet that came to mind. There was no apparent reason why this crumbling jigsaw of moss-covered stone should promote such a reaction, but it did. I looked at it all again.

Behind a couple of birches, I could see a section that had been recently dug. It helped establish context. The pattern of falling stones suggested a high wall where we were standing, with its exact counterpart some fifteen yards away facing us and then another longish wall that ran parallel to the low cliff; in all making the shape of block print C.

I bent down for a more careful examination. Norton stood gazing over my shoulder in expectation. I picked up one of the stones. It was badly eroded but I could make something of it. 'Baphomet,' I said finally. 'It's only the legs and the tip of a wing but I would stake money on this being a representation of that energetic old spirit.'

'You money would be safe,' said Norton smiling. 'The other figures and representations are emblazoned on this scattered stone.'

I surveyed the tracing of stones though the bushes with a critical eye. 'I would say you had half a Masonic temple here young Norton.'

'You would be right.'

'But where's the other half?'

I mentioned the strange feeling that had swept over me on first looking at the stones. Even as Norton replied, the feeling intensified to a kind of dread.

'Over there,' said Norton quietly. He pointed to the far side of the deep ravine. I was already looking across the gulf having anticipated his reply.

I sat down, drew out a Havana, cut and lit it. I placed my chin in my hand.

'You don't mess about when you discover things, Norton,' I said after a space.

'To be fair,' he replied. 'It all emerged from the notes. My old French is tolerable, but Carst...Lubecker's is rather good.'

'Norton. I can understand your finding this place but you do realise exactly what we are facing here?'

'Quite. They either built the temple in two parts so that central gulf would be some kind of symbolic catalyst, perhaps a spiritual receiver. Or some cataclysmic event tore the ravine from the earth and split the temple down the middle.'

'And?'

'I'm afraid it's the latter, Mulholland: Some cataclysmic event - and Lubecker is over the other side of that ravine trying to determine exactly what.'

It may sound extraordinary but here was I sitting on finds of the century, the like of which would keep a chap in an obsessive trance for a lifetime, and yet all I wanted to do was meet Norton's *parfait*, Lubecker. There were mysteries and puzzles jostling for attention and I understood that, perhaps because of his relationship with the man, Norton felt that the full exposé would only merit dénouement in his presence. It was with a pang of regret that I left the ruined temple. But it had kept for hundreds of years. Hopefully, it could wait a little longer.

There was no easy way across the ravine. The bottom was a soup of ancient bramble under which nettles, frogs, toads and bones - of what I hoped were sheep - were all scattered amidst the rotten mould of leaves. It was incredibly dark. The pitch of the ravine cut out the light in an almost unnatural fashion. Botanically speaking, there should be no brambles in such a place but I supposed that a force that could rip up hills could do what it liked with ecology. Under the auspices of ravaged temples a bit of gloom and absurdity might be anticipated and at least the rain had ceased.

Norton and Lubecker had cut a path through the brambles. At times the makeshift path went under vast bowers of them and I imagined the effort it must have taken to do this simple piece of labour. The route up was fairly tough but it was helped by some rather large blocks of masonry from you know where. As we reached the opposing ledge, Norton cautioned me to silence.

'Lubecker will be working and we must be careful how we approach'.

The site was almost a mirror of that left behind. But to the west, there was a large tent that I nearly missed, camouflaged, as it was, with bushes. The tent, just tucked under a slight overhang, was illuminated by an inner light and one could vaguely discern the shadows of two men, one seated, one standing. I raised my eyebrows. Norton advanced. The world seemed like a tightrope walker about to tumble. For some reason I went before Norton and under the tent awnings pulled back the flap to reveal a sight that I will never forget.

Lubecker was sat on a campstool, his face a picture of studied concentration, so intent, that I could only term it a meditative trance. All around him were Tilly lamps revealing a stack of papers on a desk to the rear of the tent: A stack so large that leaves of paper had fallen from its heights and were strewn across the tent floor; leaves covered in archaic symbols, cabal, Aramaic, Greek and Latin but most predominately, a virtual cornucopia of mathematical equations. The Lamps also emblazoned a large table and fell upon the strangest thing I have ever seen; on the table before Lubecker, the object that I had mistaken for a man.

You might have seen those anatomical drawings in the medical books or perhaps that dreadful body sculpture that was paraded around Europe. Try to imagine that. Add what you see under a very good microscope, an eclipse and lots of moving mayflies trapped in a glass. Laugh if you like. I can get no closer to an explanation of that dreadful thing. It stood, about half the size of a man, surrounded by bits and pieces of itself. Lubecker was holding a part of it in his hand.

For the thing was not complete. It is possible to say what it was *not*, it is possible to say what it *might be* but the one certainty is that it was far from complete. The pieces of it were stuck together like a very unfinished three-dimensional jigsaw. But some of the pieces, though in the correct place, and this the truth, were simply hanging freelance in the air.

Lubecker gave us one glance. He was a hard looking man, dark hair cropped close to the skull, gaunt cheekbones and five days beard. He looked powerful, with a kind of latent ferocity, and perhaps it was just that he was clearly a bit occupied, but he didn't look like a man to argue with. The glance said it all. Norton tiptoed in. Left the breakfast box on an empty chair and then we both left in a silence that lasted all the way back to the cottage.

It was past lunchtime when we returned but neither of us displayed much interest in food. Norton cut some logs and got a fire going. We retired to the 'map' room. Norton cracked open a bottle of Smokehead. I relit my cigar.

'How long has he been at it?'

'Well, it's been months since we discovered Liebniz…one tends to lose track of time.'

'I can imagine.'

'The puzzle itself -'

'-You call it a puzzle? I was thinking in terms of alien life force, thing from the deep, creature of another dimension, devil incarnate'

'Yes, it is a puzzle Mulholland. It's possibly all those things you suggest and more but fundamentally, it's a puzzle.' Norton took a careful sip of the Smokehead and placed the glass carefully on the table. 'Lubecker, as you are aware, is perhaps the foremost mathematician of his times. There are a few others but…well….Lubecker is just Lubecker. If that thing were Satan and his host of dark angels, Lubecker would still have to solve it… Lubecker and I…'He flushed here. 'Well, we're very close -'

'- Norton,' I said quickly, 'that thing could well be Satan and his several hosts of dark angels. If Lubecker unlocks the puzzle, we might be talking immortal souls. I presume that you want me to stop him?'

Call me arrogant, as many do, but I really thought that was why Norton had called me out. I was shocked when he said 'Damn it no. You have to help him solve it.'

Then I understood. Or at least I think I did. Just say you were a great ladies' man and you were in love with a beautiful girl. You wouldn't be terribly happy if someone said you can't have her but you can take any number of those plainer girls. It's the necessary condition of great lovers, the *need* to obtain *that* lover or live or die in unhappy circumstances. So, it looked like Lubecker, potentially the finest mathematician of his time, didn't simply *want* to solve the puzzle, he *needed* to solve it.

Bit of a dilemma for poor Norton; no slouch himself at adding up and clearly keen on his German colleague. It was all or nothing and in the last analysis, he hadn't been able to contribute as much help to his friend as he wanted.

Norton began to fix up a good student's meal at the fire. Pasta, chopped raw onions and dried tomatoes laced with Parmesan. I offered to help but he asked me to start on the notes. It was no task. Lubecker had prepared a translation of the French and presumably had little problem with his archaic but native German. I kept jumping back between his translations and the papers. Occasionally, Norton would glance over. Once he quietly filled my glass with Glenlivet.

Some say I have an eidetic memory. I'm not sure but I am a quick reader and I remember things where others don't. I skim-read most of the tracts by the time the pasta was boiled. I won't plague you with unnecessary details.

Liebniz was a polymath – he did everything, from the design of a more efficient wheelbarrow to the invention of differential calculus. But Academia often neglects mention of Liebniz's first job as an alchemist. The occult remained, for him, a perpetual fascination. These letters put the seal on all that. The first batch was to his cabbalistic friend, Van Helmont and they more or less confirmed what we all knew: Liebniz was steeped in occult learning. The rest of the letters were to an unnamed group. The language was highly symbolic, riddled with cipher and allusion. But we knew now that our merry party had seen the symbolism come to fruition on that spirit blasted gully. Liebniz had designed the temple to specifications for some English breakaway lodge, probably the owners of the ruined mansion in the next valley. No doubt, some fragments of their bodies were strewn amidst the nettles over the gully and what little was left of their souls inhabited the peacocks in the grounds.

The remaining stuff held the most fascination. It was in essence, a treatise on puzzles. Everything from the Egyptian Dogs and Jackals game to backgammon. But it was more than that. It was written with an unusual twist of humour, much in the style of Aleistair Crowley, the Great Beast. One couldn't help feeling that Liebniz was laughing somewhere out of earshot.

Norton placed the food on my lap. We both ate mechanically in silence.

Finally, Norton said, 'the title 'Episcopus'. Interesting?'

'Very. Nothing in the text refers to it.'

'Did you cope with the maths?'

I laughed. 'Not a bit.'

'It differs slightly from what is generally known of the man. There are some tangential steps in infinitesimal calculus. Quite brilliant. We would regard them as dead ends now I suppose.'

'Perhaps not.' I raised my eyebrows.

'You have something?'

'I can't read this damned French properly. Look at the second word of each line in the first chapter though. The choice of the words seems intuitively wrong to me.'

Norton threw his plate to the floor. For a few seconds he poured over the words. Then he began writing in French. 'Your right,' he said finally. 'It's a diastic. In the first sentence, the first letter makes the first letter of the first word, the second, the second letter and so…' He scribbled away for a bit. I could see him think rapidly in two languages.

Then in a fit of disgust, he threw the paper into the fire. 'Damn,' he said. 'It would have been too easy just to tell us.'

I waited for him to calm. He took another shot of whisky and calmly began to write again. Then he handed me the paper.

One English, one French; each the same, each derived from the same Latin mother, yet not one part in common.'

'Well, that's simple enough, Norton' I said. 'Bishop. In French, "évêque", both derived from the same Latin root.

'Yes, but where does it leave us?' Norton rose to his feet. 'It's been months, Mulholland: Months of sudden inspirations and blind alleys. Transcribing and transliterating notes; research in Leipzig, Hanover. The temple took us an age before we even stumbled on it. The dig itself was endless. I can't tell you how long it took to find the chamber on the second shelf. When we got down there was a tiny room. It seemed…unnaturally preserved. The remains of a man sat in a chair slumped over a small table; his skull rested among the scattered pieces of this damned puzzle: The puzzle that he died trying to solve. And Carsten… He's up there and I can't stop him.'

Norton was at breaking point. He carried on in a voice bordering the hysteric. 'Mathematics, Mulholland. The beautiful science. The elegance of numbers and their relationships. Every paradise can become an asylum. I'm losing-'

'-Sit down Norton. You're going to snap unless you find some inner reserve. Already you're talking nonsense.' I poured us both a glass of whisky, thought again and made it a double. 'There is only one issue here. Forget everything else. Forget the temple, the letters, the research. There is only the puzzle. You could make your fortune on what you already have - You'd make more than a footprint in the sands of time with half of this stuff - But your friend Lubecker has fallen for the oldest trap in the book. He's been offered something he doesn't have and now he believes he needs it. The puzzle mustn't be solved. It's got to be destroyed.'

Norton got out of his chair quick enough. He looked half-mad. I suspect he was.

'Destroy it and you destroy him.' He clenched his fists and fell back into the chair.

After a moment, Norton rose to his feet. From a small cupboard, he took a large box, scarred and pitted with age. It had all the appearance of an Arabian container for chessmen, something of the Alhambra about its design. You could see immediately that it belonged to the puzzle.

'We could go back this evening,' I said.

'Mulholland, it just won't work. Carsten has a mind like a computer – a beautifully constructed machine; the balance of its parts is infinitely delicate. If anyone can solve the puzzle, it's him. He's been at it five days and night…'

'I didn't see much, Norton but that figure was very far from complete. I'm very intuitive and my intuitions tell me he's going to fail.'

'Then help him for God's sake Mulholland.'

Well, not much a man can do really. Appeals to friendship, loyalty, the old school – not many to common sense. I have always been a sucker for the underdog and the tryer.

'Give me a look at those papers Norton,' I said finally. 'Somewhere in this encyclopaedic cribbing, you must have found something. I want to see what you have on the puzzle itself. What about the box, for example. Is there a relationship between the box and the pieces? Just how many pieces are there?'

'Liebniz states there are forty seven pieces. 'He handed me the box. We found forty forty-eight. Presumably he miscounted.'

'I looked keenly at Norton. 'Miscounted? I would think adding would be a bagatelle for someone who could juggle quadratic equations.'

'You never know,' said Norton. Sometimes the mundane details are lost on genius.'

'Forty seven. That's a cabbalistic number of significance. There might be something in that. Perhaps even deliberate misdirection. Let me see the rest.'

I paced around the room a bit to get the blood moving. 'There's something intriguing about the two halves of that temple. Something telling. No, no, it's all in the title of that treatise. Damn you Norton it's called Episcipos – 'Bishop' but its all about bloody mirrors. Why?' I stopped pacing. Norton stared at me with his pale blue eyes. 'A genius might slip up over a number or two but this is Liebniz we are talking about. He wouldn't have mistitled a whole treatise on mirrors, nor would he have interpolated a secret diastic into the text unless....' I paused and then it hit me. Norton saw. He knew. He leapt to his feet but couldn't bring himself to speak. I drew myself up.

You'll think this ridiculous, especially when the story plays out, but I *did* know. Perhaps my dealings with the occult had given me more of an insight, I was certainly no mathematician. I couldn't have solved the puzzle myself if you'd given me a hundred years but now I knew how it *could* be solved.

'Right.' I said. 'I have it.'

'Thank God,' said Norton. 'But what have you?'

'Not sure it's God we should be thanking young Norton but one thing is certain. I am divulging nothing until you bring Lubecker down here. He needs a decent meal, a bit of a rest and we'll approach the thing together.'

Norton argued. I think he wanted it all over with at once and I'm pretty sure he didn't want to disturb Lubecker through fear, or perhaps because he thought he wouldn't come. But I was adamant. I can be a rock when I choose and on this occasion, I was adamantine. I wouldn't even accompany Norton. Deep down, I wanted to give him a bit of companionship out in the darkness; the whole area around that temple stunk of darkness, but I thought it better he brave out his friend alone. Eventually, Norton accepted it and I was left to stare at the fire.

About eleven o'clock I walked out to the front door. Far away the peacocks were crying in the night and as though it were all prearranged. I heard the bell again. This time I knew it was no cathedral. It was a temple bell, a summons of some kind, and I guessed now for whom the bell tolled.

I was lighting up a second cigar when the footsteps sounded over the hills and I saw two shadows approach. I congratulated myself that I had managed to contrive a success when Lubecker came towards me in an aggressive pose.

'You better be correct, Mr. Mulholland,' his accent was mild but his voice brimmed with restrained violence. 'I was on the threshold of the solution and…'

'Rubbish.' I said firmly. 'You were going around in circles.'

He paused as though weighing up whether thrashing the life out of me would be useful. He decided not. '*Es tut mir lied*. I have …'

'No need to explain. Come in. Put your feet up beside the fire.'

We huddled around the fire. I had already boiled up a kettle and some hot cocoa was just what the doctor ordered. Norton took an age to persuade Lubecker to sit down. The German looked like a zombie. The strain was clearly kicking in. He refused any food with a look of disgust. Eventually Norton got him in the easy chair and stood behind him, massaging his neck and shoulders. I thought I better put him out his misery.

'It's quite simple really Herr Lubecker. What you have is

some infinitesimal calculus on your hands. I couldn't solve it if you gave me a thousand years but I believe you can. I don't do maths, only intuition.' He nodded. 'All that I insist upon is that you have a nights rest.'

'No!' he said.' You must understand-.'

'-Oh, I'll tell you the answer or at least the road to the answer, but give me your word you will sleep on it tonight. You know it makes sense.' He nodded again reluctantly.

I threw a log on the fire. The flames burgeoned and sent shadows flicking across Lubecker's drawn face.

'It's all in that simple diastic.' I said after a space. 'I assume Norton pointed it out on the road back.

One English, one French; each the same,
 each derived from the same Latin mother, yet not one part in common'

The word of course is bishop, 'Bischof' *auf Deutsch,* I believe, but the treatise to which it refers is on mirrors and nowhere is this bishop mentioned. Why?'

'It's all about mirrors my dear Lubecker. By placing a convex and concave mirror on either side of the object, you will have two different illuminations from the same root yet neither will be connected to each other. You will then be able see the puzzle in itself and as an object of both repeated reflection and reflections in two mirrors. Your abundance of mathematical knowledge will take over and utilising this you will create the 'bishop' – the esoteric figure or, as it is termed in some cases, the first the leader or foreman. The bishop, of course, is that damnable figure.'

Lubecker leapt to his feet. I could see him visualising reversed infinitesimal equations in his head; that wonderful brain making a host of neural connections that had been obscured because he had attempted, in effect, to solve the puzzle 'upside-down'. It was an ephinanous moment.

I knew better than to say anything. He was straight over to the map room, playing with the mirrors and drawing circles and equations everywhere.

I turned to Norton who looked less enthusiastic. I said softly 'In occult terms, Norton, there are far too many 'coincidences' here. There are too many echoes of this triad. You two, the *parfait,* and me the catalyst, the chasm that divides two sides of a temple, the two mirrors making their ethereal contact with the thing in between. This puzzle is a triactic equation and its solution has me intensely worried. What is this 'bishop'?'

Norton had no answer. He couldn't take his eyes off the older man whose hands were now flickering over the table.

Much later, in the deep of night, I heard the door open. Lubecker had given his word but under the dreadful compunction of those infinitesimal equations, had broken it within three hours.

I heard his footsteps retreat into the night and again I heard that phantom bell.

+

Mulholland put his whisky down. The Oxford bar had emptied and we were alone with our thoughts. 'Can you use it?' he said.

I laughed. 'Perhaps,' I replied, 'but it's not quite finished is it?'

Mulholland smiled quietly. 'Come,' he said. 'We might as well walk back together.'

A fog had settled. The New Town streets were deserted and silent. 'I'll tell you what we'll do,' said Mulholland. 'Stop at mine tonight. You may as well kip on the couch. That way, I can show you the puzzle.'

It was at this point that I thought Mulholland must be joking. There's a kind of gulf between hearing a bizarre and impossible tale of terror and then having the bloke put the severed head or phantom coach in front of you. I had believed Mulholland when he told the tale but now I didn't quite believe him anymore.

We paced up the streets in silence and then reached the door of his Georgian house on St_____Square. He threw open the door, advanced through the darkened hallway to a small anteroom surrounded with bookshelves whose regiments of leather tomes glistened by the light of a fading wood fire. There he produced some Glenlivet and then with an almost flippant disregard for theatrics, placed an unusual box on the table before us.

'That's it,' he said. 'Liebniz's lost puzzle. Quite something.'

I can't adequately describe that box except to say it was about the size of a brief case and apparently made of shimmering wood. Suffice it to say I am reduced to Mulholland's description of the ruined temple. It felt strange, *very* strange. I took a long sip of whisky. Mulholland lit a cigarillo. Embers glowed in the dying fire.

'Norton got me up fairly briskly in the morning,' he said finally. 'We'd both had a bad night as one hell of a storm kicked up in the early hours. When we got to the tent we found Lubecker -not a mark of violence on him but he was dead and slumped over the table with the pieces of that puzzle scattered everywhere. I had a terrible job getting the body back to the cottage. It was absolutely clear that we couldn't leave it there and naturally, Norton was so distraught he could hardly function. Anyway, the deed was finally done. We had to walk to the village – no mobile phones or email in those days – we eventually raised the police and they came to the cottage. There was a fair amount of suspicion kicking around, Village police, outsiders and all that. Although they never thought to search the hills - thank God - they asked a lot of questions and poked around a fair bit. So much so that I was fairly certain that we were going to be up for murder. Not a pleasant prospect.

In the police cells - and yes it did go as far as that - Norton and I were kept apart. We waited a day or was it two? I could hear Norton weeping most of the time but couldn't do much about it. And then Norton was standing there with a police officer who looked rather strangely at me. I can recall the conversation perfectly although at the time I misheard the officer's reply when I asked if they'd established a cause of death.

You see, I thought he said 'heart attack', which would have been feasible. But Norton corrected me later.

'Not a heart attack,' he said sombrely. 'They opened Lubecker up and his heart was simply missing; as though it had never been there.'

Naturally, the police hushed the whole thing up. That kind of thing can get you in an asylum and perhaps all sorts of records went to secret government offices and lots of things were changed, but I'm not sure they even did that. It was only later that I realised something quite significant.

You see Lubecker's heart had disappeared. I can't emphasise that enough: *Disappeared*, literally transported from his body. I got to thinking not of how that could happen but where it could have gone.' Mulholland stubbed out his cigarillo. 'I think you have guessed have you not? That unknown man whose skeleton still rests in the little chamber beneath the temple? He hadn't died trying to solve the puzzle. He died *solving* it. If you look at the pieces, you'll find there are not forty seven now or, indeed, forty-eight but *forty-nine*. Mulholland smiled. 'But then I really wouldn't look at the puzzle.'

It was hours later after a succession of double malts, that Mulholland got to his feet. He intimated that his man would serve a late breakfast and bid me good night. I sat for a while after he had gone to bed. I looked to the couch with its comfortable blanket and then back to the puzzle box that Mulholland had inadvertently left on the table; Liebniz's last puzzle.

I confess it held something of a magnetic attraction.

BIG CUP, WEE CUP

Breathless and shaking with nervous excitement, Milne of the Order, topped the stairs of the Gorgie tenement. He was a slim man in his mid twenties with a balding pate, and a pale, narrow face now beaded with sweat.

The door to the flat was open. He surged in, shouting at the top of his voice. 'Mulholland, Mulholland!!!'

There was no reply. For a few seconds he stared around the hallway, barely taking in the sumptuous and elegant décor, the fine furniture and the luxurious carpets. 'Mulholland!'

Milne hesitated. From somewhere a voice could be heard, apparently singing. It sounded like Mulholland, although the resemblance to singing was tenuous. Whoever was making the noise appeared to be inebriated. Milne tried first one door and then another. In the second room, a quaintly furnished bedroom overlooking Gorgie Road, he found him at last. The older man was sitting in the frame of the open window with his back to the room. Milne could tell it was Mulholland by the excessive velvet jacket and the bottle of laphroaig which he was waving wildly in his left hand.

'Mulholland! Don't do it.' Milne advanced tentatively. 'For God sake, don't jump!'

The singing continued, the words unintelligible. The melody, recognisable to Milne from his days with the Chapel Choir, was apparently a variation on the Westminster Quarters. Mulholland, with a whisky glass as baton, was conducting some kind of outdoor orchestra. Incredibly, the crowd, which had been gathering for some hours on Gorgie Road, seemed to be joining in the song.

'Come down from the window,' said Milne hoarsely. He observed as he advanced, that Mulholland's jacket was an exquisite shade of dark maroon; a matching tartan scarf hung around his neck despite the blazing sun. The bottle of laphroaig was virtually empty.

'What?' Mulholland paused in the performance.

'The window; come away from the window. It's just not worth it.'

'Worth what?' said Mulholland. He turned to look at Milne in bewilderment.

'Not worth jumping.'

Mulholland laughed. 'Get yourself a tumbler from the cabinet. Who on earth would commit suicide on a day like this?' Laboriously, he swung his legs from the sill, made an unexpected ejaculation of approval and shook his fist in triumph to the invisible crowd below. Outside, a spontaneous chant began to take life. The volume of noise grew with each passing moment.

'Mulholland! Get a grip. Where have you been all for the last two days!?'

'I left a message with Simpson,' said Mulholland airily.

'Yes, that you were not be contacted, that you would be unavailable, indisposed, hidden, incognito and on some utterly indispensable personal mission. We managed to torture the information out of poor Simpson half an hour ago despite your instructions that he inform the members tomorrow at the earliest.'

Mulholland found a glass and tumbled the dregs of the bottle into it. 'Poor Simpson,' he said sadly. He drained the glass.

'Never mind Simpson,' said Milne. 'What have you been doing? It was the Graal symposium; the single most important meeting in the last century of the Order.'

'It was the cup,' said Mulholland, his eyes briefly alight.

'Cup? You call the Graal a *cup*?'

'Heart of Midlothian versus Hibernian. The *Cup*. You must have seen the crowds outside. Today's the parade.'

'Crowds - I could hardly get through them - I didn't see any Hibernian fans though - Can you not concentrate for a second?' Mulholland had already drifted back to the window and was swaying to the chanting below.

'Pardon?' He wasn't listening.

'Would you get this stupid game of soccer out of your head for just a second-'

Mulholland had turned, dropped the empty glass to the carpet, and was now holding Simpson upright in his powerful arms. His face poked into Simpson's and his single eye stared with peculiar malevolence at the younger man.

'Stupid game of *soccer*? This is Heart of Midlothian we're talking about, the team with the finest sporting history in the world. And soccer! It's called football where I come from - the noble game, the great endeavour.' Slowly, he let Simpson down.

Simpson brushed his collar. 'I appreciate you're keen on…football; but The Graal, the convention, the Order.'

'Stuff the convention. Stuff the Order.'

'You can't be serious, Mulholland. It's the Holy Grail! What about those who died for the Order. Bartholomew's bones are still bleaching somewhere out in the Sinai Desert. The archaeologists assassinated in Antioch. Gerardson killed in that cathedral fire in Valencia. Poor Mathews rotting in a private asylum along with three assistants, his brilliant mind destroyed by the Templar cipher. The long years we've spent looking. It's in our grasp – you were meant to report-'

'Shut up for a second would you.' Mulholland had returned to the window. 'The team bus is arriving!' Mulholland began shouting in an inarticulate croak. Outside, the crowds roared. Milne could see a sea of maroon scarves and tops; vast numbers of singing people held back by the Edinburgh constabulary.

'Mulholland for God sake. The Graal! It's almost in our hands. Babbington seems certain that it came up through the borders. The Roslin Chapel conundrum, the parchment at Holyrood, the missives under the Tron Kirk. You were supposed to be on the case. Your findings-'

'-The Graal's gone,' said Mulholland. 'Nip to the cabinet and get another bottle, there's a good fellow.'

'Gone. What do you mean *gone*?'

'Well, not actually gone. Melted down.'

'But… but…'

'I established it beyond doubt.'

'But the Holy Grail, the silver. Where?'

The crowd out side had hit a pitch of excitement. The Lothian bus with its freshly painted signs coasted into view. A sudden chant broke out in deafening volume. Mulholland began flexing his body in a weird bowing ritual, shouting at the top of his voice. For a few seconds Milne could only hear the corrupted melody of the Westminster Quarters. Then in a kind of stupor he deciphered the words as they echoed out across the street of Edinburgh like the toll of the Great Clock of Westminster: 'Big team big cup, wee team wee cup…'

The bus drew next to the window. There was a second of awed silence as the sun caught the silver sheen of the glittering upheld cup. Milne looked at Mulholland and then the cup.

'It couldn't be' he croaked.

Mulholland smiled a beatific smile.

GIFTS

Well, Christmas eve again and the old routine right on time. The reindeer have been fed, the sleigh is packed with goodies, the pixies and goblins are exhausted but cheerily so. They've worked hard and earned a rest. The sky is bright with that hollow crisp feel you get when the evening has just fallen. My, the stars look scintillating and the moon is casting a benign glow over the endless snow. One last check over the bridles and halters; breath misting up. Gloves on, a cheery wave and it's off to deliver the presents.

There's always a certain calm contentment when I take the air. The wind seems to sparkle on the lips like cold gin and tonic, the sky expands and becomes a heavenly bowl. Far below the little workers wave and become a dark huddled mass on the ice. The tiny lights flicker and the cold vacuum of space becomes my only world. Below the ice flows and the frozen sea, too dark to distinguish, above the spinning heavens.

I never question it really – the swift travel, the time paradox, the impossibility of it all. I just do what I have always done – deliver the presents to the little children over the world. I never even see their faces and they rarely catch a glimpse of me. Oh, some do, but only briefly and they soon forget as adults. I suppose it's the good ones who are lucky but maybe not. My instructions are always the same, ubiquitous and unseen from the great unknowable. He has his ways and I am merely a messenger of hope, a simple creature who does his job and always will.

There below, the first of the city lights, distant like a string of pearls, coming speedily into view. Soon the roof tops, the chimneys, the hearths and the Christmas trees. The gifts strewn across the floor and my final delivery, the tiny boxes, one each for the good children.

I suppose I have been here since the beginning; someone long ago once said I was Dionysus, another said Bran, some ancient god, no doubt bringing his Cornucopia to spill over into the homes of men. I suppose I will be there at the end of the world bringing the last gift for the last children.

The first house; eerie, silent, shrouded in snow. As I approach I finger the first of the little boxes that will be delivered to each home. They are always the same. It is always the same. Nothing has ever changed in all these long years. I feel a sense of calm only disturbed by one curious reflection.

This year, for a reason beyond my ken, He asked me to dress in black.

The little box seems strangely heavy. I wonder what it contains?

Afterthoughts

Timeless Love
Yes, it's a poem, something I churn out occasionally despite opposition. Published in 2007 in *Filthy Creations #2:* Edited by Rog Pile, and born in a dark yet paradoxically optimistic place where love triumphs even in the abyss. (I hope).

Synchronicity
Published in 2008 in *The Third Black Book of Horror*: Ed: Charles Black and receiving an honourable mention in Ellen Datlow's *Best Horror of the Year*. This was my second contribution to the now famous series and the first where I discovered Daniel Mulholland, the anachronistic antiquarian battling against evil, dastards and school bullies. At the time I had no idea I would fall in love with him.

The Glowing Goblins
On the 24th of August 1991 I hopefully submitted this short summary of my bad childhood dreams to *Auguries #16:* Editor: Nik Morton. To my knowledge at the time it was my fourth accepted story and gained me a neat £1-50 before seeing the light in 1992. That cupboard under the stairs still haunts me.

New Teacher
This story is based largely on my experiences of school in Edinburgh in the 1970's. Not so much a horror story but a grim depiction of the times. Published in 2010 in *The Seventh Black Book of Horror* Ed: Charles Black.

The Janus Door
Originally called *The Door* I decided only to correct a couple of typos in this story which was finished in July 1992 and rejected by *The Edge, Interzone,* and indeed, everyone else.

The Heavenmaker

A novelette published in 1988 *in The 29th Pan Book of Horror Stories*: Ed: Clarence Paget who unfortunately forgot to tell me. In 1999, after discovering the story on the internet, a short bitter correspondence with my lawyer extracted £600 from the publishers which could well be the highest fee paid to a Pan author. Still didn't cheer me up much at the time.

The Waiting Game

On the other hand this did. Published in 2010 in *Back from the Dead: The Legacy of the Pan Book of Horror Stories*: Ed: Johnny Mains. A welcome return to the company of Pan Authors.

The Art of Confiscation

I finished this revisit to Bellport High in 2011. The staffroom is populated by caricatures of teachers I remember fondly from my youth.

Farmer Brown

I lost a short section from the start of this story written around 1992 describing the perils of reincarnation but the rest is more or less as it was.

Not Waving

My brother quite liked Mulholland and the smoking room tales so he sent me a manuscript in 2011. I brushed it up. Poignancy is a key element in the best horror stories and his idea presses the cry button with a forceful finger.

Spanish Suite

Charles Black was pivotal in my return to horror and I knew he liked humour. So I spent some time trying to think up the most gruesome scenario for him and *The Sixth Black Book of Horror* (2010). Pants down, apparently copulating with a corpse as the funeral cortege of the town's most important dignitary arrives seemed to fill the bill.

The Anninglay Sundial
M.R. James was always a favourite and I sent Mulholland scurrying after him in 2011 for a G&S competition, which I failed to win. If I'd known the redoubtable John Llewellyn Probert was also writing a sequel to the Mezzotint this story would never have been born.

Soup
'Quite possibly the most beautifully written example of cannibal torture porn I've ever read!' Demonik, Vault of Evil. One of the nicest things anyone has ever said about my work. First appeared in *The Fourth Black Book of Horror* published in 2009.

A Game of Billiards
This Mulholland story is based loosely on the experiences of my Grandfather, Jock Herbertson who was out there in India in WW1. Saw the light in 2009 in *Tales from the Smoking Room*: Ed: Benedict Jones: It must be one of my rarest stories; I don't have a copy myself, Benedict.

The Navigator
Someone once said The Navigator aired in the *Big Vault Advent Calendar 2011* was the first horror story about a GPS Navigator.

The Tasting
As a musician I spent a lot of time working in restaurants and seeing things in the kitchen. I am Laphroaig man, I've been up there in Glencoe and I've felt the bitter winds which are only cured by the beautiful drink. I finished this story of two rival whisky tasters in 2011.

Steel Works
There is a Steel works down the road from me and that infernal

noise follows you all the way down the river. Never been in it though. Finished in 2011 for an online competition – You've guessed it.

Liebniz's Last Puzzle
I'd made the honourable mentions for Ellen Datlow's best horror before and I thought this story, published in 2009 in *The Fifth Black Book of Horror* might crack the magic ceiling. It was nice get to get a mention again for this Mulholland story of magical puzzles.

Big Cup Wee Cup
Sorry, I couldn't resist this.

Gifts
And a Merry Christmas to you all. Took me eight minutes to write but I rather liked it. It appeared just in time for the presents in *Big Vault Advent Calendar 2011* selected by Demonik of the Vault of Evil.

Acknowledgements
Janis Mackay is an Award-winning children's author
http://www.janismackay.com/

Cover art:
'The Heaven Maker' Acrylic, collage & mixed media 85 x 60 cm 2012 Brian Keeley BA (Hons), MA